THE CALL

GAVIN STRAWHAN

ALLEN&UNWIN
AUCKLAND · SYDNEY · MELBOURNE · LONDON

First published in 2024

Copyright © Gavin Strawhan, 2024

Allen & Unwin
Level 2, 10 College Hill, Freemans Bay
Auckland 1011, New Zealand
Phone: (64 9) 377 3800
Email: auckland@allenandunwin.com
Web: www.allenandunwin.co.nz

83 Alexander Street
Crows Nest NSW 2065, Australia
Phone: (61 2) 8425 0100

A catalogue record for this book is available from the
National Library of New Zealand.

ISBN 978 1 99100 679 0

Cover design by Luke Causby
Text design by Megan van Staden
Cover images: Diane Keough/Getty Images (beach);
alexanderstoic/Unsplash (motorbike)
Set in Garamond 13/18
Printed and bound in Australia by the Opus Group

10 9 8 7 6 5 4 3 2 1

MIX
Paper | Supporting
responsible forestry
FSC
www.fsc.org   FSC® C001695

For Adele, Charlie & Gloria

1

THE 10K RUN AROUND THE town and along the beach had been fine, the decision to tackle the summit track at full tilt not so much. Lungs burning, hunched over her knees, she forced herself to stand, and raise her freckled arms to the flat grey sky. *A bull at a gate*, her mother was fond of saying. Under an oversized tee and flannel shorts, she felt the puckered flesh around her spine resisting, tugging at her skin, as her lungs tried to expand. She pursed her lips, slowing her breath, distracting herself with the view from the rocky heads, around the graceful curve of the deserted sandy beach, and down to the pale shards of sandstone of the sheer cliffs at the other end of the bay. Views from the first seventeen years of Honey's life.

Skinny, eight years old, mandarin curls in a saggy bucket hat, out in the bay in her father's old boat, pulling in snapper and gurnard by the bucketful. Building sandcastles, running races, swimming and boogie boarding, making best friends forever in the few weeks over summer as the camping ground filled up. Friends to be replaced year after year until she learned better. Lonely, misunderstood tweens. Squatting on an oyster-studded rock, watching translucent crabs cautiously emerge, imagining she knew how they felt.

A first kiss over there, first heavy petting there, first actual sex, clumsy and embarrassing in a battered black Nissan parked by the boat ramp. Down there, also, the bench seat on the little strip of green before the beach, where her mother had taken her and her sister the day their father didn't come home. Fourteen years old, running to the beach, furious after seeing their mother flirting with the weekend fishermen at the golf club, all cleavage and lipstick, so obvious. And then the other, darker thoughts — the kind the counsellor wanted her to deal with.

Bugger it.

Honey willed her body into motion again and ploughed down the track, jumping patches of sand tussock and pigface in pink flower, then on to the beach again and away.

'HEY MUM!' HONEY CAME IN the back door, gulping the last of the water from her bottle.

'I'm back,' she added unnecessarily.

Still nothing. An irritating whisper of concern. Would she ever be able to walk into a house and it just be walking into a fucking house for chrissake. She placed her bottle down on the kitchen counter and padded down the passage to the living room. Rachel was stock-still, staring at a pad of Post-it notes, a pen in her left hand.

'Mum?'

'What's it called? That thing. That you put the magazines on?'

'The coffee table?'

'Yes, the bloody coffee table.' She typed it into her mobile phone. 'Also known as *kāfēi zhuō*.' This in a faux singsong accent. Vaguely racist but what was the point. Honey watched her mother carefully write down both versions and stick the Post-it to the edge of the coffee table.

Rachel's white hair, recently thick and naturally dark, was the texture of dry grass. Her face was lined, deeply etched, her hands too, the crinkle-cut skin of a lifelong smoker. Ironic.

Rachel had been a lifelong health worker, a community nurse in a community that still revered her, even after her forced retirement. She'd been in decline for some time, but nobody had wanted to admit it, least of all Rachel herself. Oh, she'd felt a bit rocky, she'd concede, ever since Ron passed. He'd been a weekend fisherman who ended up staying nearly twenty years before a series of strokes stole away his speech, his mobility and finally his life.

Nearly every family in the district owed Rachel some debt, had stories of how she had helped them or their loved ones. She lunched with the mayor, harassed the regional health board, was quoted regularly in the *Bay Advocate*, provoked immunisation drives, was a sharp-tongued advocate for those who needed it. In the end, it was Wiremu from the garage who rang Honey to say that something needed to be done.

Ti-i-ming.

Honey was convalescing after *the incident*. She reassured Wiremu that she'd sort a few things and drive up to Waitutū as soon as she was able. But the moment she put down the phone she had to fight the urge to cry, though it was hard to tell if it was for her mother or for herself. Funny, considering she hadn't cried during or after the beating that had nearly killed her. Apparently, fists, bats and knives had nothing on her mother when it came to making her feel inadequate.

'She's an amazing woman, your mum,' was the first thing Wiremu said when Honey pulled in to fill her Mini Clubman and do some preliminary reconnaissance.

Wiremu's garage had been there from the beginning of time: two pumps, a shop that sold everything from bait to bread, and an attached workshop. He'd come waddling out as she was still unfolding herself. It was only a four-hour drive from Auckland, but she'd been weaning herself off the painkillers.

'But it was getting out of hand,' he went on, 'her forgetting appointments, losing stuff, denying she'd done this or that. And her temper, oh, boy, she called Henry Scott up at the school every name under the sun when he tried to persuade her to see the doc.'

'No, that's fine, I'm glad you called,' she said.

'I'm just grateful you could come, Honey. Considering everything . . .' Wiremu let that linger like a question.

Honey just smiled and shrugged. 'All good.' Though of course it wasn't.

'Well,' Wiremu beamed, 'bet you're glad to be home.'

Everyone who stayed in Waitutū thought it was the best place in the world. Everyone who disagreed got out as soon as they could. Honey had left a few days shy of her eighteenth birthday. She never regretted it. Too many ghosts, not just her sister's, she told her counsellor, offhand, but of course that was her hoping to avoid having to go into the details. The counsellor had kept digging until Honey stopped going to appointments. And here she was anyway, back at the source.

'Yeah, it's great. Apart from the bit where my mother has dementia.' She smiled wryly to show he didn't need to tiptoe around her.

But Wiremu stiffened slightly, as if he detected some criticism lurking. 'She'll be pleased you're here,' was all he said. 'Everyone needs their whānau with them at times like these.'

Honey really wished she could agree.

NOW, THREE WEEKS LATER, HER mother was putting bilingual Post-it notes all around the house. Table. Chair. Teapot. Some days she was unable to remember the thing in her hand with the sticky sweet dark coating (chocolate biscuit/*qiǎokèlì bǐnggān*) but she wasn't going gently. She applied her formidable will to the task of not getting to the point where Honey, with a clear conscience, could have her assigned to supported care. Or sent to the knacker's, as Rachel would have it.

The internet was a wonderful thing. It had guided Rachel to daily aspirin and turmeric supplements. It inspired her to learn another language to exercise different parts of the brain. She finally kicked smoking and started yoga classes at the local hall. Honey wasn't sure it made any difference. She'd done her online swot too. There were dozens of possible causes for the plaque that was clogging up her mother's brain and would lead to her death long before her heart stopped beating. As the specialist tried to explain, 'It's like the floor to your garage is wet and getting wetter, so you try to find ways to mop it up, but actually there are numerous holes in the roof, and you have to find vastly different ways to stopper up each of them. Imagine the water on the floor is the plaque in your brain and . . .'

Until Rachel snapped, 'You don't know what causes it, haven't got a clue, so why don't you bloody well say so!'

Rachel never asked Honey how long she intended to stay — it was a topic both were keen to avoid. Honey had injury compensation and had rented out her little house for a ridiculous amount. Her mother had savings and a pension, so there was no great financial pressure. She figured she'd stay until she couldn't care for Rachel any longer. That's all.

Part of Honey's concern was that, while she felt haunted in

Waitutū, and bearing witness to her mother's deterioration was exhausting, she couldn't muster much enthusiasm to return to Auckland. Her 'couple friends' had mostly sided with Tony after the break-up; the rest had busy lives. Until recently she'd been the busiest. They mostly kept in touch through social media and the occasional phone call. She could do that just as easily from here. The bosses had assured her she could take her time returning to work, even to light duties; they appreciated what she had been through, how hard it must be. Honey was glad of the support, but the truth was she didn't know if she'd ever want to go back. She had loved her job, been bloody good at it too, and it had very nearly killed her. It had almost certainly killed Kloe Kovich.

2

SOMEWHERE IN THE DARK A phone was grating, vibrating insistently against a bedside table. His or hers? She listened a moment. Tony wasn't moving. So, he wasn't on call.

'Damn.'

'Huh?'

'Never mind.' It was her phone. *Unknown caller*. She swung her feet out from under the duvet and perched on the edge of the bed.

'Hello, Detective Chalmers.'

Silence.

'Hello?'

'You give me your number, eh.' It was a woman's voice. Almost a whisper.

'Okay.' Honey could feel Tony shifting beside her, but fuck it, he got his share of late-night callouts too. 'So, what can I do for you?'

There was no response.

'Do you want to give me your name?' Honey ventured. She wasn't overly optimistic.

'Later, maybe.'

Another long pause.

Tony sighed loudly and turned away.

'The Knights are coming up for a big meeting, eh,' the caller said at last. Another pause, then, 'You interested in that kind of stuff?'

'What kind of stuff is that?'

'Meth. A shitload of it.'

Honey was Serious Crime and this was Drugs but yeah, she was interested.

At the kitchen table the recording app on her phone blinked red. She also opened her notepad.

'Okay, the Knights are coming up. You said it was for a meeting? Can you tell me who they're meeting with?'

Another pause. And then, 'The Reapers.'

Honey took a moment. The Reapers were blow-ins from Australia, 501s named after the clause in the legislation that allowed New Zealand-born residents to be deported if they had done prison time or were deemed to be of 'dubious moral character'. An Australian senior Minister had called it putting out the trash. Well, treat people like trash, no surprises what happens next. The Reapers had brought with them a new level of violence and no respect for tradition. They'd made enemies, Knights included. A fatal shootout at a funeral had led to a cycle of bloody paybacks.

The caller seemed to anticipate Honey's doubts.

'They got some new arrangement.'

'What sort of arrangement?' The criminal world was rife with rumour and lies, most of them not worth getting out of bed for.

'Reapers maybe want to talk about Tauranga.'

'Do you know where and when this meeting will be?'

'Can probably find out.' There was a sudden change of tone. 'I gotta go.'

KLOE KOVICH SAT ON THE back step, smoking, staring into the night. It was too cloudy for many stars, but a nearly full moon poked through. It hurt every time she inhaled.

Fucking Jason had cracked a couple of ribs this time, for sure, and there was a big lump on the side of her head where he'd shoved it into the door frame. After that she'd just lain on the floor, curled up, while he sank in the boot. She should probably go to the Emergency Department but what good would that do? They wouldn't give her any decent drugs anyway, not with her history.

All she'd done was ask for some money to treat the kids to some fish and chips. That was the thing about Jason: another time he might've enjoyed being the big man, thrown some cash on the table — 'Go on, have a big old feed on me.' Maybe he was stressed about this deal with the Knights. They didn't fuck around and Jason wasn't the most reliable. Kloe had heard him on his phone, talking in some kind of code, as if they were talking about delivering a load of dog food or some shit. As if Jason was important enough for the cops to bother bugging his phone.

Kloe used to think he was cool. Okay, he was a bit of a dick, with a boom in the boot that shook the whole car, but she loved the way he could take the piss and make her laugh. Now, nights like this, she wished she could put a gun to his head and pull the trigger. Then she'd laugh all right.

He had this dumb-arse habit of repeating most of what was said to him, so it wasn't hard to work out both sides to the conversation. He'd been trying way too hard to sound confident, when she could tell he was wetting himself. It was right after that he got stuck into the piss. And then he'd got stuck into her.

'What's to eat?'

'There's some bread and peanut butter.'

'A man needs real food, bitch.'

'A man should've given his bitch the money she asked for, so they could've got some fish and chips then.'

'What did you say, woman?'

'You deaf as well as stupid?'

If Shyla hadn't come through from putting the baby down and screamed at him to stop, it could've been way worse. Now who was laughing. It felt good to know she could drop him in it any time she wanted.

Detective Sergeant Honey Chalmers. Funny name, a pigshit called Honey. Kloe flipped over the card. On the back was chicken scratch scrawled in blue biro, 'Anytime you want to talk', and another number. She shoved it back deep into the pockets of her jeans, but then had second thoughts and dug it out again.

It wasn't likely that Jason would go through her pockets, though you never knew. Or maybe she'd be pulling out a lighter and accidentally the card would come with it. Even if she put it in the rubbish and Jason was taking it out because it was the only useful thing he ever did around the house and somehow he noticed it . . . She was overthinking it, but now it was a worm in her head and she knew it wouldn't let her sleep. On impulse she shoved the card through a crack between the warped, faded timbers of the back step. As she let it go, something else struck her, made her smile. This Honey might be pigshit, but it was kind of choice to have someone to talk to.

HONEY HAD PUT THE KETTLE on, listening to the recording, making notes. New Zealand accent. 'Street' if there was such a thing. Maybe Māori or Polynesian, maybe not. She counselled herself not to jump to conclusions. Institutional racism starts at home, and from what she knew of the Reapers, they were colour blind, recruiting displaced Kiwi-born Australians. For some reason she didn't think the voice sounded rural. Thirties, maybe older? Anxious but not terrified. Not exactly. Tauranga presumably referred to the port, the busiest in New Zealand. The Knights were a criminal gang known to be active there.

Honey closed her eyes and let her mind go blank, waiting for whatever else would bubble up. The caller wouldn't give her name but said 'later, maybe'. So, it wasn't only about the information. She might be seeking to make a connection. Maybe she just needed someone to talk to. But there was something else in her tone. Honey couldn't put her finger on it right away. She went back to the start of the call. 'You give me your number, eh.'

Honey thought back to women she'd given her number to over the last few weeks. There were quite a few. She had recently wrapped a long investigation into a horrific case of child abuse resulting in the death of a two-year-old girl. The family, four generations under one rusted roof in the backblocks of Henderson Valley, unemployed, a history of domestic abuse, crime, alcoholism, drugs, violence and all-round fucked-up-ness, was quite naturally distrustful of the police and had closed ranks. Honey was sure they knew who was responsible, but no one was saying.

Honey and her team had worked closely with local community reps and social workers. She'd been patient, which, it's fair to say, was not her natural condition. There had been heartbreaking moments, like a teenager claiming to have done it, until Honey sussed it was a cry for help, that the girl would rather be locked up than live the way she was. Honey probably shouldn't have been so free and easy with her private number, but she'd been frustrated by the lack of progress. Eventually an anonymous tip-off led to a forty-eight-year-old grandmother and her twenty-two-year-old mentally disabled boyfriend being charged and convicted. It wasn't the kind of win that made anyone feel better.

Honey rubbed her eyes, sat back. The Reapers' clubhouse wasn't far from Henderson Valley so there could be a connection, but her card could've just as easily been passed on, left in a pub or dropped on the street. The phone was probably an untraceable burner and, anyway, what would be the point? Nothing she could do but wait.

She was making herself a cup of chamomile tea when it struck her, the thing about the caller's tone. She added a word to her list. *Vengeful.*

3

A COUPLE OF WEEKS LATER, Honey still hadn't heard back from her mystery caller. She'd had a word with Spud, Inspector Greg Peely from Drugs. Spud doubted the Knights would get into bed with the Reapers, there was a lot of bad blood — literally — but stranger things had happened. He'd look into it and keep her posted.

It wasn't as if Honey didn't have enough on her plate. Apart from her usual caseload of woe and misery, a yachtie had found a suitcase floating in the Waitematā Harbour. Inside the suitcase were body parts that, when reassembled, made up most of a Chinese teenager who had been missing from her student accommodation for a week. Word was the pressure of study had got too much and she'd fled back to Mainland China. Word was wrong.

Honey was working closely with the Asian Liaison Unit, trying to break through to the student community, but it was never going to be easy. The girl had been quiet, well behaved and studious. There was nothing to link her, or either of her parents, to organised crime. They came to Auckland to take the pieces of their only daughter home — the incomprehension on their faces was heartbreaking. Honey had spent long nights combing through transcripts, hoping the translations were accurate enough to pick up on subtle differences and contradictions in the mountain of statements.

Fortunately, Tony had been training for the annual Coast to Coast, running up a mountain, kayaking and cycling, on top of his punishing schedule as a urologist. Most nights he was too fucked to fuck and his interest in Honey's work was nil.

'We need more peanut butter and bananas.'

'I just bought a whole lot.'

'We need more. And can you pick up some more tinned tuna and eggs while you're there?'

Duly noted. 'Anyway, how was your day?' It was a struggle to sound interested. There was something about short and long muscle fibres and his BMI, but by then Honey had drifted off. She needed to put more pressure on the Chinese student leaders. She was sure they knew something they weren't saying.

'Managed to get in 12 k at lunchtime. Resting pulse rate is 56.'

'Great. Look, I might just read through these. Night.'

It was like having a self-obsessed flatmate with a limited outlook and no interest in her whatsoever. A part of Honey quite liked it. When she'd jokingly complained to Michelle about being a triathlon widow, her friend reminded Honey they were way overdue for a girls' night out.

'DAMN THAT CREEPY MO-FO! I swear I am going to shove an office chair down his throat!' Michelle and Honey were at a window table of a faux olde English pub with a waterfront view, already into their second bottle of pinot gris. It was the kind of muggy February night in Auckland where you didn't so much breathe the air as drink it.

The Viaduct would not have been Honey's choice, but Michelle vibed the general sense of desperation. She said it made her feel better about herself. And Michelle was right — Honey needed to get out more. Sitting at home reading files that catalogued the worst humanity had to offer was not healthy.

'Robbo is such a tool.' Michelle was a civilian data inputter in the police's File Management Centre, or as she put it, an *un*glorified typist. She was venting about her supervisor. 'A fucking A-grade absolute shit-for-brains tool. And he tried it on at the Christmas party, dead set. I would rather eat my own anus,' she said, matter-of-factly.

Nights out with Michelle were always entertaining. And exhausting. She was gorgeously excessive in every way. She was also tragically and dramatically single. Unlike Honey, Michelle was kept awake by the ticking of her biological clock. Her last serious relationship had ended when she'd finally realised he was serious when he said he didn't want kids. Two years later he was hooked up with someone else and expecting their first child.

'Let's go to karaoke after this!' Michelle glanced around in disgust at the room full of twenty-something men in striped cotton shirts and chinos. 'I don't know why I ever let you bring me to this shit-hole.' She sighed. 'They're all about twelve and anyway I'd break them. Fuck the wine, we need tequila. Line 'em up!'

Then things got hazy. A strange little honeycomb of rooms somewhere off Queen Street. A bored old Korean guy who took their money and sold beer and terrible wine. They crashed someone's party. Michelle — Pasifika's answer to Adele — broke the ice with 'Rolling in the Deep'. Honey remembered performing a passable rendition of 'Hotel California'. At some point there was 'Stayin' Alive', which Michelle performed in perfect sync with two gay guys Honey vaguely thought she might have seen on a local soap back when she was at Police College and desperate for something to talk about with the other women.

Around 3 a.m. Honey poured Michelle in a taxi and dropped her home. At last she crawled into bed beside Tony. Twenty minutes later her phone rang. Tony groaned theatrically and rolled over, but Honey couldn't summon the will to get out of bed again. The phone kept ringing.

'Are you going to get that?' he said.

The phone stopped. Then it started again.

'Honey Chalmers,' she croaked.

'You didn't answer your phone.'

'Sorry?'

'I tried calling earlier. You didn't answer.' Honey's mystery caller was back.

'Yeah, I was out somewhere . . . loud.'

There was a long pause. Honey could feel herself falling. 'Look, it's really late, early or whatever, can I help you?'

'They put off the meeting, the one I was telling you about. Some shit went down, the ship was delayed or cancelled or something.'

Honey struggled to drag herself back. 'You're talking about the meeting between the Knights and the Reapers?'

'Yeah.' She sounded pissed off.

She wasn't the only one. Tony stalked out of the bedroom taking his pillow with him.

'Look, no offence, but I've got no reason to believe you actually know anything of interest to me.' She'd had enough of tiptoeing around. There was a machete in the back of her head.

'I know shit, all right, but I don't know if I want to tell you.' The caller sounded defensive.

'Okay, okay, then how about you give me your first name, that's a start.' For a moment Honey wondered if it would be seriously pushing it if she called out to Tony to bring her some water. She went on: 'I mean, you know my name, right?'

'Kloe,' the caller said at last. 'Your name really Honey?'

'It really is. But what do you want to talk about, Kloe?' She really hoped it was nothing important. She really hoped Kloe would hang up and call another time, preferably during office hours.

'You got kids, Honey?'

'What?'

'Kids, you got any?'

'Er, no, not yet.'

'I wouldn't have nothing if I didn't have my kids. Not that he gives a fuck.'

'You're talking about your, um, husband?'

'Fuck that, woman, we're not married.'

Honey felt like she was having an out-of-body experience.

'You married?' Kloe sounded like she was settling in for a chat over a cuppa at the kitchen table.

'No, but I have a partner.' The partner on the couch probably not thinking kind thoughts.

'Bet he doesn't give you the bash.'

'No, he doesn't.' Although she couldn't guarantee he wasn't wishing it. Still, Kloe was giving her an opening, and she took a tentative step through it.

'Is that what your fella does, hit you?' She tried to sound sympathetic but not judgemental.

'Sometimes. Not tonight . . . I . . . It's not about that.'

'Because if he does, I could recommend somewhere . . .'

'Are you not listening, bitch? I said it's not about that. What kind of cunt doesn't come to his own kids' school concert?'

Honey strangled back a laugh. Was she really having this conversation?

21

'They were real good, too. The youngest, she's only six, but she looked wicked dressed like a fairy in a costume my eldest girl made her, real feathers on the wings and everything, dancing in a circle with the other girls, and my boy and his mates did this rap, sunglasses, arms crossed, talk about a crack-up. We was all of us laughing and crying, but where the fuck was my old man? Down the pub, playing on the pokies, fuck knows. Wouldn't care myself but the kids were expecting him and he let 'em down, like always.'

It took a moment for Honey to realise that Kloe had finished her story. It was now 4.23 a.m. She was going to have to suck up to Tony so bad.

Kloe interrupted her thoughts. 'Anyway, I better let you go.'

'Hang on. Kloe?'

'Yeah, I'm still here.'

'Was there anything else?'

'Nah.'

Honey could hear the hiss and crackle of the tobacco as Kloe drew back, the elongated sigh as she exhaled.

'Yeah, nah. That meeting I told you about? Just found out it's happening tomorrow arvo out at this warehouse place the Reapers've got. Out Ōnehunga.'

KLOE PUT THE PHONE DOWN, and stayed in her usual place on the back step, smoking and watching the vid of the kids' performances again on her phone. She was proud fit to burst and was pleased to have her new friend to talk about it with. Okay, she was pigshit, but her name was Honey. You had to love that.

Still, she hadn't been entirely honest. She'd known about the meeting for weeks. She hadn't intended to say anything, but fuck 'em, fuck Jason, how dare he not come to his own kids' performance. She'd make him sorry.

HONEY WANDERED THROUGH FOR WATER and to find her notebook while she could still remember the gist. She'd have to call Spud first thing. The thought of it made her groan. She went back to bed and died until 6.30 when Tony came through to the bedroom and very noisily got his sports stuff together for his Saturday training regime.

At 7.30 Honey let Spud know about the call. He sighed theatrically. He was supposed to be taking his kids to rugby. But he said it concerned him that none of their usual sources had wind of any meeting. Maybe this Kloe person was taking the piss? Honey had to admit it was possible. She was just passing on what the woman had said; it really wasn't her problem. Spud admitted the bit about a Reapers warehouse in Ōnehunga was correct. He kept her on the line while he thought it over. Finally, he decided on limited covert surveillance, on the off chance.

It would be a couple of weeks before Honey learned it was Kloe with a K. Eventually she would know way more about Kloe Kovich than she ever wanted to.

4

DINING OUT IN WAITUTŪ MEANT one of two places. There were a couple of tables at the Chinese takeaway, but it wasn't licensed so that didn't count. There used to be a halfway decent Indian place, but that had closed along with the haberdashery and the hippie crystal and bead place where teenage Honey took a five-finger discount while her little sister gazed at the dreamcatchers. Now half the main street was for lease. After the plague, the floods had been the final straw.

The pub did a tolerable roast of the day, but it was Friday night, and that meant an eighties covers band, under-aged kids hanging around trying to get in on their older siblings' ID, the odd hippie dancing ostentatiously, a few middle-aged couples determined not to stay at home with a movie again, and a sad parade of single men wandering between the lounge bar and the pokies before finally buying a box of premix and heading back solo to the safety of the bush, bach or farm. Too loud for Rachel, still too raw for Honey.

That left the Waitutū Centenary Golf Club. Breeze block, low ceiling, cream-painted walls and mission-brown trim, a good view of the course through the ranch sliders on the hardwood deck, a grill counter where meals were ordered and a row of stainless-steel salad containers sat under clear plastic covers. The dark-timber bar dominated the wall closest to the entrance. Honey thought the place reflected the character of the town. It was basic, functional, and little money had been wasted on unnecessary comforts. And after three weeks dining with her mother on anything just so long as it was cooked in coconut oil and involved turmeric, garlic and whatever else the long-lived, Alzheimer's-free inhabitants of a certain Indian village ate, a surf'n'turf or serviceable pasta of the day was appealing.

Thanks to Rachel's status they were given a table with a view, and Honey had to admit the golf course looked gorgeous in the sunset. All golden-green and impressionistic. Beyond the course was a stand of rewarewa; beyond that, the river that gave Waitutū its name wound its way to the untameable sandbar across its mouth. It was the sandbar that had prevented the town from becoming a major trading port and consigned it to inevitable decline after the closing of the meat works.

Honey had plenty of time to admire the view as locals paid homage to Rachel. None was the least bit curious about her own life outside of Waitutū. It used to infuriate her on her occasional trips home. She would dutifully enquire about old friends' work and marriages and building projects and boats and offspring and pets for god's sake, and in return they'd tell her how glad she must be to be home.

'Nobody gives a fuck about anything that happens outside Waitutū and they certainly don't give a fuck about me!' she'd complained to her mother. She was a few years out of Police College and on the fast track to promotion.

'Nonsense, they're always asking after you.'

'Then how come they don't ask *me*?'

'Because they ask me.'

Now Honey appreciated her sort-of anonymity. People didn't ask. She didn't tell.

Given recent events, that was a win.

SHE WAS WAITING TO ORDER another beer when he appeared on her left, resting dark, muscular and heavily tattooed forearms on the bar.

'Kia ora. How's it going?'

It took a moment. 'Marshall, oh my god. Hi.'

Oh, my fucking god I don't believe it! was what she meant. The last time she'd seen Marshall was at her sister's funeral thirteen years ago.

'Long time, no see.' It was an effort to keep her voice casual.

'Sure is.' His voice was deeper, slower, different. He reminded her of someone else. He grinned. 'To state the fucking obvious.'

Honey smiled back, relieved. He sounded like the Marshall she remembered.

'Rumour has it, you're the Po Po.'

'Rumour is correct.'

'Fuck me.'

'Not if you paid me,' she retorted, an old joke, a reflex.

He laughed — a machine-gun in the back of the throat laugh that was very distinct, very familiar. Honey was fifteen again.

She finally managed to get the barmaid's attention. Marshall insisted he buy her beer as well as his own.

'I heard you were back looking after your mum,' he said quietly, nodding over to where Rachel was holding court with Ganesh Bhana, a science teacher from the area school.

'Yeah, I guess I am.' She shrugged. 'Although she's okay most of the time.'

'That's good then.'

'Yeah.'

They both sipped their beers.

'You were shacked up with a doctor, yeah?'

'A specialist, actually. Tony.' Part of her was pleased he was interested, part of her wondered how he knew. She doubted her mother would give Marshall the time of day.

'Ooh, get you.'

'But not anymore.'

'That good or bad?'

'It is what it is.'

They sipped their beers again in comic unison.

'How long have you been back?' Honey said at last.

'A while. Been staying out at the old place. Don't come to town much.' He glanced around the room. 'Haven't been *here* for a long, long time.'

Honey could feel the patrons on either side at the crowded bar straining to keep their distance.

'I was sorry to hear about your dad.'

She'd been doing a postgraduate forensics course in Canberra when she heard Marshall's father had died, but she probably wouldn't have come to the funeral anyway. Way too much water.

'Yeah, well, he'd been crook for a while,' he said. 'Stubborn old bugger wouldn't see a doctor.' He shook himself. 'I heard about Ron, too. Bet your mum was gutted.'

She shrugged. 'You know Rachel.'

'Keep calm and carry on?'

'That's the one.'

He looked at her closely for a moment. 'Fuck it's good to see you.'

'You too, Marshall.'

He laughed his rat-a-tat laugh and looked away again. She could tell he was as uncomfortable in the surroundings as the surroundings were with him and wondered if he had deliberately sought her out. She took a sideways glance at him. Marshall Keller was exactly one year and one week older than her, something she knew for a fact because they had shared birthdays when they were growing up. He was more solid now, and broad of shoulder. His dark hair was cropped short and just beginning to recede, and his face had a weathered, outdoor look, with fine lines around his eyes. He reminded her of someone else, not Marshall, as if he'd grown away from himself.

Over the years Honey had heard snippets and rumours: he'd been in the army, he'd been to prison, he was married, he'd moved to Oz. Maybe all or none of the above were true.

'Heard you got done over, really bad,' he said softly, finally breaking the silence.

'Yeah, pretty bad.' Her eyes met his. He had been a part of her life that had gone on forever until it hadn't. 'Actually, I died.' Playing it cool. As if *the incident* hadn't changed everything.

'No shit? In the line of duty, right?' Concern in those brown eyes with gold flecks.

'Yeah, I guess you could say that.'

Then he grinned. 'Did you see a light at the end of the tunnel?'

'Turned out it was just a train coming the other way.' Another old, shared joke.

'Something like that happens, kind of makes you realise how fragile you are, how ... temporary ... everything is, eh? Can be kind of liberating.' He was still smiling but his eyes were serious now. Honey guessed he was speaking from experience.

In the years between eight and seventeen, Honey couldn't imagine her life without Marshall in it. Best mate, big brother she never had; after her father left, the only significant male in her life. Then he went south, to Otago University to study medicine, assisted by an iwi scholarship, having somehow pulled out all the stops in his final year of school while she was distracted partying and behaving badly. She'd been left behind, had a god-awful final school year before escaping north to Auckland. They'd sworn they'd stay in touch. That arrangement lasted until Honey's first serious boyfriend. Fault on both sides.

Meantime, Honey had heard from her mother — insert heavy disapproval here — that Marshall and her sister Scarlett had hooked up during one of his visits home from university. Honey had mixed feelings. Part of her was delighted, genuinely; another part peeved that he had chosen her sister over her. At the time she was living with a guy she thought she loved, an angst-ridden musician, her first crack at cohabiting.

Then seventeen-year-old Scarlett Chalmers air-walked off the South Head cliffs and everything changed.

'I should probably let you get back to your mum.' Marshall nodded to the table where Rachel was now sitting alone, glancing around as if uncertain where she was or what she was supposed to be doing.

'She does that, goes in and out. One moment she's fine, next . . .'

Marshall nodded. 'It was great to see you, Honey.'

'You too.' She started to move off, turned back. 'Call me, we can have a proper catch-up.' She held out her hand, and he looked at it as if confused, as if she wanted him to shake it.

'Your phone, dummy, give it to me. I'll put my number in.'

'Great, except I don't have a phone.'

'You are kidding me?'

'I'm kind of off the grid.'

Immediately Honey's cop brain wondered what or who he was hiding from. She reached into her bag, found a pen and wrote her number down on a coaster.

'WHERE HAVE YOU BEEN?' RACHEL asked when Honey sat down.

'I was talking to Marshall. You remember Marshall?' She nodded towards the bar where he was draining the last of his glass. There was still a vacuum around him.

'Of course I remember Marshall,' Rachel said. But she looked bewildered. 'That's not Marshall. It's his uncle. That terrible man.'

'No, that's Marshall, but he does look a bit like his Uncle Jim.'

They watched as Marshall put his glass down, gave a nod in their direction and headed out.

'Why would you talk to him, after what he did to Scarlett?'

'Mum, don't start.'

'He treated her like dirt, and she couldn't live with the pain he caused her!' Rachel was getting louder; people were glancing over in their direction.

'No, Scarlett made her own choices. He was as cut up as anyone. More.'

'What the fuck would you know, you weren't even here, you slut!'

'Mum!'

Rachel stopped.

'It's okay, I know you didn't mean it,' Honey said. 'Shall we order dessert?'

'I think I'd like to go home now.'

But Rachel had not been completely wrong. Something *had* happened between Scarlett and Marshall. He'd barely talked to Honey at the funeral and left immediately after. That was the last time she had seen him, until tonight.

She collected her bag and stood to leave, but Rachel was staring out the window. Honey knew her mother would never blame anyone for Scarlett's death half as much as she blamed herself. Maybe that was the perverse blessing in her disease. One day she would forget.

5

THREE DAYS LATER, MARSHALL STILL hadn't called. Honey lay on her back on a lumpy pull-out bed in her old bedroom that now doubled as Rachel's sewing and out-of-sight-out-of-mind storage space, and listened to dogs and chainsaws and trucks with busted mufflers, thinking how everything sounded so much louder in the country. *Fuck this for a game of soldiers.*

She kicked off the investigation by booking her Mini Clubman in for a service.

Wiremu was the gossip el primo, his garage the Central Intelligence Agency of Waitutū.

He was contemplating pies in the warmer when she arrived at 8 a.m., chose steak and onion and put it away with half a dozen bites as they chatted about the weather (nice when it's not raining), the fishing (big concerns the government was going to declare a marine reserve) and local politics (the community divided on the need for speed bumps on the road outside the school).

Wiremu didn't do any mechanical work himself; the thought of him squeezing his body under a car was as amusing as it was unlikely. That service was provided by Malcolm, a thin, stooped Brit with a greasy ponytail. Rumour had it Malcolm had been a sought-after session musician in London before something broke him and he eventually washed up in Waitutū. Now he drank rum and Coke alone in a rough bush hut where trampers sometimes heard a saxophone wailing along to jazz classics.

'How's your mum doing?' asked Wiremu, inevitably.

'Yeah, good, most of the time.'

He waited for details.

'We went up to the club the other night. Saw Marshall Keller there.' She dropped this casually, like berley off the side of a boat.

She wasn't disappointed. Wiremu looked like a concerned gummy shark.

'Well, that's a surprise. How'd your mum take it?'

'Not that well. She seems really down on him, even after all this time.'

He nodded sagely. 'Some wounds will never heal.'

'You know what?' She said it casually. 'I didn't even realise she still blamed him. I mean, I knew there was something going on, but we never talked about it after Scarlett . . .'

'Your mother's a bit of a closed book, but there's a lot going on between the lines.'

Honey waited. Wiremu did not disappoint.

'You know your sister went to see Marshall the day she . . . passed?'

'No, I didn't. I don't think anyone ever mentioned it.'

'Didn't come out until later. Janice and Ian Scott saw poor Scarlett crossing their fields, and Janice asked her if she was okay. Scarlett said she was looking for Marshall at his Uncle Jim's place. Janice said she was quite upset. If only they'd known . . . but you don't, do you.'

There was absolutely nothing wrong with Wiremu's recall of events from more than thirteen years ago. Honey felt a stab of shame. Her own memory of the days surrounding her sister's death was much less acute.

'We've got no way of knowing if she actually saw him,' Wiremu continued, 'but it seems the poor girl was still stuck on Marshall and went to see him to plead for a second chance and he turned her away — at least that's what most people think.'

Honey wanted to steer him back to the present. She tossed off a little more bait. 'To be honest, he was the last person I expected to see at the club.'

'I'd be surprised if Marshall Keller got a warm reception anywhere in this town, except maybe the marae. He was spotted there mucking in after the floods, so perhaps he stays in contact with his mother's people.' He sniffed. 'Who was he with?'

'No one. We had a drink and then he left.'

'You had a drink with *him*?'

'Just the one. He said he was living out at his dad's old place.' She fished a little more. 'Must be lonely out there on his own.'

'Well, he's got no one to blame but himself. Him and his uncle both, they were never the kind we wanted around here. And Marshall with all that iwi scholarship money — a lot of good that did anyone, and what has he got to show for it? A prison record!'

'I think I knew that. What did he go to prison for?'

'It was over Western Australia. Someone said it was for violent assault, but I don't know for certain.' An uncharacteristic gap in intelligence. 'Couldn't you find something like that out with your connections?'

'Not without a good reason.' She was tempted to add that the force frowned upon the use of the police resources for gossip but instead moved the discussion on. 'Where's his Uncle Jim these days?'

'Up at the hospital, in hospice. Lung cancer. I'm surprised Marshall didn't mention it. They say it's in his liver and spine and everywhere else. I want to say I'm sorry, but to be honest I can't find it in me.'

Honey knew that Wiremu was a happy clapper: there was a flier for his tithe-grabbing church in the window. Not very Christian after all, she thought, even if he was a useful one-man Google when it came to local knowledge.

It was a relief to see Malcolm pulling up in his battered ute, giving her an excuse to move. 'I won't need the car until tomorrow,' she said over her shoulder. She had plans.

HALF AN HOUR LATER, HONEY was running steadily along the firm sand at the low-tide water's edge. Her playlist was mostly indie country: Lucinda Williams, Ryan Adams, the obligatory Townes, Cat Powers and Wilco with some Johnny Cash from his Americana series, and a nod to Marlon Williams' almost too-good-to-be-real voice. She had a light running pack with a drinking bladder containing two litres, and some energy bars. Marshall's place was roughly a half marathon in distance, and if she kept up a reasonable pace she could be there in a bit over two hours. If he wasn't home to give her a lift back, the return run might be considerably slower.

It struck Honey as one of life's ironies that she'd been so rude to Tony about his tightly structured training regimes. She'd always kept fit, though in a slipshod, magpie kind of way. One year taekwondo, the next gym circuits, then she fell in love with boxing. But she'd spent her convalescence in a much more ordered way. Her physio had built a programme for her, and she'd stuck to it. Another irony: she was fitter than she'd ever been, despite losing a bucket of blood and a few centimetres of her bowel. After the initial crisis when her heart had stopped, it was the peritonitis that nearly killed her. Having to deal with her own shit was how she liked to put it. There wasn't a day now when her body didn't hurt, but she'd come to appreciate it like an annoying but consistent workmate.

As she settled into her run, she picked over what she had learned from Wiremu. It was senseless, tragic, that Scarlett had felt her only option was to kill herself, but she wasn't going to blame a twenty-two-year-old Marshall. Not based on current evidence. God knows, if she were held accountable for all the dumb decisions she'd made, she'd be judged just as harshly. But now she knew what the locals thought of him, Honey felt guilty for not having made more of an effort to stay in touch. She hadn't tried hard enough to talk to him at Scarlett's funeral, assuming there'd be time for a catch-up over a bottle of vodka later. Instead, he disappeared, and she went back to her city life. Meeting him again made her realise what she'd been missing. No one knew her essential self the way Marshall did. Even Michelle only knew the grown-up Honey, and in her secret heart Honey wasn't sure how real that woman was.

As a child, Honey had found it tough relating to other girls. They seemed to think differently, speak a different language. She'd had girlfriends, usually temporary ones from the camping grounds, but they never stuck. Her mother used to say she was a tomboy, but Honey thought most boys incredibly annoying. With Marshall it was different. There was no need to talk if they didn't feel like it. They'd sit for hours fishing off the wharf in companionable silence. They were even convinced they could communicate through ESP. And when she was eleven, Marshall saved her life.

After her husband left, Rachel intended to sell his boat but hadn't got around to it and instead rented it to another local. So

Honey — in an obvious expression of grief — decided to take the boat out and lay some pots. But the motor had stalled, the wind was picking up, and the boat was being blown towards the rocks of the South Heads. She began to panic. She wasn't sure if she should put on a lifejacket and abandon the boat or keep trying to start it and hope. Finally she gave up and jumped overboard and tried to strike out for shore. But the tow had other ideas, sapping her strength. She felt herself being dragged towards the rocks where her father's boat had already foundered. The lifejacket was barely keeping her afloat and she was spluttering and coughing as she took in mouthfuls of seawater.

Marshall, by some sixth sense, glanced out to sea from his uncle's shed where he was supposed to be repairing a net but was in reality strumming on his guitar. Within minutes he was racing towards her in his uncle's old runabout. Moments later he hauled her aboard. He told everyone that her dad's boat had broken free from its moorings and that he and Honey had tried unsuccessfully to save it. Later, Honey learned that his Uncle Jim had given him a thrashing for taking his tinnie. But Marshall stuck to the story and she knew he would never betray her.

She'd dined out on that story all through her twenties. Tales from her wild youth. Men usually felt the need to chip in with their own stories of danger and bravery. But women would nearly always ask, 'What happened to him, to your hero?'

'You know what? I have no idea,' she'd say with an exaggerated shrug, aware that it was a deeply unsatisfying coda. 'We just lost contact.'

So, she stopped telling the story and didn't think about it for years. Until she told it to Kloe Kovich.

'YOU STILL AWAKE?'

She was. Binge-watching a French thriller full of impossibly gorgeous cops. There was no danger of waking Tony. He'd shifted out the last of his stuff over the Anzac long weekend. Fortunately, the television had been hers. So was the house — another source of great frustration to Tony. He'd wanted her to sell and for them to buy a place together, somewhere more befitting a successful medical specialist, somewhere *not* a shabby Sandringham do-up. Bet he was glad *now* that she hadn't gone along with that little plan.

'What's up, Kloe?'

Kloe Kovich, common-law wife of Jason Curran, a Reapers gang associate, mother of his two kids, as well as her older daughter from a previous.

'Not much. Just feeling a bit, I dunno, like talking to someone — your bad luck it's you, girl.' Kloe gave her raspy laugh. For once Honey didn't mind. 'How's it going with that fella of yours?'

Kloe had by now been calling sporadically over a couple of months and she knew nearly as much about Tony as Honey knew about Jason. Honey knew that to win Kloe's trust she had to share, and it was too easy to trip up with complicated lies, so she stuck as closely to the truth as was comfortable.

'Actually, not so good. He's moved out.' Honey was surprised to hear her own voice catch a little. Damn, she thought Tony was a bit of a tool, but she cared about him. When he'd led with, 'We need to talk,' she wished she'd said it first.

'That's a bit shit.'

'Yeah, well, so it goes.'

'The bastard screwing someone else?' was Kloe's not unreasonable next question.

'Not that I know of.' But Honey had to admit she wasn't sure.

38

'If he was, it would be a recent thing,' she said. 'I think I'd know.'

'Yeah, you always know in your guts. You got to trust your instincts, eh?'

Honey had the impression that Kloe was enjoying the shift in power, feeling like she was the one with her shit together for once, comparatively at least.

'How about you? Jason treating you okay?'

Spud's team had established that Jason, like Kloe, was Kiwi born and ill-bred, had never even been to Australia, was not privy to deep club secrets, but he was still the best way in they had. There were rumours that the Reapers/Knights arrangement had been a success and millions of dollars of crystal meth, P for Pure, would soon be hitting the market. The team had encouraged Honey to exploit her connection with Kloe to the hilt.

'Yeah, not too bad. His mum's been a bit crook with this thing, lupus? It can't be cured. You heard of it?'

'Yeah. I think they can treat it these days, though.'

'Drugs make her feel sick as a dog. She's a nice old bird, staunch as. We always got on okay. It's kind of shook Jase, y'know? Knocked the shit out of him. Now he's being real nice. Promised to take the boy fishing down Westhaven on the weekend.'

'Hey, I'm glad to hear it.' And part of Honey meant it, even though she knew it was unlikely Kloe would pass on anything of value when things were sweet between her and Jason.

'Ever been fishing, Honey?'

That was when Honey told her the story of being rescued at sea by her friend.

There was an appreciative silence on the other end of the line when she'd finished.

'Cool story. What happened to your friend?' asked Kloe.

GOOD QUESTION, THOUGHT HONEY AS she continued along the beach at a steady eight to nine ks. Maybe today she'd find out.

6

AN HOUR AND A HALF into her run, and well past cellphone coverage, Honey began to see a flaw in her plan. She wasn't exactly sure where the old house was.

Back in the day, Marshall usually stayed in town, closer to school, helping his Uncle Jim with the boat and fishing-related chores. Honey remembered a dark, poky dump, with a longdrop out the back and a wood stove that had to be lit whenever hot water was required. Electricity came courtesy of an old diesel generator, but diesel cost and it was rarely used. Marshall's father Walter was an odd, suspicious man, a German-born wanderer who finally put down his roots in the back blocks of Waitutū. He was already middle aged when Marshall was born and had always seemed ancient to Honey.

Marshall's mother had died of meningitis when he was three. It was her family land the house was built on, but Walter had fallen out with them as well.

Honey kept returning to thoughts of Scarlett and Marshall together. They would have made a gorgeous couple. With her black wavy hair and dark eyes, Scarlett could've had Māori ancestry herself, much more so than pale, freckled Honey. In fact, their paternal grandma was reliably rumoured to have had an *understanding* with a Māori/Norwegian merchant seaman, which would mean they were around one-sixteenth to one-thirty-second tangata whenua, as Marshall had once calculated.

Honey recalled staying over with Marshall and some of his

mates only once when his dad was away. She couldn't remember what she'd told her mother. No doubt some overly complicated story of staying at a fictional girlfriend's holiday bach. They'd drunk cider and told ghost stories by lantern light and later when she'd gone out for a pee round the back Gary McDermott had tried it on with her. She let him feel her breasts, it seemed only fair, he'd been trying so hard all night. She thought she saw a flicker of jealousy on Marshall's face when they returned, but she might've been imagining it. Poor Gary McDermott, dead at nineteen, his prized Subaru wrapped around a tree.

Oh, well, thought Honey, if it comes to the worst and I can't find the house, I'll just turn around and head back. In the meantime, the morning clouds were breaking up and the sun pushed through. She stopped to skinny dip in a sandy little cove fringed by low-hanging pōhutukawa. The sea was bracingly cold and clear, nothing like the murky *E. coli*-infected waters of Auckland Harbour. As she stood waiting to drip-dry enough to put on more sunblock, she heard and then saw a pair of tūī crashing around in a clump of flax, and felt something inside of her give. She laughed out loud and then felt like crying. It took her a moment to analyse the feeling. Pure joy. She was finally happy to be back. Maybe she should put an announcement in the *Bay Advocate*.

She glanced down at the scars from the knife on her belly, more dramatic but less bothersome now than the ones around her spine. You're one fucked unit, she thought. Her mind threatened to go back *there* but she willed herself to stay in the present. *Not today, buddy.*

Honey decided to play it safe and cut along a track away from the sea until she found the road. Fifteen minutes of steady slogging along the rutted gravel and she was confused. There was just a turn-off to a track that wound inland through thick mānuka and kānuka scrub towards some hills in the distance which looked vaguely familiar.

Where twenty years ago an old piece of pipe served as a letterbox, now there were a couple of beautiful, scary, carved pou on either side, humanlike figures with extended tongues, and mere and other traditional weapons in hand, and repeated swirls and the familiar fern-leaf motif. Honey walked quickly between them and down the track. If it was the wrong place, she could always ask.

A couple of hundred metres further along and the scrub opened to reveal a green paddock leading up to the cottage. A battered grey Land Cruiser with a flat wooden tray was parked out front. To one side was a well-cared-for veggie garden and small glasshouse; to the other an orchard of fruit and olive trees. Hens and ducks wandered the orchard, where Honey could see a couple of tethered goats. It was the old house, but not as she knew it. The tin roof was painted forest green, and there were timber-framed skylights and an array of solar panels. The old fibro walls had been replaced with freshly painted weatherboard. The steps leading to the veranda and deck were wide and solid, unlike the narrow rickety ones she remembered. A chimney made of large blue-grey stones set in concrete was built into one corner wall. What had she been expecting? A hovel? Somewhere she could come riding to the rescue? She slowed and then stopped.

In her head it had all been so simple; now she was having serious doubts she had any right to even be here. If she had driven her car, she might have turned around, put it off to another day or never. Then a figure in shorts and singlet came around the side of the house, looking at her quizzically, and that settled it.

'YOU RAN ALL THE WAY here?' Marshall shook his head as he handed her a mug of black tea.

'Most of the way, yeah,' she said lightly. 'It's not that far.'

'If you say so.' He sipped his tea and regarded her over the rim of a mug that read 'Fuck I Needed That'.

'Well, since you haven't bothered calling,' she added.

'Told you, I don't have a phone and I haven't been back to town. Anyway, I kind of lose track of time out here. There's a lot to do.'

'Yeah, yeah, excuses, excuses.' She could have left it there, but why pretend? 'Talking to you the other night, it made me realise how much I've missed you.'

For a moment he looked like he was going to agree, but then he stopped himself, turned away, mumbled, 'You want something to eat? You must've burned up a truckload of calories.'

Her cop brain noted the change of subject.

'What've you got?' Her eyes met his, a playful challenge.

What he had was the most delicious sourdough bread Honey had ever tasted, along with golden butter, fresh goat's cheese, honey, sundried tomatoes in olive oil, garlicky black olives, dill gherkins, the freshest salad, boiled eggs and slices of mānuka-cured ham. When pressed, Marshall admitted he'd made the bread himself, and that he'd grown, made and/or preserved nearly everything else on their plates.

He sounded embarrassed and Honey could understand why. The Marshall she'd known lived on fish and chips and burgers sans tomato and lettuce. It was a disconcerting reminder that although she'd known nearly everything about the early years of Marshall's life, she knew next to nothing about the years since. Apart from the fact he'd picked up some very useful skills.

She stood up and moved towards the solidly built wooden bookcases that covered two of the living-room walls. She was conscious of Marshall watching her.

'Still hard to believe you're a cop. Do they actually know who you are?'

'I guess they're not fussy,' she said lightly, wondering if she knew him at all.

She was relieved to see familiar signs: old hard-covered copies of the complete works of Conrad and Hardy stood in a neat row with some shabby paperback thrillers and books of a nautical nature. Shipbuilding, navigation and the history of the Pacific all comfortably belonged in the known world of Marshall. But they were surrounded by intruders, books on building your own eco home, growing vegetables in Aotearoa, home handyman hints, curing your own meat, fermentation, cooking and eating for health and for pleasure, and a series called 'The Great Philosophers'. There was almost an entire row dedicated to Māori culture, history and language, right next to books on yoga, meditation and tai chi.

'Have you had enough to eat?'

'Yes, thanks, that was amazing.'

Marshall started clearing up the plates, putting the open food away.

'A real renaissance man, I see.' Her tone was joking but she was impressed to the point of feeling inadequate. Her own shelves contained books and periodicals on forensic science, the law, policing and the occasional chick lit novel borrowed from Michelle. A thought crossed her mind that someone else was involved. She'd already spotted a yoga mat rolled up in the corner. But the rest of the house lacked any touches she would have called overtly feminine.

'Is this all your own work?' she said, forcing casualness.

'All mine,' Marshall said, stacking the plates back up on an elegant timber drying rack that hung above the sink. 'Doesn't mean I've actually read them all. Maybe I'm just doing a "Great Gatsby" — y'know, uncut pages, all for show.'

'You see, the fact you know that's a "Great Gatsby" is in itself disturbing.'

Marshall looked up at her for a moment. 'Why are you here, Honey?'

'Do I need an excuse?'

'I dunno. Yeah, maybe.'

She thought he looked pissed off, distraught even. But was it with himself or with her?

'Fine, I can just go if you like. Thanks for the lunch, it's been *real*.' She was amazed at the sudden intensity of her anger. She grabbed her pack, adding tartly, 'Okay if I fill up my water first?'

'Go for your life,' he said, but lightly, and she looked back to see he was smiling.

'Oh, yeah, friggin' hilarious. Laugh, I nearly started.' She tried to sound scathing but just felt foolish.

'Fuck me, the look on your face, priceless.'

'Yeah, well, I thought you were going to cry like a baby, so, whatever.'

'Whatever? What are you, fifteen?'

She glared at him. He moved towards her, arms held open in supplication.

'Look, I'm sorry, it's just I wasn't expecting you and it's been so long and it was so fucking crazy at the club the other night, I could feel everyone wishing me bad. I shouldn't've even gone in, but I was driving past, and I saw you going in with your mum and

I thought, What the hell. It seemed like a good idea at the time . . .' He gave a wry shrug. 'Like most dumb ideas do.'

'No, I was glad you did.'

'Really?'

'Yes really, you idiot.'

Marshall looked so relieved that Honey felt like crying.

'Now come here and give me a hug!'

She let herself sink into him for a long moment. When they finally broke and looked at each other, their cheeks were glistening.

'Oh my god, you're bawling, that is so gay.' She gave him a playful shove to cover her confusion.

'No, Honey,' he said sternly, 'I think you'll find that when two men — or women — are in love or have sex, that's gay. When two people hug and cry to express their feelings openly and honestly, they could be gay but not necessarily.'

'Stop it, you're scaring me now.' She was only half joking. His closeness was disconcerting.

'Got anything to drink?'

He smiled. 'Funny you should ask.'

They sat on the veranda, drinking homebrewed apple and pear cider from their mugs.

'At least you haven't gone all wowser on me,' Honey said. 'This is really good.'

'Actually,' he said, 'I gave it up for a few years, even joined AA.'

'The Automobile Association?'

'Nope, the real deal. Kia ora, my name is Marshall and I'm an alcoholic.' He smiled, and it took her a moment to see he wasn't joking. 'But all that higher power stuff annoyed me, even though I know it really works for some people. For me, not so much. In the end I understood my problem wasn't the booze, it was the reasons I drank.'

Honey got the feeling he was struggling with how much to tell her. She gave him a little push. 'Oh yeah. For example?'

Marshall regarded his cup for a moment. 'Let's not put that shit on such a beautiful day.'

Honey filed it away. She had to agree: it was a beautiful day and not just because she was hanging out with her old buddy in paradise with a cider glow on. A few white clouds hung over the hills, but the sky was an intense southern blue and a nice breeze leavened the warmth from the sun.

'Okay, so the last eighteen years, give me the headline notes,' she said. 'Or is that going to shit on our parade too?'

'Maybe.'

'You could just tell me the good bits but that would be boring.'

Marshall grinned but was starting to move. 'More cider?'

'Hang on, mister, we need to get ourselves reacquainted before I'm gonna let you get me drunk.'

'Okay.' He sighed heavily and sat back down. 'First of all I have to say this.' He stopped, and she could see him almost trying out different words in his mouth. 'I wasn't sleeping with Scarlett. I mean, we were close, but we didn't have a relationship, not like that.'

'But ...' He'd gone straight to the point, as if he knew her secret, wicked heart.

'I know what everyone says, but it's not true,' he said, holding her gaze. 'A few months before she ... I was back home on semester break. Uncle Jim was away, and I had his place to myself and I was intending to hole up there and swot. Scarlett started dropping around. I didn't mind. She'd just sit and sketch or read or listen to

48

my music on her headphones. One night we got a bit drunk, and she told me she was being hassled at school by the other girls and that her mum was giving her a hard time, and she showed me . . .' He broke off, searching for the right words. 'She'd been cutting herself, self-harming. I told her she needed to get help, to talk to someone, and she looked at me strange — you know that slightly crossed-eyed look she had — and said, "But I have got someone, I've got you."

'It was kind of intense, but I felt for her. It's hard being the odd one out in a place like Waitutū. Anyway, the night before I was due to head back down south, I went out for a few drinks with some mates. When I came home, she was in my bed, naked. I told her it wasn't right, she was too vulnerable, too young, and she cried but eventually said she understood. I just felt fucking relieved, to be honest.'

Honey wondered. Your average twenty-two-year-old red-blooded boy coming home drunk to a beautiful naked and willing girl wouldn't normally have such iron-clad scruples. But maybe Marshall wasn't average. She decided to park it.

'Okay. So then what?'

'Then . . . I went back down south, to uni. Thought nothing more of it until I started hearing that Scarlett was going around saying that we'd hooked up, that we were in love and so on.'

Honey found herself automatically comparing his story to the known facts. She couldn't find any obvious gaps, but she sensed some missing pieces. At the same time she felt a terrible wave of sadness for Scarlett.

It was cool in the shade of the veranda, but Marshall was sweating now, and wiped his forehead with his tee-shirt. 'Scarlett started sending me poems, drawings, her innermost thoughts.

I tried to be friendly but detached. But she wanted more. Things came to a head when—' He stared into his mug for a moment. 'I let her think I had a girlfriend. It wasn't true — I mean, I had a kind of university fuck buddy but nothing serious. It was just my cowardly way of trying to get Scarlett off my case. She stopped writing and I thought I'd got through to her, but when I came back at the Christmas break she wanted to go on acting like we were a couple. I should've confronted it, but I figured I'd only be in town for a couple of weeks, so I just tried to ignore her. That's when . . .'

Honey could see how it all played out. No wonder he felt so guilty, no wonder he hadn't been able to tell anyone.

'I tried to find you after the funeral, but everyone said you'd already left,' she said, surprised to find the old hurt still lingered.

'Yeah, I was in no state, eh?' He put down his mug. A struggle was going on and Honey was afraid he'd close up again.

'It's okay. With hindsight, shit, we all would've done things differently, but I don't blame you, I want you to know that.' He didn't look convinced, so she resorted to another old gag: 'Look at me, look at me, look at me.'

He did, and she pulled a face. He smiled broadly, and she saw that at least one of his teeth was dentistry. She'd been with him when he'd slipped on the pipe crossing the creek and broken it.

'Yeah, okay, thanks, that means a lot.' He gave himself a shake. 'Enough about me, what about you? How'd you go from wannabe journo to instrument of state oppression?'

'No way, mate. You went back to uni, what next?'

He looked away and stared off over the orchard, anywhere but at her. 'My heart wasn't in medicine. I tried changing majors to English and History, which fucked off everyone and invalidated my scholarship. I was drinking, smoking a lot of weed, wasting

50

everyone's time including my own. So, one day I decided to pull finger and went and signed up.'

It took a moment to register. 'You joined the army?' She'd heard the rumour but never believed it could be true.

'As a medic. Ended up going to Afghanistan.'

'What an incredible experience,' she said, regretting it immediately, hearing how inane she sounded.

'If by incredible you mean opened my eyes to how fucked up the world is in general, and by imperialism and colonialism in particular, then yeah. It *is* amazing to think that the same British Empire that screwed over my country also screwed over that part of the world and everyone's still paying for it.' There was pure anger in his voice.

Of all the conversations Honey had imagined she'd be having with Marshall, this was not one of them.

He took a breath. 'Bugger it, if we're going to do this, I need more cider.' He refilled their mugs. 'Anyway, I did four years, which was more than enough. Then what? A couple of years in Sydney, behaving badly.' He gave a rueful shrug, leaving Honey to fill in the blanks. 'Then I tried to clean up my act by going bush. Ended up in Western Australia. Got some work with a mining company driving heavy machinery.'

'You never thought about coming back home?'

'Couldn't think of a good reason. Shit, there are still people who'd lynch me if they thought they could get away with it. After a couple of years of digging up the outback I'd saved a packet of money, and I was even thinking of buying some land over there.'

'Turning into an Aussie, traitor!'

'You know the Maussie diaspora; first we took Bondi, now we're coming for the rest.' He paused.

'What?' she demanded.

'So anyway—' He put on a lighter sing-song voice that Honey understood was his way of distancing himself from the story. 'I was having a few beers with some mates one night at a back yard barbecue and I decided to walk home. On the way I came across this big white guy beating the shit out some skinny Abo.'

'Are you allowed to call them that?'

'I can, you can't,' he said, po-faced. 'This native son of Australia was only a kid really and this white guy was a bloody rhino. So, I politely suggested that he desist.'

'You know what, I almost believed you up until then.' She smiled.

'Okay, I told him not to be a fucking prick and pick on something his own size, like a fridge. He said the kid had pissed on his car. Literally pissed on it. I said, "Woah, is this your car, bro?" It was a flash Holden Camaro V8, bright yellow, screamed wanker.'

'The kind of car you would've killed for once upon a time.'

'Yeah, when I was that kind of wanker. He said yeah, and so I walked around as if I was admiring it, then I unzipped and started to relieve myself.'

'Classy.' It sounded completely like the Marshall she knew and loved.

'It took a moment for him to realise what I was doing, and the kid took the opportunity to skedaddle. Then the big guy came at me and I hit him. That slowed him down but didn't stop him, so I hit him again.'

'Hang on, was this with or without your cock hanging out of your pants? With us cops, it's all about the details.'

'Now that you mention it, I may also have pissed on his shoes. As I said, I'd had a few beers. Anyway, third hit lucky, and he went down in a heap.'

'I like a happy ending.'

'Yeah, not quite.' Suddenly he dropped the facetious tone. 'I was holding my keys at the time, so they ripped up his face pretty bad.' He paused then for the punchline. 'Turns out the reason the kid was pissing on this car in particular was because he *knew* the guy was one of your mob. A cop.'

'Oh shit.'

'Oh yeah. I got three years. It would have been longer, but this particular cop already had a terrible reputation for First Nation relations.'

Honey was prepared to be outraged on his behalf, but Marshall was strangely chilled.

'You know how people say the worst thing to happen to you can turn out to be the best — well, I wouldn't want to make a habit of it, and sometimes shit is just shit, but in my case, it was the kick up the arse I needed. I met a cool old dude inside, Tamati, and he helped me turn my life around.'

Honey realised she was holding her breath. Was he going to tell her he'd joined some nutty church?

'Long story short, he pushed me to carve, guided me to learn about myself and where I come from. Funny that I had to go all the way to Western Australia to reconnect with my tikanga, but that's what happened.'

He paused and held Honey's eyes for a moment. She felt a stab of what? Jealousy that he'd got his shit together and found his purpose while she was still floundering at home with her mother for fuck's sake? Regret that she'd had no part in his transformation? Small mean thoughts she didn't want to have.

'I did eighteen months, with good behaviour. Oh, yeah, and then I married Tamati's daughter.'

'You're married?' Honey was stunned: the town gossip had been right on the money. And there had been a woman involved in the transformation of Marshall.

'Yeah, her name is Miriama. She's originally from up north.' He grinned. 'One of those scary Ngāpuhi women.'

'That's so great!' Honey hoped she didn't sound disingenuous. 'Where is she now?'

'She fell out of love with me and in love with someone else.' He shrugged. 'Shit happens.'

Honey hoped she looked sympathetic.

'What about you?' he said. 'Got a significant other in your life?'

'Nope.'

'Seriously?'

'It's a long story and we're still talking about you.'

He gave her an amused look, but then continued. 'Western Australia had lost its appeal. Also, you're probably aware the Immigration people are not so kind about us New Zealanders with criminal records . . .'

Honey knew only too well. Her lower back was throbbing. She was overdue her painkillers.

'Anyhow, I came back for Dad's funeral, stayed to sort his shit, then just . . . stayed. Because of the land, because I didn't know what else to do.'

He stopped, waiting for her to say something smart, but Honey was teetering on the edge. Mention, no matter how oblique, of 501 deportees had triggered her to the edge of panic. She took a few deep breaths, steadying herself. For a moment it was like she was outside of herself, watching, irritated that she was unable to control her racing heart.

'You okay?' He reached out and gently touched her arm.

'Some other time, okay?'

'Sure.'

Honey sensed he was relieved it was about her, not him. She drained her cider and looked at the bush, the darkening shadows. A moment of quiet, apart from the sound of goats and chickens and a weird rusty-bedsprings noise from the orchard that she thought might be duck sex. It was enough to bring her back to herself.

Marshall finally broke the silence. 'So now you know way more than you probably wanted to know.'

She shook her head. 'No, but my god, it's all so — wow . . .' She sounded like an idiot, but she was genuinely lost for words.

'Wow?'

'Yes!'

'Which bit?' He was laughing at her.

'All of it, and shut up anyway.' She meant it. It wasn't just the story of the last eighteen years, the edited highlights no doubt; it was that she *knew* it was only the tip of the iceberg. She could sense this huge looming mass below the surface, not in detail, but in essence. She shivered.

'Are you cold?'

'What? No, I'm fine.'

But Marshall was looking over to where the sun had already gone behind the hills. 'What time do you have to get back?' he asked.

'Good point.' Reluctantly she dragged herself back to the here and now, and the fact that Rachel would be worried if she wasn't back in time for dinner. She reached for her phone before realising: 'No reception.'

'Nope.'

'Bugger. I really need to get back to Mum.'

'No problem, I'll give you a lift. Unless you've got your heart set on running it?'

'Thank you, no, a lift would be lovely, sir.'

'Next time I'll cook you a proper meal and you'll tell me your life story and we'll get properly drunk on moonshine vodka.'

'If you say so.'

She really liked the sound of next time.

MARSHALL PULLED UP ONTO THE berm across the road from Rachel's house. It was just a Lockwood and double garage on a quarter acre, but Rachel kept a nice garden, with a bed of roses and some vegetables and an obscenely fecund plum tree out the back. A neighbour mowed the front lawn for her. Honey had a sudden image of playing there under the sprinkler with Scarlett. She wondered if it was a true memory or if she'd mixed it up in her mind with a schmaltzy TV ad for a telco.

'Do you think she's going to have to go into a home, your mum?'

'Unless I put a pillow over her face first.'

'Is that legal?'

A shared smile.

Honey saw the curtains across the road twitch. A couple of vehicles slowed down as they passed. She had no doubt that Wiremu would soon be getting a fresh transfusion of gossip.

They sat in companionable silence a little longer.

'Well,' Marshall said at last.

Honey was pleased at how reluctant he sounded. 'Yep.'

RACHEL HAD MADE A CHICKEN curry, heavy with turmeric and tamarind, which wasn't awful, but Honey couldn't help but compare it with the meal she wasn't having with Marshall.

'How was your day?' she asked. 'Did you get into the garden?' Rachel looked surprised at the question. She didn't reply, concentrated on her food for a moment. Honey suspected she was trying to remember exactly what she had done with her day. Well, no biggie, Honey had had plenty of days like that too. Then Rachel looked back up at her.

'You saw Marshall.' It was a statement, not a question.

'Yes, he's done amazing things to the old house,' Honey ventured. She didn't want to upset her mother again but it seemed wise to lay the groundwork.

'I know you think I'm wrong to blame him for what happened to Scarlett, we all have to take responsibility, but if it hadn't been for him, she'd still be alive.'

'You can't say that.'

'I bloody well can!'

'Mum, please, okay, please, let's just not talk about it.'

They ate the rest of the meal in silence. They watched an old rerun of *Midsomer Murders* and even made their old joke about what a dangerous part of England that was to live in.

Later, Honey was brushing her teeth when she saw her mother in the mirror, watching her from the doorway.

'I am glad you're here, Honey. I know I don't always say so, but I am.'

'Me too, Mum.'

SHE WENT TO BED, HEAD buzzing, feeling lighter, more herself, than she had in years. But as she dug in, turning over Marshall's story, inconsistencies wormed to the surface. The bit about not having had sex with Scarlett, for example. As she replayed it, she saw him hesitate, heard the tone of his voice shift. And when and where had he told Scarlett he was seeing someone else? Dunedin is a long way from Waitutū, and she couldn't imagine him volunteering it over the phone: he was a boy, he would take the course of least resistance unless his hand was forced. Then there was the way he'd rushed over the details about the weeks immediately prior to Scarlett's death. He might not be flat out lying, but she felt there was some serious avoidance going on. But then again, seeing the worst in people was par for the course for a cop. Maybe Marshall had good reasons to hedge around the facts. Sometimes you just don't want to go back.

She tried willing herself to sleep by thinking good thoughts, reviewing moments from the day — the darkly green pōhutukawa reaching from the bleached cliffs towards the sea, boisterous tūī with their flash of blue-green bronze and white poi on their chins, clear salty waters, and a gorgeous green-roofed cottage beneath a startling blue sky. Then she saw herself moving self-consciously under Marshall's gaze and into his embrace. 'Fuck it,' she thought, and quickly masturbated herself into a deep sleep.

7

SHE'S BACK IN HER SANDRINGHAM place and she can hear sounds from out back in the little courtyard garden. She remembers that Kloe has just called — strange because it's mid-morning and Kloe never calls in daylight hours — but she's hung up without speaking. She'd been tempted to call back, but now the sounds out back are getting louder... She should get her arse out of bed and investigate...

HER PHONE WAS BUZZING IN the dark. There was only one person who called her at 4 a.m.

'Kloe, is that you?'

She could hear sobbing.

'Kloe, you need to talk to me. Are you okay?'

'It really fucking hurts.' Her breath was ragged, she was whimpering. 'Think the bastard broke my wrist and now I'm scared he's gonna find me and kill me.'

'Where are you, Kloe?' A long pause.

'Out the back of one of the neighbours.'

'Can you get yourself to the hospital?'

'I'm too fucked to drive and anyway he'll hear me.'

'What about a taxi or an Uber?'

'Are you fuckin' kidding me? I haven't got any money or a card or nothing. I just had to run. Oh, fuck, fuck, I think there's bone poking through, I'm gonna...' The unmistakable sound of gagging and vomiting.

'Kloe?'

'Yeah, yeah, I'm still here.'

'Can you get yourself to a road far enough away from the house so that Jason won't see you?'

'I don't know, maybe. Oh, fuck.'

'Hang on, hang on.' Honey was checking Google Maps. 'What about Te Oho Drive? Can you cut through up the side?'

'Yeah, maybe.'

'I'll meet you on Te Oho Drive in twenty, okay?'

KLOE WAS SLUMPED IN A bus stop, a terrified possum in the car's headlights. When Honey got out to help her into the passenger seat, Kloe apologised for the smell. She'd pissed herself.

It was only a fifteen-minute drive to Middlemore ED. Jason had considerately picked a quiet Tuesday night to stomp all over Kloe, but it was still a couple of hours before she was finally ushered into a cubicle and triaged.

'Good to finally meet you, police lady,' Kloe said when at last the meds were kicking in.

'Likewise,' said Honey, making a mental note to update the photo in Kloe's file.

She had brittle, shoulder-length hair, dark except for yellowing tips from a bleaching that had nearly grown out. Her eyes were dark, narrow, over sharp cheekbones. There was a cluster of pimples around her chin, and she kept her mouth closed when she smiled. Honey guessed it was because her top teeth were missing. It was sobering to remember that Kloe was only a few months older than she was.

While Kloe was having her wrist set and — Honey hoped — a

ward bed prepared, Honey went about trying to find emergency accommodation and organise for Oranga Tamariki to uplift the kids from the house as soon as possible. It was a bugger to be losing her informant, but Honey was pleased with the result. She went back to report the news. Kloe was gone. She'd left a one-word message with the nurse: 'Sorry.'

THEY'RE COMING FOR HER NOW. She's standing in her courtyard, frozen to the spot, urging herself to run and going nowhere. And she knows how it's happened. She'd left Kloe in the car outside the ED for a few minutes while she went in to get help that night. That must've been when she rifled through the glovebox and found the old shopping list Honey had stuffed in there. The shopping list written out on the back of an envelope with her address on it. She'd let Kloe get too close. And now she'd put herself in danger too.

THAT'S WHEN SHE WAKES UP. Back in her old room, in her mum's house, in Waitutū. Hardly able to breathe because she knows exactly what happened next. It's a matter of record.

The bag went over her head.

'What do you know, bitch?' A harsh Australian accent.

'I'm a police officer.'

'We know that, bitch. What do you know?'

'What about?'

A crippling blow to her back made her drop to her knees. A hand twisted the bag and grabbed a fistful of hair.

'Who you been talking to?'

'I don't know what you're talking about!'

'Who told you about the drop-off?'

'What drop-off?'

Another blow, immediate agonising pain in her back. It felt like something had broken. Still she was conscious of trying to work out how many voices there were, any details that could be useful.

'Please, I don't know what you want!'

Another voice in her ear, a different one, softer, a New Zealand accent: 'Go better for everyone if you just tell us, eh?'

'Nothing! I don't know anything!'

She was vaguely aware of knocking in the distance, a voice calling. Not the same soft voice that was whispering in her ear.

'We just need a name. C'mon, no one will know it was you.'

'Listen to me, listen! It's not too late, I haven't seen you, walk away.'

'Fuck this. Do it!' The harsh Australian voice again.

A punch to the guts this time. As it turned out, a knife not a fist.

A sound in the distance. Banging. Someone calling her name. It was Tony come to borrow the camping gear they'd bought together and that she'd refused to let him have. Her car, he said later, was out the front and he'd thought maybe she was in the garden so had gone around the side, calling her name so she wouldn't think he was sneaking around.

It must have been enough to persuade the intruders to cut their losses. They stabbed her in the belly again for the hell of it, and left her for dead. Just dumb luck she wasn't. They took off as they came, via the back gate.

IF YOU'RE BLEEDING OUT AND about to go into cardiac

arrest due to shock exacerbated by blunt force trauma, it's best to be found by a medical professional — at least that was Honey's experience. Poor Tony. As the ex in a recent break-up, he was prime suspect. 'For Christ's sake!' Tony was outraged. 'I saved her life, why would I do that if I wanted to kill her?'

'Last-minute remorse,' suggested the interrogating officer.

'Are you a complete moron?'

It was days until Honey was in any position to confirm Tony's innocence, so he'd had a shit time before the cops worked out they were barking up the wrong tree and moved on. The next most popular theory was that Honey had disturbed a burglar who was known to be operating in the area. Wrong place, wrong time. The cops pulled out all the stops and on the positive side found a guy with a lock-up full of stolen goods. Unfortunately, that suspect also had a watertight alibi, backed by CCTV footage, that he'd been at the Avondale TAB at the time of the home invasion.

Honey knew all this much later, well after death and resurrection. She had watched the tapes of all the interviews, hoping for a clue someone else had missed. But it was academic, because she knew who was responsible. She just couldn't prove it.

Attempted murder of a police officer is big, and her colleagues went hard. In the end, a gang prospect, a young Reaper, coughed to it. But Honey doubted he'd even been there, guessed he'd confessed to earn his patch. Eight years inside and he'd only be twenty-seven when he came out with a fuckload of cred. And he was already in custody and couldn't take credit when Kloe went missing.

That was on Honey.

8

THE MORNING WAS OVERCAST BUT warm with the chance
of a cooler southerly change, showers, or sunshine, or all three. In
other words, typical Waitutū weather. Honey groaned, swung her
legs over and sat on the edge of the bed. Rachel, in her unsentimental
way, had done a big clean-up after her daughter moved out, so there
were no Green Day or Beastie Boys posters Blu-Tacked to the walls
to remind Honey what a wannabe cool kid she had been.

She'd spent a lot of time in this room feeling misunderstood,
hating her mother, her life. Her escape pod was always going to
be journalism. She'd started at Victoria University but couldn't
settle. She dropped out and drifted: crap hospo or office jobs,
Wellington to Auckland, bad choices in men, occasionally
women. The only thing she knew was that she never wanted to
go back to Waitutū. But if you'd told nineteen-year-old Honey
that twenty-four-year-old Honey was going to be a cop, she
would have laughed in your face.

In a strange way, *that* was on Scarlett and maybe even Marshall.

Honey had returned from Scarlett's funeral feeling sad and
guilty about being a terrible sister, upset by her mother's unspoken
accusations, pissed off with Marshall's disappearing act. She broke
it off with the musician once and for all. He left her with an old sofa,
a better taste in music and a mild STD. She began cold-calling ad
placements for a suburban newspaper. She didn't have great work
stories. One night — high, it must be admitted — she saw an ad for
joining the police and, once she'd figured enough time had passed

for the THC to clear her system, she applied. It was a good time for a smart young woman with life experience to join the force. There had been scandals, male cops calling the female colleagues 'front bottoms' and worse. She was a quick student and lucky in her mentors. By thirty she was virtually a veteran Detective Sergeant, and by thirty-four almost an Inspector.

A shadow crossed the room, just a cloud over the sun. Honey rubbed the goosebumps on her arms, told herself to move.

She wandered through to the kitchen in her floppy Felice Brothers tee-shirt and knickers and prepared her stovetop percolator. She'd brought a sack of good coffee with her from Auckland. Call her a JAFA, she didn't care; life without good coffee was a life less lived. She was never an early-morning person and Tony had been so perky and full of his own beans she had wanted to strangle him. Now she found herself wondering about the new Marshall. She suspected he'd be up at sparrow's fart. She also suspected she'd find it in her to forgive him.

Her smile faded. She recalled the hesitation in his voice, the gaps in the narrative. There were at least three sides to this story — Marshall's, town gossip and Scarlett's. The truth probably lay somewhere in between.

Honey was standing at the benchtop, savouring her first hit of caffeine, the crema clinging to her upper lip, when she remembered the journals.

From her early teens, Scarlett had been a committed archivist of her own life. She'd filled notebooks with jottings, poems, sketches, cuttings and the occasional feather or pressed flower. Honey had been envious. She wanted to be the kind of person to keep a diary, but it had never stuck. She'd start in January only to give up by April or sooner.

Whereas Rachel had done a thorough job on reimagining Honey's old bedroom as a sewing room-cum-unwelcoming guest room, Scarlett's was largely untouched. Honey stood in the doorway for a moment, waiting for a wave of melancholy to pass. The bed had a bright, childish duvet cover in pink and blue with teddy bears and dolls. Far too young for seventeen-year-old Scarlett, but she'd marched to her own drum. There were stuffed toys and a fluffy faux fur cushion. There was a black painted bookshelf she'd inherited from Honey. Amongst the books of poetry, art, old school textbooks and an *Illustrated History of Witchcraft* was a neat line of hard-cover notebooks. Honey hesitated for only a moment.

She pulled out the last notebook. It was bursting with scribbles and essays and long and short poems, some dark and gloomy, some surprisingly funny and observational, terrific sketches of the bay and boats and close studies of flowers and leaves. There was a drawing of a mouse skeleton with many of the bones labelled and its head partially reconstructed. One full-page pen drawing of their mother in three-quarter profile captured perfectly her look of weary judgement. The look that said, 'You have fallen short of my expectations, but I'm not surprised.' Honey looked more closely and saw that within Rachel's pupils were tiny tombstones. With a stab she realised she had no idea how darkly talented her little sister had been.

Scarlett was sixteen when she filled this notebook — a whole year before she killed herself. Surely she hadn't suddenly stopped? Yet there was no sign of another diary. Honey rechecked to be sure. But the journal she so badly wanted to see, the one covering the period of her relationship with Marshall — that one was missing.

RACHEL WAS STANDING AT THE kitchen bench, facing away from the door.

'Good morning, Mum.' Honey tried for bright and breezy.

There was no reply.

'Mum?'

There was just a subtle shaking of Rachel's shoulders. She was crying.

'Mum? Are you okay?'

She went over and put her arms around her mother's shoulders, and tried to remember the last time she had seen her cry. Not at Scarlett's funeral, certainly. Or Ron's either. The word stoic had been invented for Rachel Chalmers.

'It's bad enough not being able to remember the name for a thing, but when you can't even remember what they're for. That's not fair. It's not.'

Rachel had been looking at the Magic Bullet she'd bought a few months earlier. It was obviously a complete mystery. The specialist had said there were no hard and fast rules, but the memories that were last on board were often the first to go.

'I can remember the pressure cooker your father bought me when we were married, exploding devil that it was. I can remember the little Japanese hibachi I got for Ron for cooking fish. Very trendy. But for the life of me — what is this *thing*?'

Honey knew this wasn't the time to ask her mother about Scarlett's missing diary. Instead, she filled in the blanks, sat Rachel down and made a cup of tea. She waited at the bench for the kettle to boil, and felt overwhelmed by the responsibility. Overwhelmed and inadequate. Her mother needed her.

And then another thought. Kloe Kovich had relied on her too, and look how that had worked out.

9

HONEY HADN'T BEEN ABLE TO bring herself to admit that she had been waiting for Jason to do something heinous so Kloe would call again. Thanks to her connection to Kloe and Kloe's connection to Jason, and his connection to the Reapers, she had been seconded from Serious Crime to Drugs for Operation Pachyderm. The names for police operations were computer generated and assigned randomly, but Honey thought it pretty apt: there was a huge fucking elephant in the room called 'What Happens To Kloe If They Find Out She's Been Talking To A Cop?'

Spud had mentioned witness protection. But New Zealand was a small place. There was a reciprocal arrangement with Australia, but given that most of the Reapers were from there, that was no safe bet either. Either way Kloe would have to cut all family ties, and Honey couldn't see her doing that. Try as she might to shove the issue into the part of her brain called 'Not My Problem', after all these months of late-night chats it wasn't that simple.

When the call finally came, Honey had been out celebrating with Michelle in a K Road bar. Post-Tony, she had been tying it on a bit. But she had good reason to celebrate. Two Chinese students initially sought for questioning about the body in the suitcase found floating in the harbour had left the country. They had no criminal records and anyway, because of the dead girl's high-profile parents, the investigation had focused on Triad operations in New Zealand, much to the joy of the Auckland Tabloid, as Honey called the only daily newspaper still operating in the country's largest city. But the investigation had gone nowhere. Now Honey's persistent work in the community had paid off. A tip led to student accommodation and the two nineteen-year-olds who had returned to New Zealand to recommence their studies. Under Honey's interrogation, it didn't take long for them to blame each other. They'd just meant to kidnap her, but the girl was asthmatic and had suffocated before they'd even sent the ransom note. It was tragic and senseless, but the case was solved and Honey hoped that at least the girl's parents would find some peace.

A few more wines into the night, Michelle returned from the bar with a good-looking forty-something architect in tow. Honey played wing until Michelle, looking only slightly embarrassed, whispered that she was going to check out his designs. Honey wished her luck and ubered home alone. After an unnecessary nightcap of tea and whisky, she fell into a deep, deep. . .

'KIA ORA, HONEY BUNNY!' KLOE sounded very drunk, but who was Honey to judge.

'What's up, Kloe?'

'Not much, I just thought I'd, y'know, say hello. It's my birthday!'

'Congratulations. Had a good day?' She was hoping not, but—

'I'll say. The kids made me a real flash card, and Shyla bought me breakfast in bed. And me and Jase, y'know what they say?'

'No, Kloe, what do they say?'

'My Auntie Lil reckons you get it on your birthday whether you want it or not!'

Honey laughed obligingly, but she needed to get Kloe to a less happy place.

'How's the wrist, Kloe? Still giving you trouble?'

A moment's silence, just background music from the party — rap, Honey thought, though it wasn't her specialty topic. She just hoped it was loud enough to block out prying ears.

''S'good, cut the plaster off myself,' Kloe said. 'Wasn't worth going into the hospital.'

Honey thought it was more likely she didn't want to answer questions about how her wrist managed to break itself.

'Anyway, lady, better get my arse back to the party.'

'Hang on—' It was time to shift it up a notch. 'The thing is, Kloe, I had to tell my boss about these chats we've been having, and my boss wants to talk to you too.' She tried to keep her voice even and friendly, but Kloe wasn't so drunk she didn't recognise the danger.

'Fuck that, not gonna happen.'

'Yeah, that's what I told him.'

'You're not wrong.'

'He wanted me to say that in return for the right information, we could find you a new place to live, a fresh start for you and the kids. Somewhere away from all the shit.'

'Not fucking happening I said!' Kloe's voice was louder now.

It was time to go hard, get mean. 'Yeah, the trouble is, if we picked you up now, and brought you in for questioning, say to talk about what was going on between the Reapers and the Knights, and it came out that you've been calling me, well, that wouldn't be good for you. I mean you can see how it would look. How you might need some support.'

'You can fuck right off, ya bitch!' Kloe disconnected.

HONEY MADE HERSELF A CUP of tea while she waited. She leafed through a women's fitness mag. Tony had given her a subscription last Christmas. She'd joked it was really for him — unkind, but a little bit true. There was a woman with an abdomen that looked like it was made up of two rows of hard little apples. For god's sake . . . She was just about to give up and go back to bed when the phone jangled again.

'It's me.' Their talk had apparently sobered Kloe up, fast.

'Hi.' Honey figured it was a matter of less being more. Give Kloe some space to reach out, as they said in the new police speak.

'What does he want to talk about, your boss?' Kloe's voice was barely above a whisper, but the music was more distant and Honey figured she was now deep in the back yard.

'We know the Knights are bringing the meth through Tauranga, that the Reapers are organising distribution. But we need to catch them in the act, so we need to know when the next shipment is, and when the handover's happening.'

A long pause. Honey could almost hear Kloe's brain hurting.

'Kloe?'

'Yeah, I hear you. I don't know none of that shit, 'cos they don't even tell Jase.'

'I'm just asking you to keep an ear to the ground, let me know if you hear anything.' She knew Kloe was far more connected than she let on.

'I told you I don't hear shit.'

KLOE WAS BEING ONLY HALF truthful. The Reapers didn't tell Jason much, but Kloe had been at a lunch with some of the WAGs when her sister Renata let something drop about the

71

hassle of cash. All that drug money — you couldn't just buy a house or a car without drawing attention, so some of the wives and girlfriends were regular winners at the racetrack. There'd been talk about buying into a trendy Ponsonby Road bar so they could shovel lots of imaginary customers through.

One thick-armed bitch with a pink streak in her bottle-blonde hair and an Aussie accent that could cut glass had complained that they had 200K in a suitcase buried out the back and soon there would be a fuck of a lot more. Lucky her bloke was Aussie born so they could retire to the Gold Coast, no sweat, but you couldn't carry more than 10 thousand without declaring it. That's if she could ever get her old man to give up the life.

Kloe had made sympathetic noises, but it pissed her off that Jason was so fucking unmotivated. 200K! Some days she was lucky to find lunch money for the kids. She knew she could always ask Renata, but she didn't want her sister's pity.

'Kloe?' Honey's warm, encouraging tone brought her back. 'I want to help you, but you've got to give me something or my boss is going to do this without me. He's likely to ride in there and pick you up in front of everyone and there won't be anything I can do about it.'

'I dunno, okay. I think it's happening, but I don't exactly know when.'

She was playing for time, she knew. There had to be some way out of this, but there'd been a fuckload of piss and a chocolate-chip dope cookie wrapped in a bow. She thought of Honey as a friend, and yeah, maybe she was trying to do the best by her, but she was still a pigshit and that meant she couldn't trust her. Or could she?

The music from the house was pulsing with an almost subsonic bass and her head was starting to hurt in rhythm.

'Kloe, are you still there?'

'Yeah, give us a sec, will ya. Trying to think here!'

'Can you find out about this meeting? Can you do that for me, Kloe, so I can keep my boss off your back? Do that and I promise you I will do my best to look after you, okay?'

Kloe thought she could hear someone calling her name. She needed time to think, to find a way out of this mess.

'Kloe?'

'Yeah, I can try.'

HONEY HAD RECORDED THE CONVERSATION, of course, but she'd sat up for a while longer, making notes for team Pachyderm. Kloe was an informant, not a friend, Honey told herself; she was annoying and needy. After the hospital incident she'd joked darkly to Michelle that she'd almost felt like giving Kloe the bash herself. But now she'd pushed her directly into the line of fire and there was no going back. The thought of what the Reapers might do to Kloe kept Honey awake for a long time, and when she finally fell asleep her dreams were of dark forests and shovels full of pine needles and dirt.

10

"Kloe, are you still there?"

"... yeah, gwon, I'm ... wiri ... listening to this ... Carol."

"... day you ... turned on this machine? Can you see that? And ..."

Kloe ... "I can keep my ... and you haven't. So that I ... but you know ... you will have a ... best to look after you ... blue."

SHYLA WAS WORRIED. SOMETHING BAD was gonna happen, she could feel it. It was like Kloe wasn't even her mum anymore, she was just pretending, like her real self had been kidnapped by aliens, leaving only the shell behind. It was like that trick her Auntie Lil had shown her, how to put a hole in each end of an egg and blow out the insides. Her real mum was lippy, said what was on her mind and a whole lot of shit besides, but this woman was empty, going through the motions of being Kloe but not really.

When Jason was going off his head at her, real Kloe would stand up to him, even if she got the bash for her troubles. Real Kloe was a mangy old alley cat with sharp claws.

Pretend Kloe backed down, scuttled away, a little grey mouse.

When Shyla had gone to her mum to say she was pregnant with Tama, Kloe hadn't asked about the dad, except to confirm he wasn't around. That was good enough for Kloe. Shyla had never met her own biological father, and Kloe wasn't certain anyway. Given her daughter's kinked dark hair, dark eyes, and a spray of freckles around her wide nose, Kloe guessed he was a Māori dude from Taranaki but couldn't swear to it — she'd been very popular back then. She'd had three abortions since, so knew what she was talking about when she promised her daughter it was no big deal.

Shyla had never even had a real boyfriend, wasn't really interested in guys in *that* way. The baby's dad was a shy, quiet guy she knew from touch rugby — had to be, they'd been at a party and got so wasted on weed and premix they didn't really

74

know what they were doing. When she realised she was pregnant they'd met at McDonald's and he'd cried and said his parents would kill him, that he would support her when she went for the termination but they couldn't tell anyone, please! She'd looked at him and thought how he was just a kid, sobbing and shoving fries into his mouth, and decided then and there that, whatever she did, she'd do it without him.

That was the last time she drank or took drugs of any description. She stopped playing touch, too. She knew a termination was the sensible choice, but as the weeks passed and she could feel her body change and her baby inside her, she kept putting it off until it wasn't a choice anymore. Kloe agreed to take care of the kid while Shyla stayed at school.

Now Shyla was worried about leaving her mother alone with Tama. She was supposed to be cramming for her mock exams, but what if Kloe tried to top herself or drove into the oncoming traffic or just sat on the back step and never got up again? The thing that bothered Shyla was that nobody else seemed to notice. Certainly not Jase the arse, and Auntie Renata hadn't said anything, either. Shyla had asked her, flat out, 'Do you think Mum's okay?' and Renata had just shrugged and said, 'Sure, she's fine.' But Shyla knew she wasn't. First she thought maybe the broken wrist had scared her in a way the other beatings hadn't. She'd been to hospital, even called Shyla to say that she was gonna find somewhere for her and the kids away from Jason. But then she'd come home again, even joked about it a few weeks later when Shyla helped her cut off the plaster. It was tatty and getting in the way and Kloe said it didn't hurt anymore and she didn't want bits of it in *her* dinner. So, Shyla knew it wasn't just that.

She went to her room, a section of the front veranda that had been closed in, unlocked the padlock on the old sea chest she'd scored from the op shop, and took out her carved box of precious things. Inside were some strands of Tama's birth hair, along with other treasures, like a broken pounamu koru she'd got from her Auntie Lil, and a fine, broken silver wrist chain with some tiny bluebirds. Buried underneath a drawing of a bright smiling sun from her little sister was the cop's business card.

She'd been sitting on the back step with Tama, updating her social media while she distracted him by letting him play with the gold chain around her neck. But he'd given it a sharp pull and the little gold disc of Saint Anthony had gone flying. She could see it, stuck in the gap between two boards, but when she'd tried to lever it out it had slipped through. She put Tama down and, using the light from her phone, crawled under to retrieve it. There were all kinds of other shit there — like scratchies and an old plastic supermarket club card — but the business card stood out, propped up against a post, sheltered from the weather. On the front was printed 'Detective Honey Chalmers' and an Auckland number. On the back was written something, maybe 'call me anytime' and a different number. It could be nothing, but in her guts Shyla knew it was more than that. It was a thing her mother did, smoking on the step, absentmindedly pushing stuff from her pockets through the gaps.

One night, after she'd put Tama down after his feed, Shyla went outside and called the number on the card.

A woman picked up immediately: 'Detective Chalmers.' She sounded sleepy but not annoyed, as if late-night calls from unknown numbers were just part of the job.

Shyla had meant to ask how she knew her mother and if she was in trouble, but somehow it wouldn't come out. Eventually, the woman who called herself a detective asked, 'Who is this? Are you okay?'

Shyla was touched by the concern in her voice. Was she okay? Not really.

'Sorry, do I know you?'

Still she couldn't think of anything to say, so she hung up. And she didn't answer when her phone rang back half an hour later. The next day she threw it into the creek and told everyone she'd lost it. She just knew this Detective Chalmers woman was the reason her mother wasn't like her mother anymore and it had all started the night of Kloe's birthday. Shyla had seen her on the back step, talking on her phone. Her mother had looked shit-faced happy at first, but then something had gone wrong and she'd disconnected.

Later, Shyla checked Kloe's call history. The number from the card was there — twice from that night. It was those calls that had sucked the insides out of her mother's shell.

NO ONE ANSWERED HER CALL to the unfamiliar number, so Honey went back to bed. The next day she put through a request to trace it, and was disturbed to learn the phone belonged to Shyla Kovich. Shyla was only sixteen and, as far as she could tell, a good girl. A miracle given her environment. Her social media profile said she didn't smoke, drink or take drugs because 'that was how the state oppressed and controlled them'. Honey thought Shyla was probably right. Apart from going to school and being mother to a toddler, she was a member of an artists' collective based in the community centre and sold gorgeous handpainted runners from their website. Some brains trust had made a note on the file that they were 'radicals query dangerous', which made Honey feel weary. Some gonzo cops were desperate to find dangerous terrorists lurking among artists, animal rights activists, Māori self-determination advocates, anarchists and anyone who thought outside of the mainstream. It would be funny if it didn't fuck with people's lives.

Honey decided the most likely explanation was that Shyla had found the number and called it out of curiosity. Now that she'd done so, she knew, at least, that her mother had been talking to a cop. It was a worry but there was nothing Honey could do about it.

Meanwhile, Operation Pachyderm was heating up. They weren't just relying on Kloe coming through. She was only a cog in a much bigger operation, but if she could corroborate the information the police had from other sources it would help keep the investigation on track. And of course the bust was only a part of it. When it came to securing convictions, her testimony could be vital.

KLOE FELT LIKE SHE WAS crumbling. She was made of dust, and a gentle wind would tease her apart and blow her away. After the calls to Honey on her birthday she marvelled as she watched her body going about its business, making school lunches for the kids, putting Tama down for his nap, going to the supermarket. Meanwhile, her *other* self was perched on her left shoulder like a wicked goblin, watching, making rude comments about how useless she was. How she was going to get caught. Now and then she'd try to formulate a plan, but her goblin self would laugh and call her a loser, while her body kept going through the motions.

She was so busy trying not to give anything away, she couldn't remember how to be. It was like trying to walk down steps. It came naturally to you, until you tried to deliberately put one foot after the other. That was when you stumbled. Shyla had noticed something, asked her if everything was okay, if something was wrong. Shyla would: she was too smart for her own good, that girl. But Kloe had tried to put her off, not to engage, and Shyla hadn't pushed it. Kloe was relieved, but the problem of how she was going to get the cops off her back remained.

Funnily enough, it was Jason trying to be nice that moved things along. He'd come home from the pub and out of the blue announced they were all going to Fiji for a holiday. Kloe wondered what they'd use for money. Jason laughed, the big man, telling her he'd take care of it, they'd take the kids, and Shyla and the baby. No problemo. They'd sit around a pool, drinking; maybe they could swim with the fucking whales or some shit.

While Kloe was getting her head around that, he said that some of the other guys were taking their families too — maybe they should hire a whole fucking island. Kloe guessed the big payday was coming soon. Her goblin chuckled. Time to pull finger. After the days in limbo, she was cheered at the thought. She felt her body becoming solid again.

Maybe she could do this after all.

11

OVER AN ANTIOXIDANT-RICH BLUEBERRY SMOOTHIE —
and no mention of the magic blender — Honey cautiously steered
her mother around to Marshall and Scarlett, and eventually the
diary. The subtlety was wasted. Rachel required little prompting
to poison the waterhole. She said that Scarlett had been hopelessly
infatuated and Marshall had taken advantage. That his callous
treatment was the trigger that led Scarlett to do what she did.
Marshall was older and should've known better. Scarlett was such
a young seventeen-year-old. When Honey cautiously suggested
that some of it might have just been in Scarlett's mind, Rachel
snorted, and Honey noticed a fine spray of blueberry on her
mother's cream blouse.

'She was staying with him over at his uncle's house for two
weeks. I pleaded with her to come home, to think about what she
was doing. She laughed in that way of hers and said, "Don't worry,
mama, we've got plenty of condoms".'

'She could have been winding you up.'

'Scarlett wasn't like that. She was so honest sometimes it hurt.'

Honey knew what her mother meant. She was grimly pleased
to have another tick on her list of inconsistencies in Marshall's
stories.

'You know she was working Saturdays in the Four Square,
saving up for art school,' Rachel continued. 'As if she'd spend all
her hard-earned money flying down there if she didn't think he
cared.'

'She went down to Dunedin to see Marshall?'

'That's where she found them — in his room, in the act.'

'You mean Marshall and another girl?'

'Of course she was distraught, and the coward didn't even go after her. He let Scarlett hitchhike home alone from one end of the country to the other. A seventeen-year-old girl. It was a miracle she wasn't killed.'

The silence wrapped itself around the unintended irony.

'Did Scarlett tell you this?' Honey asked.

'I can't remember.'

'You remember *what* happened in absolute detail but you can't remember *how* you know?'

'That's what I said, isn't it?' It took a little longer for Honey to wheedle it out that Rachel had peeked at Scarlett's journal. She hadn't seen all of it, because Scarlett had sprung her in the act and made a terrible scene, and she was adamant that the last time she'd seen the final journal it was under Scarlett's pillow. It wasn't there when she'd tidied up after the funeral, so sometime in the months between Scarlett's return from Dunedin and her death it had gone missing. Lots of people had been through the house in the days afterwards, including Marshall.

'If anyone had a motive to cover up *his* part in it . . .'

Honey thought it more likely that Scarlett had hidden her journal from her prying mother. But now Rachel turned the tables and began quizzing Honey about her intentions towards Marshall. She had seen the two of them sitting out in his truck last night. She wasn't serious about taking this *friendship* any further, was she? Honey told her the truth. She honestly didn't know.

She didn't say she was going to need more information.

LATER, HONEY DROPPED HER MOTHER at the Waitutū Institute for her morning yoga, and politely declined the offer to join in. Rachel was meeting friends for coffee after, so that gave Honey a good three hours for phase one.

Honey drew up a rough house plan. She figured that *if* her mother was telling the truth and the journal had been missing since Scarlett's funeral, it wouldn't be in the kitchen, which had had a bit of a makeover since. She'd leave that room till last. Still, it was a big *if*. It occurred to her that Rachel might actually have destroyed the diary, and the whole search was pointless. She pictured the old kerosene-drum incinerator behind the garage, the illustrated pages curling and burning. Well, only one way to find out . . .

The three-bedroom Lockwood had been a holiday home until Geoff Chalmers disappeared into the place where dissatisfied, unhappy men go when they don't want to play families anymore, and Rachel sold the family home and moved in with her two girls. Honey found it staggering that of the five million people living in New Zealand, more than ten thousand were reported missing every year. The mentally ill, the bewildered or drugged out, the ones having passionate affairs and lost in a fug of hormones, over-dramatic teens or those with dementia like her mother were usually soon found. But a few, especially middle-aged men with families, went away and never came back. With no evidence of foul play, the police didn't look too hard to locate them. It wasn't nice, but neither was it against the law to want a new life. When she thought about it, and she rarely did, she wondered if her dad was alive, if he was still connected to the sea, maybe an oyster farmer down Bluff or taking tourists out for crocodile safaris in Queensland or, fuck knows, living in Thailand with another wife and family. It hurt to think he didn't love her enough to stay. Were there any women she knew who *didn't* have daddy issues, though? Her counsellor told her, 'Just because it's the simple answer, doesn't make it not true.'

Honey forced herself back to the task in hand. Scarlett's room was the obvious starting point. She looked in all the obvious places, then resorted to tapping the walls and feeling the mattress before reminding herself this wasn't a drug bust. Forty-five minutes later, she put a neat cross through the room on the plan and moved on to the laundry. An hour and a half and several more crosses later, she figured it was time to call it a day and to think about dinner.

She parked her Clubman in the new bitumen car park behind the New World, feeling a twinge of guilt for driving past the old Four Square on her way. Scarlett had worked there weekends, and for years it had been the only show in town, but the selection was limited and, after the opening of the new supermarket, the turnover slow. At least quinoa and instant miso had come to Waitutū.

'Honey! Hey!'

The woman coming towards her at a rapid clip was around the same age as she was, and of a similar height and build. She had startlingly blue eyes, her blonde hair was cut into a stylish but sensible bob, and she had slender muscular legs and a pale-peach tunic-type dress that showed her sculpted shoulders and arms. A lot of time in the gym, probably with weights and pilates, was Honey's immediate thought as she tried to place the face.

'Oh, my god, Gemma, hi!' The name came to her in the nick of time.

To be fair, the last time she'd seen Gemma she'd been a chubby, mousy-haired girl most often found perched on top of a horse. She had lived with her grandparents on a farm out of Waitutū and had been insufferably bossy. One summer she decided to make Honey her friend and let her ride her pony. At the beginning of winter it was all over and Gemma told her next new best friend embarrassing stories about Honey that were only partially true. By the following summer Gemma's parents had reconciled and she had gone to live with them somewhere out of Hamilton, which was punishment enough for anyone. Honey had never heard from, or thought of, Gemma Rowan again.

Her confusion showed because Gemma laughed. 'It's okay, I *know*. I'm way different now!' She put a hand under each full breast as if making a presentation and laughed again. 'So, do you like them?'

'Um, yes, they're very nice.'

'It's all my husband's doing, he's a plastic surgeon. Ex-husband, I should say.'

'Oh, I'm sorry,' Honey said. She noted that Gemma's nose had also had work.

'Don't be, he was a total cheating bastard. But I did very well out of the settlement, thank you very much, and I don't have to worry who he's rooting tonight. What are you doing now?' Gemma hadn't paused between sentences and it took Honey a moment to realise she'd asked a question.

'Not a lot, just looking after Mum, really.'

'No, I mean now, right this minute? Do you want to get a coffee? There's a place inside the supermarket that's not too bad.' She didn't wait for an answer as she strode off.

Honey laughed. Gemma Rowan might look different, but she was still bossy as hell.

'I NEED A CHEESE SCONE,' Gemma declared as they stood at the counter. 'I've just come from the gym and by god I've earned it.' It was still weird to Honey that Waitutū now had a big enough sedentary population to support a gym. 'I'll get you one too. My shout!'

They sat down, and Gemma launched into her life story.

'So, you know I had to leave Nan and Pops' farm to live with my parents in Hamilton, which was pretty shit, actually, because they still fought all the time, then I ended up going to Waikato Polytechnic and graduating as a beautician, can you believe? That's how I met my husband — at a product launch party I had to lie and beg to get invited to. He was twelve years older and an actual doctor and I thought he was so fucking sophisticated. Ha! Talk about lipstick on a pig, or Chanel aftershave or whatever. Appearances can be *so* deceiving.'

Honey wondered if she was being deliberately ironic. Decided probably not.

'So anyway, we got married and I worked as his receptionist and then I started up a little side business, pushing organic creams and potions. It absolutely took off. We had a big old house in Remmers, I was living the life and didn't want to wake up and smell the roses. When I finally did, I hired a private investigator. Theoretically, divorce is no blame and a 50/50 split, but if you've got *extremely* incriminating photos of your husband shagging his theatre nurse he is much less likely to argue the toss. Although I'm not sure I should be telling you this. You're still a cop, right?'

'That I am.'

'That's crazy! I want to hear all about it.' But evidently not right away, because Gemma continued, barely pausing for breath, 'Then Nan died, did you know about that? She went in for what

85

they said was routine surgery and never came home. Pops was kind of lost without her, so I came back to help out and really got into riding the horses and being busy on the farm. I've even toyed with the idea of having these taken out' — she poked out her chest to make her point — 'but they'd probably flop around my knees if I did! Where was I? Oh, yeah. Last year, Pops went out to plough a patch of turnips and . . . Heart attack, they said. Now I do a homestay for a select clientele and take horseriding treks. It's pretty cool, actually.'

Honey realised Gemma had stopped and was waiting for feedback. 'Wow, that's . . . a lot.'

'Of what?' Gemma laughed, but she was staring at Honey with her intense blue eyes which Honey saw were helped by tinted contact lenses. The pupils were huge, and Honey wondered if she was on something.

'I bet your story is just as interesting,' Gemma said with a stab at sincerity.

Honey wasn't about to make it a competition. She gave a brief synopsis, along with a smidge of man-tossing to make Gemma feel in good company, though she felt a bit guilty for dissing Tony. After all, he had saved her life and, as far as she knew, hadn't cheated on her. Now, she told Gemma, she was taking extended time out, her mother needed looking after, so it had all worked out really.

Gemma knew what Honey had been through and thought she was a saint to be looking after her mum after such an ordeal. She respected Rachel, she said, everyone did, but she was not an easy woman, was she?

'It always really upset me that she broke up our friendship.'

'I'm sorry?'

'When we were about ten or eleven, I thought you were so

86

cool, but then you weren't allowed to come out to the farm anymore.'

'No, you broke up with me,' Honey said, startled at her own petulance. 'You started hanging out with different girls.'

'Because your mum told Nan and Pops I had to stay away from you.' Gemma shrugged. 'I know it's silly, it's so long ago, but I just wanted you to know that it wasn't my fault.'

'Thanks,' said Honey, not knowing what else to say.

'It's amazing how these things lie quietly in your brain and then suddenly come bubbling up. The other thing I wanted to say is, I'm really sorry I wasn't around for Scarlett's funeral. I was actually here for the holidays when she died, but Mum and Dad had already arranged to pick me up so I couldn't stay.' She gave a strangely inappropriate little giggle.

'As you say, it's all a long time ago.'

'Must make you think about it, though, living in the same house.'

'Does a bit, I suppose.' Honey shrugged, giving Gemma nothing, but acutely aware she had just spent the morning tearing the house apart looking for Scarlett's journal.

But Gemma wasn't giving up. 'Must be especially weird seeing Marshall here as well, given everything.'

And there it was. Her mind flicked back to the night at the golf club. Had Gemma been there? No, but someone could have easily told her.

'No weirder than seeing you, Gemma,' said Honey coolly.

'Hey, I didn't mean anything, I just . . .'

'You want to trash Marshall like everyone else because it's easier to blame him than it is to accept that everyone let Scarlett down and sometimes shit just happens!'

'Oh, god, I've really upset you, haven't I? I am so, so sorry.' Gemma sounded genuinely contrite. 'It's been so great to see you, I'm sorry if I've spoilt it. Forgive me. Please?'

Honey sighed. 'Yeah, sure, I'm sorry too. I guess I'm a bit sensitive about it.'

'I get it, totally. And for what it's worth, I don't blame Marshall at all, despite what people say. I always liked him.'

'Okay. I didn't even know you knew him.'

'I didn't when we were at high school. You guys always kept to yourselves back then.' Gemma smiled to show she was teasing, but Honey heard an edge there. 'After you left, I'd stay with Nan and Pops for uni breaks, and when Marshall came home we'd hang out a bit. He came out to the farm sometimes. He was a total natural on a horse.' She laughed a little too loudly then, and said, 'Not like that! I mean, Marshall wasn't interested in the old-flat chested, try-hard me. And let's face it, Scarlett was so beautiful, why would he look at anyone else.'

For a moment Honey could hear something catch in Gemma's voice, something raw and real, before she covered it with another forced laugh. 'Maybe he'd like the new improved Gemma now. Do you think I should try?'

'Go for it, absolutely.' Honey smiled brightly, trying to lighten the tone.

Gemma gamely picked up the ball. 'He's looking quite hunky, don't you think? He's a bit of a hermit but he came out to the farm once to ask about buying a horse and, actually, I saw him outside the post office the other day. We had a nice chat. He seems good in himself, sort of calmer, I dunno, kind of Zen.'

Honey had to agree but it irked her unreasonably that Gemma seemed so knowing.

'He was always cute, y'know, but now he's a real man, solid, but not in a bad way.' Gemma was definitely crushing on him.

'What about after Scarlett and Marshall broke up,' Honey asked. 'Weren't you tempted then?'

Gemma shook her head. 'They never really broke up, not according to Scarlett, not until, well, you know ... and then Marshall went away so ...' Gemma lowered her voice. 'Did you know she got pregnant?'

Honey felt a twinge in her guts around the old knife scars. The darkness was well and truly back. 'Scarlett? Are you serious?'

'Oh, crap, I honestly thought you knew.'

Honey could only shake her head.

'Oh, god, I've put my foot in it again, haven't I? I honestly thought ... forget it, none of it matters now, does it?'

'Except to Marshall, maybe. If he knew what people were saying ...'

Gemma stared at her. 'You think I'm just spreading nasty gossip? I'm not. I swear you're the only person I've told after all this time. Cross my heart.'

Honey stared back, and it was Gemma who broke first.

'You remember Denise at the pharmacy? She was my closest friend and at the time she told me, which I know she shouldn't have, but she was really upset and feeling a bit guilty about not helping Scarlett more, and she knew I was leaving town, so maybe she felt she could unburden, anyway she told me that a few days before Scarlett ... passed over ... she came in and wanted to know if the morning-after pill would work if she was already pregnant. Denise told her she'd need to see a doctor and do it properly if she wanted a termination and Scarlett got upset and left.'

89

Honey thought she sounded genuine. But she'd heard enough, and began gathering up her bag.

'Hey, look it's okay, Gemma.' She tried to be reassuring. 'I believe you, or at least I believe that's what Denise told you, and anyway, you're right, it's all ancient history, but I have to go.'

'Are you pissed off with me? You are, aren't you?'

'No, honestly, no, it's good to see you, Gemma, but I've got stuff to do and I've got to get home.'

'Of course, your mum, I'm sorry, I've been going on, dragging up all that old stuff when really, all I wanted to do was catch up and . . . and connect with someone who actually knows life outside of Waitutū. Forgive me?'

She looked about twelve years old despite the breasts, and Honey assured her there were no hard feelings. Gemma gave her a hug and they made loose arrangements to catch up again soon.

Shopping on autopilot, she thought about the timeline and what Gemma had said. She could accept that Marshall might have fudged one drunken night when he found Scarlett in his bed, but she couldn't believe he lied so adamantly about not having sex with her at all. That was a good three months before Scarlett went to Dunedin and found out about his fuck buddy, and nearly five months before she died. So, if Scarlett was pregnant just a few days before she died, who was the father? Did that have anything to do with her decision to kill herself?

Honey reached her car and was about to load her shopping in the back, but then stopped. Maybe all this curiosity about her sister was a sign she was mentally on track again and should be sorting out her mother's future and getting herself back to work where she could be doing something useful. Or, if she was to be honest with herself, was it about wanting to clear Marshall's name so she could ... what? Jump his bones with a clear conscience? Drag him back to Auckland? Only one of those scenarios seemed even remotely possible and she wasn't sure it was what she wanted, much less how Marshall might feel about it.

If she hadn't stood still at that moment, grocery bags in hand, lost in thought, she might not have noticed the black low-slung BMW with tinted windows parked behind the mini skips at the back of the supermarket, right where the narrow service road fed into the car park.

She could just make out two figures wearing caps and dark glasses. One of them was huge, filling up the driver's side. As she watched, the car started to move, and she felt a sudden surge of fear verging on panic. But the vehicle quickly veered off up the service road and disappeared from view. Honey tried to calm herself, tell herself it was nothing. The Reapers were Auckland based, they couldn't know she was here and anyway she was no longer a player so why would they even be interested? Her logical self knew all this, but she resented the relief she felt in closing her own car door.

Bubbling away like the toxic dairy waste that filled the rivers and lakes, hiding behind the clean, green, natural beauty served up with a hearty 'kia ora!' for the tourists, rural New Zealand was rife with gang turf wars, hidden dope plantations, methamphetamine manufacturing, guns and extortion rackets. There had been Wild West-type shootouts on the main streets of numerous country towns. Waitutū had been largely spared. A few years ago, she heard, a gang had tried to rent a property, but the local iwi had shown them the road out of town, and they'd never come back.

Perhaps the dudes in the black BMW were just day-trippers, visiting relatives or here for a wedding or a funeral or any number of reasons. Fuck it, gang bangers can have holidays too. But she couldn't shake the feeling that her subconscious had noticed them earlier and they'd been watching her car, waiting for her to return to it.

As she pulled up in the driveway, another worrying thought intruded. In all the late-night and not always sober conversations she'd had with Kloe — like when she told her about the time she smashed her father's boat on the rocks and nearly drowned and had been rescued by Marshall — had she ever mentioned Waitutū by name?

12

THE ANZAC DAY PICNIC WAS the perfect opportunity. Armed with a big pack of chops and sausages and her famous potato salad with extra spring onions, secret agent Kloe Kovich was ready for action.

As usual, they converged on the gas barbecues at the Long Bay reserve. It was one of Auckland's most popular beaches, for good reason, with a long wide sweep of golden sand flanked by a wide, grassy, tree-studded park. The place was already filling up, but families who'd tried to nab a prime spot early got the message and moved away when the boys on their Harleys rolled up in convoy. The thunder was deafening and strange, and it still thrilled Kloe to hear it. Hammer's Harley was a joy to behold, literally gold plated, a big fuck you to anyone who reckoned crime doesn't pay. Jase had a pissy Honda trail bike that he used for hooning around and doing wheelies, but he wisely left it at home, and they'd all trucked north in their crappy maroon Mitsubishi people-mover.

Kloe and her sister Renata and some of the other ladies set up at a solid wooden table, buttering piles of white bread and ripping the scab off the first beers of the day. It was just after ten o'clock; the older kids were off with their boogie boards, the littlies down digging holes in the sand, and Kloe was conscious of pretending to drink but keeping her wits about her. She was on a mission, after all, and the price of failure would be high. 'No, Mr Bond, I expect you to die,' she imagined Shyla saying, stroking the cat.

KLOE WAITED FOR THE RIGHT moment before casually mentioning the upcoming Fiji trip. That certainly got the girls going. There was dissent about the location, the cost, the practicalities, the logistics of taking the kids, the fact it could draw attention, who was going to end up doing all the work: there were a hundred reasons to complain and bitch. In other words, they were all very excited and looking forward to it.

'Be good if it's soon, like in the holidays,' said Kloe. 'Don't want the kids missing out on too much school, eh.'

Renata took the bait. 'Hasn't Jase said anything?'

'Nah, maybe he doesn't know or maybe he just wasn't paying attention, I really need to up his Ritalin, eh?' The women sniggered. Jokes like this were a gang-WAGS standard.

'Yeah, maybe,' was all Renata said.

'Be nice to be able to plan ahead is all I'm saying.' Kloe hoped she sounded sincere.

'Guess they've got good reasons for playing their cards close to the chest,' Renata said before stopping and casting around the loaded tabletop. 'Fuck me, where's the sauce?'

'There's heaps in the back of my car, don't get your tits in a knot,' someone said, and Renata stomped off to get it.

Bugger, Kloe thought. She couldn't keep pushing the subject or it'd look suspicious.

SHYLA WAS ON A BLANKET under a tree with the baby, but she was keeping an eye on her mother. Something still wasn't right. It was like Kloe was trying to act like her old self, but it was still acting. There'd been more phone calls, her mother tiptoeing outside when the house was quiet. Shyla's window was usually

94

open, and she could hear murmuring from down the back yard. She had no doubt she was talking to that detective woman, and that was why she was being so weird and trying too hard not to be.

If her mum really was a narc, Shyla knew she couldn't tell anyone, fuck no, but she found it hard to believe. Kloe was staunch and Auntie Renata had serious gang cred. No, it was much more likely she was being pressured and trying not to worry anyone by keeping it all bottled up, and that was making her crazy.

Shyla had brought it up with her Auntie Renata in a round-about way one night when she was over babysitting. She didn't say anything about the lady cop, she wasn't stupid, but she mentioned like she'd just thought of it that she was a bit worried about her mum being stressed out and kind of not herself lately.

Renata wanted to know more, so Shyla brought up the night Kloe's wrist got broken, and Renata went off at what a cunt Jason was and how he had to learn to keep his fists to himself or she'd sort him out herself. Shyla felt grateful that her auntie was on their side, but she still didn't mention the calls, just shrugged and said, 'Yeah, I guess,' and tried to change the subject.

But then Renata started in asking what else Shyla knew about the night Kloe had ended up in hospital, how she'd got there, why she didn't call Renata for help and what exactly Kloe had been doing lately to make her worry. Shyla felt her face burning, but her auntie seemed to accept what she said, gave some last-minute instructions concerning the kids, and eventually went out. Shyla hoped she hadn't looked too relieved as she closed the door.

Now she glanced at her mother and saw Renata come up behind her. She stood still a long moment, watching the back of Kloe's head. What Shyla saw on her aunt's face frightened her. It wasn't anger, it was pity and something else as well — like heartbreaking sadness.

LATER IN THE AFTERNOON, THE flies were thick around the overflowing bins and most people lay or sat around in groups in the shade, talking shit, while some of the guys kicked an Aussie rules football around and the kids ran in and out of the water. Kloe made herself real useful clearing up, all the while listening in to whatever conversations she could. She struck gold when Hammer got into a bit of an argument with Siz, a tall drink of water with a trim goatee, over some shit one of the Knights had done at a recent meet at the clubrooms. Apparently, this Knight had thought Siz's old lady was just another ho up for grabs, so he picked her up, threw her over his shoulder and started carrying her out towards the back room. Siz was outside but someone alerted him and there was a tense standoff. Hammer had intervened in the nick of time, extracted an apology from the offending Knight, and had Siz's old lady spirited away before there could be any further misunderstanding. But now Siz had a few in him he wanted Hammer to know he wasn't satisfied with the outcome. She heard Hammer say, 'Ten days, mate, that's all, ten days, hold your pee pee, bro, the deal is done then you can do whatever the fuck you want with that cunt.'

Ten days, thought Kloe. Surely that'd be enough info to get the cops off her back?

No sooner had she thought it than she felt a twinge of regret. She liked her nighttime talks with Honey: in another life maybe they could've hung out, been friends even. She'd been tempted to spy on her since she found her home address on the back of a shopping list in her glovebox, and she'd done a drive-by once to see what her house looked like. Nice little place, like an old state house but with a good garden, fenced-in back yard. She was sorry Honey didn't have kids. It would be a good house for kids.

What would Honey say if she dropped in one day and said she was just passing, how about a coffee? Yeah, right.

ACCORDING TO HER AUSSIE MATES, Renata was built like a wombat, with a thick mane of hair she kept long and bottle black. Their mother always insisted that she and Kloe had the same dad, but you wouldn't know it to look at them. Today, despite the heat, she wore her usual dark jeans, a black tee (Motörhead) with a man's checked flannelette shirt over the top, sleeves rolled up. She drank in moderation, didn't take drugs, pumped iron and boxed. Her mum had been a dumb-arse druggie who knew bugger-all about her background and died young and ignorant, but Renata forged her own path.

She watched her sister moving about with a stupid, vacant look on her face and thought, that dumb bitch. Renata cared about Kloe, course she did; she was her little sister and Renata felt she owed her. Twenty years ago, she'd decided, fuck it, New Zealand was too small, she wanted adventure, so she'd sold everything she had — including her soon-to-be-ex boyfriend's dope crop — and got on a plane to Melbourne. The first few years were party central but eventually she realised that what she wanted was control: over her life, over her future. She met Hammer, a Kiwi expat like her, at an AC/DC concert in Melbourne. They caught each other's eye singing along to 'High Voltage' — it was a tribute, the thirtieth anniversary of Bon Scott's death, and Hammer had actual tears on his cheeks. Hooking up with a foot soldier in an outlaw motorcycle gang from Adelaide wasn't an obvious career move, but Renata saw untapped potential.

Kloe was only twelve when Renata left, fifteen when she came home from wagging school and found their mother's body, a needle still in her foot. When Kloe got knocked up, Renata felt guilty not being there to support her, and sent money, made the occasional visit, but it was obvious Kloe was taking after their mother. Hooking up with that fucknuts Jason and dropping two of his kids only confirmed it.

Then shit in Adelaide got messy. Hammer's club was in a feud with the Hells Angels that saw a series of high-profile murders for some, unmarked desert graves for others. Their club commander had been in South Australia for a half a century but that didn't matter when Immigration came for him, exporting him and his rat's tail back to the land of his birth as a 501 under the 'undesirable moral character' category. Now the old prick was on the pension in Timaru, moaning about the good old days.

While the remaining Adelaide club members fought among themselves, Renata looked to the future. It made sense to move back to New Zealand before Hammer was forced to leave and the government seized their remaining assets.

They fortified a clubhouse out west where she'd grown up and recruited mostly ex-Aussies who, cut adrift in a strange land, were fiercely loyal to their new patch. It wasn't all smooth sailing. The shootout with the Knights had been a tactical mistake. Renata knew it was more efficient to make alliances than enemies, but Hammer had been keen for a show of strength. The local gangs had closed ranks, and too much blood was spilled before Renata was able to calm it down.

Last year or so, things were looking pretty damn rosy, though she never took anything for granted. Renata knew that Hammer was rooting some skinny blonde chick in Three Kings, a ho called Summer whose mum was some reality TV celebrity, and who got off on playing the bad girl. And on the drugs Hammer supplied to her and her friends. Renata wasn't happy about it but it wasn't sensible to make a fuss. She'd always been woman number one and Hammer needed her. But now, this cop had got involved with her sister. Kloe had well crossed the line and Renata had to do something about it.

It'd started months ago, the suspicions, with Kloe being even more twitchy and strange than usual. Renata thought at first that maybe she was back on the P, but it wasn't that: she wasn't wasted and she was still taking good care of the kids. But everything around the night Kloe's wrist got broken was wrong — why she didn't call, how she took herself to hospital. None of it added up. So, she looked into it. She knew someone whose brother was an orderly who asked someone who was on duty in A&E the night in question, and pretty soon Renata knew Kloe was brought in by a lady cop who tried to organise somewhere safe for her to go. Kloe, the silly bitch, paid her back by disappearing home again without even getting discharged properly.

So when Shyla, the lovely girl, came to her to ask for help for her mother while trying to be staunch and not give anything away about what was really upsetting her, Renata had no problem reading between the lines. Now the question was, how much had Kloe told the bitch pig and what was she, Renata, going to do about it?

As the picnic wound down, Renata watched Kloe leaning in, listening to Hammer talking to Siz with her mouth open like a retard, as if no one could see her being way too interested. She felt sad for her stupid sister and anger at the cop who'd turned her. She knew how this had to go down, was almost resigned to it. And then it came to her in a flash — a way she could maybe save her sister. Maybe.

13

THE POLICE ONLY HAD THEIR own success to blame for the strategic alliance between the Reapers and the Knights. The local methamphetamine market had traditionally been supplied by gangs importing Chinese pseudoephedrine to be transformed into crystal meth (known locally as P) by 'cooks' in home labs — but the best cooks had been locked up and a series of police raids made it impossible for the gangs to produce enough to meet demand. The Knights began importing the final product direct from Mexico, via Tauranga, but some high-profile busts involving local and international law enforcement had interrupted the supply chain and the Knights were finding it increasingly difficult to service their clientele. They had access to New Zealand's busiest port but no product. Meanwhile, the Reapers had partnered with an organisation with connections to super-labs near the Chinese/Laos border. They had access to all the P they could sell, but no reliable way of bringing it into the country.

The Reapers also brought with them a new business model. They didn't quietly bury rats in the Riverhead Forest as tradition dictated; they preferred more public displays. After one informant was shot dead in his car with his girlfriend a few doors down from the Henderson police station, the message was received. But attacking Honey in her own home signalled a new confidence even for the Reapers. They wanted the Knights to know that when it came to the cops trying to turn their own, all bets were off.

HAMMER WASN'T A BIG MAN but that didn't hold him back. In a stoush he was fast and relentless; like a pit bull you'd have to chop his head off to make him let go. He got that way by a familiar route. Born in the Hutt Valley to a struggling teenage mum, he spent his formative years in and out of a Catholic boys' home; he was eleven when his older brother hung himself from a shelf in the work shed where Father Farley abused him. His mother finally took him away, to Elizabeth, a burnt, desolate satellite town north of Adelaide, where she had relatives. A fresh start for both. It didn't take. She went through the windshield, three times over the limit, when he was seventeen.

Hammer earned his patch and confirmed his nickname in a gang brawl where he put a claw hammer through a rival gang member's head and did five for manslaughter. He learned a lot about power and control in prison, but it was meeting Renata Kovich that changed his life.

When all the 501 shit started going down, his instinct had been to dig in his heels, lawyer up, and fight the government bastards, but she'd convinced him their future lay back across the ditch. Moving to New Zealand and setting up the West Auckland clubhouse hadn't been without problems, but the demographics were in the Reapers' favour. The traditional Kiwi urban gangs were largely an ageing population who preferred four wheels to two, indulged the grandkids and were risk averse. The Reapers set out to demonstrate that retirement was for them the safer option. Now their flag was firmly planted, the alliance with the Knights was the perfect way to fund their plans for expansion.

Hammer and Renata's dream was to onsell the product to Australia, where the big money was. But big money brought its own problems. What do you do with it? Can't stick it in the bank or the IRD will be on your arse. Get busted, and the government can just take it away again — along with your cars and properties and bikes and whatever else money can buy. There was already too much cash stuffed in plastic bags and buried out behind the clubhouse and in back yards.

Renata swore the solution came to her in a dream. The Reapers bought a stake in a nightclub on Fort Street managed by a local actor who'd made a name for himself in a couple of crap American movies and a US cable show, and who was on tap to meet and greet most evenings. The clientele was a mixed bag of what passed for celebrities —local wide boys and girls, international businesspeople passing through, bankers and investment wankers who got their thrills hanging out with the mad, bad elements of trendy society. The staff were attractive and deliberately cool, and some nights there were long queues for the ordinary people.

ONE PERSON WHO NEVER HAD to wait in line was Bradley Morgan. Mid-fifties, neither tall nor short, thinning salt-and-pepper hair that flopped across his wide forehead, Bradley wasn't pretty or cool but he knew how to work a room. He was also a dab hand at making money disappear. He'd done it for thousands of mum and dad investors: now you see your retirement fund, now you don't. He was one of those who emerged from the ashes of the 2008 GFC even richer. Rich enough to afford a Herne Bay mansion and a Paris apartment, a ranch in Venezuela, and holidays in Hawaii where he golfed with ex-prime ministers and internet billionaires. Wife number two was an ex-model and influencer, and Bradley had all the trappings of success. But what he craved was excitement.

He met Hammer at the club one night. Hammer was the real deal and Bradley felt bad-ass just by association. So, when Hammer proposed he help out the club with their money problems, Bradley was happy to oblige. Setting up overseas tax havens and laundering profits was what he did best, and he wanted to show off to his new best friend. He drew up the necessary documents and got them signed off, all right and proper and legal. He even went around and explained the ins and outs to Hammer's old lady. She was a scary chick but quick on the uptake.

Hammer was grateful. They partied hard to celebrate. Then, late in the evening, Hammer grabbed Bradley Morgan by the balls and squeezed.

'Morgo, mate, we need to have a bit of a chat.'

Bradley tried to pull away, but Hammer's grip only increased.

'Uh uh. Hold still, mate. You'll do yourself a damage.'

'Fuck, man, that really hurts!' Bradley felt like hurling but had the sense to hold still.

'Just a conversation we need to have, cobber. You do the dirty on me . . .'

'I wouldn't . . .'

Hammer cut him off with a tiny tweak but didn't raise his voice. Bradley felt like he was going to pass out. His whole conscious being was focused on the small area between Hammer's thumb and fingers.

'Just listen, okay? You do the dirty on me, try and rip us off, or talk to the cops, anything like that, and this'll be like I'm tickling your balls with a feather, we clear on that?'

'Yes, god, yes, I'd never—'

''Cos no offence, mate, I like you, don't get me wrong. But you've got a rep, eh, for being a bit of a rip-off artist, and I'd hate to have to come for you.'

'You won't have to. You can trust me.'

'Yeah. Yeah, I reckon I can.' Hammer stared at him a moment longer, then released his grip, before adding, 'It's all about to happen, mate. Shit yeah. We're gonna be rich as fuck.'

He slapped Morgan on the back, brought out another little bag of the purest P, and the rest of the night was a high-energy blur.

THE OPERATION WAS A DEAD dog from the start, according to the infallible wisdom of hindsight. After Kloe's call to Honey, telling her that the gear was coming in in the next ten days, the Drug Squad pulled out all the stops, seconding staff from other operations, and keeping the Reapers and Knights under close surveillance. The twin focus would be the port of Tauranga, where the pure amphetamine would be arriving, and the warehouse in Ōnehunga from where the drug would be cut and distributed. Of course, they weren't just relying on the intel supplied by Kloe; phone taps, informants and the one undercover cop who'd managed to get relatively close to the Reapers all confirmed the story. The warrant for the raid included an excerpt from a recorded conversation between Hammer and a senior Knight by the name of TJ, confirming the details for the handover. It was a lucky break. Hammer rarely spoke in his car and when he did the music was usually at full volume. Fortunately, this conversation took place in silence while, according to the GPS tracker, he was parked outside his own house. It was late, so maybe he hadn't wanted to wake the kids. Honey felt no joy at the thought of putting their dad inside, perpetuating the cycle, another generation of fatherless sons with axes to grind, but the alternative was a truckload of misery when all that P hit the streets.

She was part of the team watching the Ōnehunga warehouse from an unmarked van while another team watched the port, focusing on the Tasman Quay entrance. Under different circumstances Customs might have broken into the container, checked the contents, then closed it up again, but the Knights had eyes all over the port, and a couple of recent operations had been botched because of leaks. It was decided to trust the intel.

The plan was simple enough. Note the container when it arrived and tag it with a tracking device, follow it from hook-up to delivery in Ōnehunga, wait for the Reapers to unpack the goods, then swoop in with the Armed Offenders and bust as many as possible, coordinating the raid with Customs in Tauranga. The Asian Unit was involved because there were high hopes that in the mop-up they might also collect the Triad-linked group suspected of organising the supply side.

Everything went like clockwork until the distributors started showing up at the warehouse. None were the usual suspects — but perhaps the Reapers were being extra-cautious. After a couple of the visitors were identified as having drug-related convictions, Spud authorised the go-ahead. The Armed Offenders went in first, gung-ho, guns pointed, screaming *Down, get down, everyone get down* — and what they found was something from *Antiques Roadshow*. A container load of crappy second-hand Asian goods: statues, bowls, cupboards, lacquered furniture, rugs and about a million fancy chopsticks. The assembled crew were mostly dealers from legitimate second-hand and Asian import stores. The Reapers were affronted by the police insinuation that there was any drug business going on. About the only thing they could be charged with was bad taste.

The raid in Tauranga was equally fruitless. All the Customs and police operation had succeeded in doing, at great cost to the taxpayer, was thoroughly document the movement of legal goods from one part of the country to another. It was several weeks before the embarrassing truth would come to light, and by then Honey was nearly dead and Kloe was missing, presumed.

WHEN RENATA ALERTED HAMMER TO her sister's situation, his first easy thought was to put a bullet in Kloe's head as a warning to both sides. He'd never warmed to his sister-in-law and Jason was a waste of space. But Renata persuaded him that the smarter course of action was to use Kloe to pull the rug out from under the pigs. She'd make sure that Kloe was fed enough information to point the cops in the wrong direction while alternative arrangements were made in a series of very secret meetings between Hammer and TJ.

Nearly a tonne of high-grade crystal meth, hidden in a container of heavy farm machinery, was thus quietly delivered to another part of the port, loaded on a semi-trailer, driven overnight to Wellington, then rerouted back up the North Island for final delivery to a big disused agricultural shed in Tāmaki. There the container was opened and emptied. Hundreds of convenient half-kilo packs were retrieved from behind the false walls of the container and parcelled out to be distributed throughout the country by a network of gang-associated dealers.

By the time Spud was explaining to his superiors why so much money had been spent on an operation that had got it so wrong, one of the largest single shipments of P to hit the streets of Aotearoa at one time was being sold from Kaitāia to Bluff, and the Reapers and Knights were in for a spectacular windfall. The gang holiday in Fiji went ahead. It was a great success, especially when it served as a smokescreen for Hammer's very secret meeting with a local exporter of coconut, vanilla and other Pacific Island-based produce to Australia.

Long before that all went down, however — in fact, on the day of the Ōnehunga raid — Renata sat Kloe down and read her the riot act, let her know how close she'd come to seriously fucking herself up. Kloe was contrite, Kloe was a mess, Kloe pleaded for mercy and promised she'd never talk to anyone ever again.

Renata was inclined to leave it there, but Hammer wasn't satisfied. The cops needed to be sent a clear message — one cop in particular. Renata was cautious — they'd be crossing a line, there'd be ramifications — but Hammer was seriously pissed off. In the end Renata thought, Fuck it, yeah. That bitch cop had used Kloe and put her life in danger, and Kloe had to help if she wanted to live to see her kids grow up.

Faced with these options, Kloe gave up Honey's address with only the briefest hesitation.

Traditionally, police and gangs kept a wary, even respectful distance from each other. A good number of them were as likely as not to be cousins, at least. The cops were generally unfussed about the gangs applying violence to each other, as long as innocent bystanders weren't hurt — it kept them occupied and stopped any one gang from gaining too much power. In turn, the gangs avoided the hassle of attacking police, knowing the hell-fire retribution that would undoubtedly follow.

So, when Honey returned from the debrief following

the Ōnehunga debacle and was assaulted in her own home, interrogated and left for dead, it signalled a dramatic shift in police/ gang relations. And while she was in hospital with her intestines leaking into her abdominal cavity, it was finally dawning on the police that the Reapers weren't just ignoring the rules. They were playing a whole different game.

14

MICHELLE CALLED WHILE HONEY WAS putting her mother's house back in order after one last methodical sweep. There was no sign of the missing journal, and she was filthy, covered in dust and grime, and had a long scratch on her arm from a poorly directed nail. She was also resigning herself to the fact that the record of Scarlett's last year would never be found.

'Come back, I miss you! Karaoke is no fun anymore!'

'I can't. I still don't know what's happening with Mum.'

'Bring her with you! We'll show her a good time in the big smoke.'

'Sadly, she's not here.'

Rachel had come down with a serious bout of the flu and was spending a couple of days under observation in the regional hospital.

'Are you saying I have to drive all the way out there if I want to hang out with my bestie? I come out in a rash past the Bombay Hills.'

'I wouldn't inflict Waitutū on anyone, least of all you.' She was only half joking.

But Michelle had gone quiet on the other end.

'Hey, 'Chelle, you there?'

'Yeah, look, sorry. There was something . . . look, you probably don't want to know, but have you heard from anyone about what's happening with the Reapers?'

Honey was pretty sure it was impossible for her scars to bleed, but that's how it felt. She tried to stay calm.

'Not a thing.'

'Shit, maybe I shouldn't say.'

'But now you probably should.'

Honey could hear Michelle taking a deep breath.

'So, interesting times at work. They busted a casual data inputter, who it turns out was having a relationship with someone in the Reapers, feeding them information and also burying or deleting files. They're trying to play it down but it's been going on for months, apparently. None of us had any idea — I mean, she seemed so boring and normal. Everyone's feeling a bit on edge about it, to be honest.'

Honey knew what she meant. Cops and criminals inhabited the same shady world, and it wasn't unknown for cops to date crims, and vice versa. No surprises there; she'd read somewhere that sixty percent of relationships begin in the workplace, and you could say cops and crims were hot-desking in the same office. Another way cops dealt with living cheek by jowl with the bad guys was to run them down, call them stupid, animals, dehumanise them. It made the job more bearable, feeling superior to the people you were at war with, but there was an element of truth: most criminals were not the sharpest chisels in the toolbox. So, the idea that the Reapers were consistently getting one over the cops, like with the botched Ōnehunga raid — or could actually have a spy working for them from within the police — would be rattling a lot of preconceptions. They weren't supposed to be that smart but here were the Reapers putting the organised into crime.

'The thing is,' Michelle continued, 'and I especially shouldn't be telling you this, but fuck it, they should've told you anyway. Thing is, when they pressured this mole — pun intended, babe — she said the Reapers were *really* keen to know if *we* knew where Kloe Kovich was or if she'd been put into witness protection or whatever. I only know this because I've been processing all the stuff they've managed to recover from her computer and I remembered you talking to me about Kloe when you were in hospital, so, y'know . . .'

Honey was unable to speak. For the last few months she'd been living with the almost certain knowledge that the Reapers had killed Kloe and she was responsible.

Michelle broke the silence. 'What the actual fuck, eh?'

'Yeah.'

'You okay?'

'I will be.'

'That's kind of good news, isn't it? I mean if *they* don't even know where she is, she could still be alive, right?'

'Yeah, could be. Thanks.'

'Like I said, fuck 'em. After what you've been through, you've got a right to know.'

Honey could barely concentrate as Michelle switched tack and regaled her with the latest from her tragic, loveless life and a few *possible* pencilled dates for when she *might* visit.

Then came a sudden knock at the door. Honey took a sharp breath.

'Hon? You okay there?' said Michelle.

Honey was trying to remember if she'd locked the front door.

There was another knock. She stayed frozen to the spot.

'Babe? Say something. You're freaking me out here a bit.'

''Chelle, can you stay on the line for a sec?' Honey whispered, forcing herself to move.

She was almost at the door when she heard his voice: 'Honey, it's me, Marshall. You there?'

She couldn't remember feeling so relieved.

'Jesus, you look like you've been dragged through the bushes backwards,' he said when at last she'd opened the door.

Honey tried to speak and started sobbing her guts out instead.

A few minutes later, after reassuring Michelle that she was fine, she and Marshall were sitting knee-to-knee on the sofa. Part of her felt self-conscious and stupid, but also felt right to be telling her oldest friend about the most traumatic events of her life. When she'd finished, they both sat there for a moment, hands on thighs, staring straight ahead. Like they were waiting for a bus.

'Shit, eh,' was all Marshall said, at first.

They looked at each other and she burst into tears again, but this time from the release of having unburdened. 'It's okay, I'm okay, really,' she said, wiping away tears and laughing at the same time. She meant it. 'Bet you're sorry you dropped in now.'

'Not at all,' he said. 'But Jesus, that poor woman, Kloe? Imagine what she must've ... I don't know ... her life — being in that world but needing to reach out to you — needing to have someone to talk to so badly she'd risk anything — with her kids and ... the violence and just the sheer hopelessness — it's so fucking sad.' Marshall shook his head.

Honey felt something shift inside her, a subtle click of a gate closing. 'She told them where I lived. It must've been her.'

'She probably didn't have a choice.'

'I think she did.'

'I just mean—'

'I know what you meant.'

A long silence, Marshall playing with his hands, Honey ripping tissues out of the box and drying her face.

'At least, I mean, now you know she might not be dead, that must be such a weight off, eh,' Marshall ventured at last.

'Yeah, it is. Although it's hard to believe she had the brains to pull it off, so it's still possible she's in a shallow grave somewhere, or pieces of her are scattered all over Northland.'

She was being unduly harsh, but was it unreasonable to expect him to be on her side?

'Do you want me to make a cup of tea?'

She bolted to her feet. 'It's okay, I'll do it.'

God knows why she didn't just tell him to leave.

As she stood waiting for the kettle to boil, she was aware of Marshall coming up behind her. Without turning she said, 'I feel sorry for Kloe, too. Sorry that her mum was a loser druggie, sorry that she's part of a dispossessed underclass with limited options, but she's still made choices all her life. Not everyone born into that world stays there, not everyone hooks up with a dropkick like Jason Curran and stays with him. The only reason she ever "reached out to me" was because she wanted to pay Jason back for giving her the bash, but she never really wanted to change her situation, even when I busted my arse to give her the opportunity. And yeah, I felt bad for her, she's been on my conscience for nearly a year, for fuck's sake, but I still think she made choices and one of those choices pretty much ruined my life.'

'That's all absolutely true from your point of view.'

'My point of view? Why can't it just be true!' She felt a real flash of anger as she turned to face him.

'Because it's never black and white.'

'I think sometimes it is.'

Marshall, the fucker, was actually smiling. She wanted to punch him.

'What?'

'Do you really want me to say it?' He gave a little shrug that might have been apologetic.

'I don't understand because I come from a nice middle-class background and my mother wasn't a junkie and I never had to wonder where my next meal was coming from, so I can't ever know what it's like to grow up on the wrong side of the tracks?'

'Okay, you say it then.'

She was glad there was no sharp object in her hand. And was surprised at the control in her voice.

'Because you did, you think that gives you some unique insight into her world, even though you've never met, and your life and her life have been completely different?'

Marshall opened his mouth, but Honey wasn't going to give him the satisfaction.

'Okay, you had a pretty shitty start too, your mother died when you were young, your father was a recluse, probably undiagnosed bipolar, but you got to go to university and maybe you went off the rails a bit, but you're back on track now.'

'Nice of you to say so.'

'Oh, fuck off, Marshall.' She hated that she could feel herself tearing up again. 'I don't want a political argument about the nature of a class society and the evils of capitalism, I just wanted . . .' She broke off, turning away again to hide her furious tears.

'What did you want?' His voice was closer now.

'I don't know — for you to care, maybe?'

'I do care.'

'Not about Kloe Kovich, about me!'

'Isn't it possible for me to care about both?'

'But you don't even know her.' She knew she sounded like a churlish brat.

'I've known a lot of people like her,' Marshall said, 'and yeah, they make choices, but it's way more complicated than that, and I know you know it. It makes me sad for lots of reasons, but one of them is that I had it way better than her, I had a scholarship handed to me, I was encouraged all the way, and I still managed to stuff it up, let people down, hurt some of them badly, especially the ones closest to me.' His voice cracked a little and Honey thought he sounded like he was going to cry too. 'Why do I deserve a better, safer life than her?'

'I never said you did,' she snapped, and then instantly regretted it.

A look of hurt and something else, maybe guilt, crossed his face before he said softly, 'Do you really think your life has been ruined?'

She stared at him. He didn't look away. 'I said *pretty much* ruined.'

'Ah, well that's entirely different.' And then, just like that, he smiled again — the bastard was actually smiling!

'Shut up anyway.'

'You shut up.'

And damn it, she was fighting hard not to smile too. 'Do you still want that cup of tea?'

'Wanna game of pool?'

WALKING INTO THE LOUNGE BAR of the Waitutū Hotel, Honey's first thought was, 'Bad, bad mistake.' It was like one of those old westerns where the stranger walks into the saloon and everything stops. Except their problem was the opposite: she and Marshall weren't strangers, everyone *knew* who they were. There was no guy in a striped shirt and shiny waistcoat playing honky-tonk piano while busty bar girls in corsets and feather boas chatted up dusty cowboys. Instead, the local easy FM station played hits from the eighties through some dusty old speakers and a group of four guys at one end of the bar were watching sport on the big screen. Honey had been at school with at least two of them.

Graeme Holmes came from a big Pākehā rural family and had made a drunken attempt to force her to have sex with him out the back of the memorial hall the night of the school ball. She'd punched him in the balls and he'd thrown up. He'd always been beefy; now he was morbidly obese. Tim Feeney was rat faced and rake thin apart from a protruding belly that made him look like a snake that had eaten a basketball. He'd been a mean little bully at school and she had no reason to think he'd changed. They made no effort to disguise the fact that they were talking about Honey and Marshall, nor did they make any attempt to greet them.

Near the picture windows to one side, a large family group had pulled together a few tables to celebrate some event. With a sinking feeling Honey recognised the elderly man with a patchwork complexion and a shock of white hair at the head of the table as Ian Scott. The dumpy, peach-cheeked woman to his right was his wife Janice. They had been the last to see Scarlett alive and the first to spread the word that she had been on her way to meet Marshall the day she died. Ian Scott's mouth hung open when he spotted her. About the only patrons who paid no notice were two middle-aged women, backpackers with identical heavy blue rain jackets hung over their chairs. They were focused on the roast of the day.

Ariki, a handsome local man in his forties, was already at one of the pub's two pool tables. He was known in the neighbourhood for planting a yearly dope crop somewhere in the ranges. He briefly raised his eyebrows to Marshall, but then pointedly turned his attention back to the game. His opponent glared at them from over a trim military-style moustache.

Barry Snydon had had a crush on Scarlett since primary school. Scarlett had shown no sign of returning or even being aware of his feelings, but he'd waited patiently, walking her to school, partnering her in the science lab, taking her on chaste dates to movie nights, confident she'd come around eventually. It must've come as a rude shock to hear she'd taken up with Marshall Keller. Even worse to learn that he'd dumped her. At the funeral wake Barry had got seriously drunk and punched a hole in the wall of the institute kitchen. He'd been looking to deck Marshall, but Marshall had already left town.

Honey grabbed Marshall's arm. 'Are you sure you want to do this?'

'Fuck 'em,' he replied. 'You set up. I'll get you a drink.'

It wasn't lost on Honey that two of the most important people in her life had both given the same advice on the same night: 'Fuck 'em.' Well, all right.

She'd put in the two-dollar coins and heard the satisfying sound of the balls going thunk when a voice said, 'What are you doing with that prick?'

She turned to see Barry, standing too close.

'Having a game of pool, what does it look like?'

'Like you're hanging out with the bastard who killed your sister.'

'You don't know what you're talking about.'

He stood there, staring hard. She glanced over at the bar where Marshall was still trying to get the bartender's attention, then back at Barry's pale watery-blue eyes. His face was flushed and she could smell the beer on his breath and a cologne that reminded her of a bag of mixed lollies.

117

She gave a little tilt of her head. 'Do you mind?'

'What if I do?'

'Piss off, Barry.'

A moment, and he moved back to his table, where she saw Ariki counselling him to be cool. As she grabbed the triangle and a pool cue, she could still feel Barry's angry eyes on her, but she wasn't going to give him the satisfaction. 'Fuck 'em' was her mantra now.

She stepped back and chalked her cue. The room had more or less gone back to normal. Nothing to see here, she thought grimly.

But Marshall was still waiting at the bar. Nobody else was waiting to be served, and the bartender seemed intent on checking the stock and stacking the glass washer.

Honey marched over. 'Hey, you! What's your name?'

The bartender glanced around. She was all of twenty, petite, pale and freckled, with her dark hair in a long braid. 'Me?' She had an accent, possibly Scottish.

'Yeah, you.'

'Katherine, or Kate if you like,' the girl stammered.

Yep, definitely Scottish.

'Well, *Katherine*. My friend's waiting there to be served.'

The girl mumbled something.

'I'm sorry, what did you say?'

Katherine looked terrified, as well she might be.

'Is there a problem here?' Just then the manager came through, carrying a crate of empties.

'I'm asking her to do her job and serve us some drinks,' said Honey.

He propped, unconvincingly. 'Are you intoxicated?'

'What? How can I be intoxicated when I can't get a friggin' drink?'

She noted that the sign near the specials board said the duty manager's name was Craig. She also saw that the men further down the bar to her right were watching closely.

Craig opened his mouth, but Honey got in first.

'Craig, I don't know what the fuck you're playing at, but my friend and I want a drink and you've got no reason to deny us. You might think you're just trying to avoid trouble, or maybe you think my friend has done something to earn him your disapprobation, but you're wrong. You know nothing about it and it's not your job to judge. We just want a quiet game of pool and a drink, but if you want to make things difficult, we can do the same. I'm guessing you know who he is from gossip, but do you know who I am? I'll tell you. Detective Sergeant Chalmers, Serious Crime Unit. Now, do you really want to piss me off?'

Craig had gone bright red, taken off his glasses and was rubbing them with a cloth as if it might help him see his way out of this. Katherine looked like she was going to cry. The only sounds were 'Eye of the Tiger' through the speakers and the faint babble of the rugby league commentary.

Honey glanced sharply to her right.

'Graeme, Tim and the rest of you, mind your own business if you know what's good for you.'

The gang of four quickly turned away to study the game on the screen with intense concentration.

In a feeble attempt to regain face and the semblance of authority, Craig barked orders about getting on with the job, then headed off with the crate of empties and didn't reappear.

'I'm really sorry,' Katherine said. 'I didn't . . . I mean . . . he told me to —'

Honey cut in. 'Rum and Coke, thanks. A double.'

She turned to Marshall who was grinning from ear to ear.

'Same as the scary lady,' he said. 'Thanks very much, kia ora.' He looked at Honey, eyes wide. 'Jesus, Joseph and Mary. You even had me shitting myself.'

'Don't mention it,' she said. 'It's your shout.'

As she headed back to the pool table she had to stop herself from sashaying. She knew with absolute certainty that Marshall was watching her every step.

AFTER THE BUMPY START, THE evening was going pretty well, she thought, while deliberately putting aside any expectations as to how it might end. She was on her third rum and Coke, a game up on Marshall (four games to three) and enjoying herself immensely. She felt at ease out in public in a way she hadn't for a long time.

'Watch and weep,' she said as she sent the black ball rolling softly down the side cushion to edge his ball out and hover over the pocket.

Just then, Barry Snydon bumped Marshall's cue as he was taking his next shot and wondered aloud what he was going to do about it. Marshall cheerfully assured him it was no problem, and Ariki cut in to suggest they call it a night. Honey assumed they'd be off to sample some of Ariki's finest, and she had no problem with that.

The backpackers had complained to each other about their meals, but had cleaned their plates, donned their blue waterproofs, and presumably returned to the camping ground. The Scott family hadn't lingered either, though Janice had paused on her way out to ask Honey about her mother, while pointedly ignoring Marshall's existence.

Honey had given her the usual bland response: 'Oh, you know, one day at a time,' and then, because, well, fuck 'em: 'Janice, you remember Marshall Keller.'

The older woman squirmed, clearly torn between her deeply ingrained sense of politeness and her loathing. 'Yes, of course, nice to see you, Marshall,' she said, and hurried off to join her departing family.

THE RURAL REDNECK CONTINGENT, GRAEME, Tim and co., had lingered for longer and Honey was conscious of their watching as she took her shots. Late in the evening, on her way to the bathrooms, she ran into Graeme in the corridor. He winked at her with a little piggy eye.

'Looking good, Honey, looking good,' he leered, and made no effort to make room for her to pass.

'You too, Graeme, you too,' she said deliberately, looking him up and down, 'and wow, there's so much more.'

She knew she was being a bitch, but he'd started it, and for a nanosecond she remembered one of his surprisingly strong sixteen-year-old hands pushing her up against a car, fumbling with his belt with the other, before she'd punched down hard and run.

Older, thrombotic Graeme hissed, 'You think you're so good, but round here we know you. You're just a slut, always have been, always will be.' He still wasn't moving.

'Graeme, get out of my way or I will hurt you. You know I will.' She pushed past him and didn't look back. By the time she returned to the bar area, he and his mates had gone.

And now it was closing time, and Honey had only the black to sink. She was surprised at how sanguine Marshall was about losing; his younger version had been way more competitive. The older Marshall nodded approvingly as she doubled off the cushion to get around his snooker and clipped the eight ball neatly in, making it six games to four.

'Excellent shot.'

'Well.' She looked at him. 'I guess that's us.'

'I guess it is.' He drained the melted ice in the bottom of his glass. The question of what next waited patiently to be answered.

It had been threatening rain, so they'd driven to the pub in Marshall's Land Cruiser. Home was only a fifteen-minute, well-lit walk for Honey, so there was no real reason she couldn't say goodnight to him now. Marshall was definitely over the limit, but he held it well and was unlikely to encounter another vehicle along the 20 k of gravel road to his place — the two cops posted in Waitutū were strictly nine-to-five, barring emergencies. But as a friend and a police officer it was her duty to offer him a safer alternative. He could always say no and that was fine too, she told herself.

The Land Cruiser was the only vehicle left in the car park. Honey was about to suggest they leave it and stroll back to hers when Marshall swore softly: 'What the fuck?'

The near-side tyres were completely flat. So were the tyres on the other side, like big rubber clown shoes that had been strapped to the wheel rims.

Honey shook her head. 'Those arseholes!'

But then, to her surprise, Marshall started to laugh. It was a real laugh that came from deep inside.

'Sorry, I just—' But he couldn't speak. Between spasms of laughter, he tried to explain: 'The thought — of those — some — poor — sad bastard — going to all the trouble — oh, god — sorry — it's just too — funny—'

Honey opened her mouth to protest, but Marshall's laughter

was infectious. 'You don't think whoever — did this,' she gasped, 'is still — still out there somewhere, watching?' She motioned helplessly into the darkness.

'I hope so! I really hope so,' he managed, before collapsing against the bonnet. 'They'd be wishing so bad that I'd lose my rag, instead . . . instead—'

'They'd be going what the fuck? Why are they laughing?'

'What's so funny!'

It took them a full five minutes to recover. Every time one regained composure, the other would set them off again. And as far as they could tell, there was minimal damage to the tyres; whoever had done it had just removed the valves. Marshall decided he'd worry about it in the morning. He could sleep in the truck, he said; he had a blanket and he had some business to take care of in town in the morning anyway. But Honey told him not to be stupid, and that settled it.

By the time they arrived at the house, they'd almost got the laughing under control, but were divided on the likely culprit. Marshall's money was on Barry; he'd been openly aggro, and it was well known he still took flowers to Scarlett's grave. Marshall could see him sitting in the car park, toking away at Ariki's finest and deciding to make a statement. The thought set Marshall off again, which set Honey off again, although both acknowledged it was in bad taste due to the mention of Scarlett's grave. In Honey's considered and trained opinion, it was more likely to be Graeme and his dickhead mates egging each other on. She recounted how she had threatened him during their hallway encounter: cue more laughter. It hurt. Honey actually had a stitch as she pointed out it was kind of a dumb redneck kind of thing to do that was right up Graeme's alley. On balance, she thought Barry had more dignity than that. Marshall nodded gravely then said, po-faced, 'He bumped my pool cue.' For some reason this was the funniest thing either of them had ever heard.

At last she regained adequate motor control to produce her extreme-occasions bottle of Polish buffalo grass vodka from the freezer, and they did shots. The conversation turned to everyday matters — what Marshall had been doing around the farm, his latest experiments in fermentation, how Honey had realised the flu had gone to Rachel's chest although she was pretending otherwise, how Rachel had insisted Honey didn't know what she was talking about but Honey had taken her to hospital anyway. Honey confessed that not having her mother around for a few days was bliss. Marshall admitted that he got lonely out at the farm sometimes.

Honey had sensed that there was something else lurking beneath the conversation, something that Marshall was waiting for the right moment to say, but maybe she was imagining it. Eventually, weary from the alcohol and laughter, they lapsed into a companionable silence, letting the Spotify algorithms decide their listening pleasure.

Honey thought how easy it would be to invite Marshall to her bed. But then what? Maybe it would be simple; they would undress each other, and she would probably keep the light off because she was self-conscious about her scars, and they would kiss and get down to it and she would lose herself for a time. They would lie in each other's arms, exhausted, find their second wind and go longer and harder. She could feel herself blushing at this extended fantasy, and a warm feeling spread from her belly to her crotch.

But immediately another scenario intruded. It would be awkward and clumsy and embarrassing, and there was too much history, and both of them would be having doubts and regrets that they were ruining their friendship and would worry it was too late to call a halt for fear of hurting the other's feelings. And all the while the ghost of Scarlett would hover over proceedings. Honey saw it all in a flash and cursed her imagination.

'What was that?' Marshall was looking at her strangely.

Honey realised she must have made a sound. 'Nothing, I was just . . . thinking.' She felt her face, chest and throat glowing like a baboon's arse. Either scenario would lead to the morning after, and that would be a whole other thing.

'About what?'

'Nothing, lots of things, I don't know.' Now she just felt too warm all over. 'Actually, I could be coming down with this flu too.' Once the words were out of her mouth, she wondered if it could be true.

Marshall leaned towards her, a serious look on his face, and felt her forehead. 'You are a bit hot.'

She wanted to say, 'So are you', but stopped herself.

His face was so close, he looked so concerned and she wanted badly to kiss him.

'You need to keep your fluids up. Vodka is probably not the best idea. Have you got any herbal tea?' he asked.

Honey nodded. 'My mother has a cornucopia of magic teas.'

While Marshall made her a ginger and honey brew, Honey decided *almost* definitely that she was in all likelihood *probably* not going to jump his bones, not tonight at any rate. Lucky escape, buster, she thought. But maybe she meant that for herself. It was all very confusing.

Then Marshall served her tea and said, sheepishly, 'I've been meaning to tell you. The other day, when you asked me about

Scarlett and I said we hadn't slept together, I was kind of fudging the truth a bit. I mean, what I said about us not having had sex that time was true, but I . . . shit . . . It probably doesn't matter, and you probably don't want to know.'

'You might as well finish now you've started,' Honey said.

'Okay.' He paused for a moment, hunting down words. 'Everything I said about coming home drunk and finding Scarlett in my bed was true. But then we did try to, you know . . .'

'You had sex, yes, I did manage to work that out.'

'No, that's not what I mean. I was so trashed and . . . We were getting there but then she told me she was a virgin and how much she wanted her first time to be with me, and that kind of brought it home — how young she was, and vulnerable, and with all the booze in me, after that I just couldn't . . . you know . . . so finally I said, let's just cuddle instead.' He trailed off, embarrassed.

Honey let the silence thicken and set.

'The thing is, I think it actually made her like me *more* for not taking advantage of her, when in actual fact, I just physically couldn't . . .'

'You're a hell of a guy, all right,' she said, unnecessarily. Feeling angry, knowing that she had no right to be angry. 'And then, later on, you had sex with her anyway.'

'No, I told you, we didn't have sex. Not then, not ever.'

'Then how did she get pregnant? Immaculate conception?' Honey snapped out the words like staples.

Marshall stared at her. 'What are you talking about?'

'I have it on reasonably reliable authority that Scarlett was pregnant, or thought she was pregnant, around the time she killed herself.'

'Christ.' He slumped, his face in his hands, then looked up at

126

her. His eyes were burning, his cheeks wet. Honey knew she'd gone too far but it was too late to shut the doors now. Part of her hated herself. Part of her felt an ugly satisfaction.

'And you thought it was me?'

'I thought it was *possible*,' she said, trying to soften the blow. 'I mean nobody's ever mentioned anyone else.'

'There must have been, or your information's wrong,' he said flatly. 'Like I said, I didn't — apart from that one time when we didn't — I didn't sleep with Scarlett.'

'Okay, I believe you. Not that it matters.'

She felt unaccountably irritated with him for sharing details that were now evil worms burrowing in her brain, but more so with her own unkindness.

They sat in silence while she toyed with her cup.

'Actually I might go to bed now,' Honey said eventually. 'Are you all right on the couch? There's Scarlett's room, but Mum's kind of funny about it and I thought probably . . .'

He gave an involuntary shudder and said quickly, 'The couch is fine, it's great. Thanks.'

Honey found sheets and a duvet and pillow, and insisted on making up the couch. Marshall hovered. 'Honey, I'm sorry if what I said about Scarlett . . . if it upset you. I felt it was this *thing* kind of getting in the way and I just wanted to be honest with you.'

'Yeah, I know.' She straightened and they looked at each other for a moment, and it was so grave and serious Honey had to add, 'I'm sorry too, for being a bitch. The fact you suffer from embarrassing brewer's droop is none of my business.'

'That's kind of you to say.'

'That's me.'

'Friends?'

'Don't be a fuckwit.'

'I'll try not to be but, you know, it's hard.'

'That's not what I heard.'

They hugged it out and Honey was the first to break, aware they were in the danger zone again.

'Good night, Marshall,' she said at the door, turning off the light. 'You should know I haven't laughed that much in a long, long time. I really needed it. Thank you.'

'Any time, Honey. You know I love you, don't you?'

'Yeah, I know. I love you, too.'

And as she slid the door closed, she knew with absolute certainty that it was true.

15

KLOE HEARD THE MUSTANG RUMBLING up beside the house, heard it stop, heard the creak of the screen door, followed by it banging shut, the step of heavy boots. Through the living-room window she could see the front lawn needed a mow, but the jacaranda was in bloom, shedding a pretty carpet of lilac. She concentrated on folding the washing.

'Klo?' It was Marty. She felt a flicker of hope. Of all the boys, he was the most considerate — polite towards her, a family friend. He had played with her kids, for fuck's sake, helped them make a fort down the back last summer, let Nico ride him like a horse. But behind him, filling the doorway, was Keg, all dirty denim and leather and Ray-Ban wrap-around knock-offs.

She smiled and ducked her head, as if focused on what she was doing, as if it was just another day. The grey Snoop Dogg tee was threadbare, but she'd never even think about throwing it out.

'What's going on, Marty?' She was surprised how calm she sounded.

'You need to come with us, eh?' he said softly.

Kloe let that hang like smoke. That's what she could do with right now, a fucking smoke. And a gun. Maybe if they let her get changed she could grab it from the Nike box over the wardrobe. But then the bullets — where the fuck did Jase put the bullets? She'd nagged him not to leave them anywhere near in case the kids found them. But, who was she kidding? She wouldn't have a clue, didn't have the guts.

'Can I talk to Renata? Let me at least call her, please?'

She reached out her hand for her phone, but he shook his head and pocketed it.

'Let's go.' Marty cocked his head to indicate he wanted her to go out the back way. Made sense. Not that the neighbours would see anything, no matter what they saw. Kloe thought about offering up what she'd found, the thing she might be able to use to bargain for her life. But if she did that, there'd be no reason for them to let her live anyway. On TV they said shit like, 'I've left it with my lawyer with instructions to go to the police if anything happens to me.' Who the fuck had a lawyer on tap?

'I want to talk to Hammer,' she said. 'I need to tell him, whatever he thinks I did, I fucking didn't.'

'We'll see what happens, Klo,' said Marty. At least he sounded sad.

'The kids will be home from school soon. They'll be here any minute—'

She was playing for time, but Marty just shook his head: school wasn't out for another hour at least. It crunched her insides to think of them arriving home and her not being here, though Nico would get him and his sister a peanut butter sandwich while they waited. That made her want to cry.

Keg was losing patience. 'You gonna shift your arse or we gonna have to drag you out?'

She glanced around. It was pretty tidy, all things considered. On the table there was even a glass jar of flowers that Shyla had picked that morning. Shyla was a good girl. Smart. Kloe thought she'd done all right there.

She stood a little straighter, nodded to Marty.

'What the fuck we waiting for?'

SHYLA HAD BEEN PUTTING TAMA down for his nap in his cot next to Renata's youngest when she heard them arguing. Both kids were nearly asleep, and she had been singing a waiata — 'Tohora nui', about a big fat whale — that was one of Tama's favourites.

Renata had poked her head in and smiled, but when she heard the roar of Hammer's Harley out front she'd tsk tsk'd and closed the door.

Renata had told Shyla more than once how proud she was of the way she was raising Tama, how she'd started looking into her own family history — something about a great-great-grandfather who'd come out from somewhere in Croatia, though it wasn't called that then, and run off with the daughter of some rich Dutchman. How she thought that was maybe where families went wrong, not having any connection with their history. Shyla had grinned and said, 'You sure you want to go there, white trash?'

It sounded like Renata had gone straight outside, because she and Hammer were talking down the side of the house — Shyla could hear low, serious voices through the open window. At first she thought Renata was telling him off for making all that racket, but then she heard her mum's name mentioned a few times. She checked that the kids were asleep and went into the kitchen to stand by the louvered window nearest to where Hammer and Renata were talking.

It took her a moment to tune in. Something about a lady cop not being dead but Hammer thought Kloe was in the clear, but then somehow the Knights had found out that someone had been talking to the pigs and they wanted proof that the Reapers could clean their own house. Renata was pleading with Hammer, which was unusual, and Shyla thought for a moment it was someone else's voice, but Hammer was saying it was out of his hands and

131

Renata told him she thought he was in charge, and he said it wasn't that simple.

'Maybe if the cop had karked it, it would've been okay, we could've said we'd dealt to it, but she's alive, and fuck knows what Kloe's told her and what might come back on us. The Knights have a point is what I'm saying.'

Renata said something Shyla couldn't catch. She leaned in close enough to see the back of Hammer's head, but at that same moment Renata stepped away from the house, so that if she looked slightly up and to the side she would see her.

'She knows what we do to rats. She fucking well knew it but she went there anyway.'

'She's an idiot, we both know that, but she's my sister, I'm s'posed to look out for her.'

'Knights don't give a shit about that. We're proving we can do what needs to be done.' Shyla saw Hammer turn his head away so he wasn't looking straight at Renata when he added, 'Can't stop it now.'

'What do you mean? When's this all meant to be happening?'

Hammer was still looking off to one side. 'When it happens,' he said.

'The fuck, you already set it up?'

Shyla tried not to breathe as Renata glanced up but gave no indication that she could see her at the window. Maybe she'd known she was there all along.

'When?'

'Marty and Keg are gonna do it. Dunno when exactly — soon. Today, at any rate.'

'Please don't do this. Call them. Tell 'em we'll find another way.'

'You know I can't do that, Ren.'

'Please, I'll get rid of her, send her away, you'll never hear from her again.'

'We both know that's bullshit. Your sister couldn't keep away.'

'What about the kids? Say what you like, she's a good mum to those kids.'

'We'll take care of them.'

'Jesus, Hammer. Please, don't do this!'

'Okay, no more fucking talking. I let you know 'cos it's your right, but you fucking pick up that phone and call your sister and you'll be the next one and I won't be able to stop that either.'

The mournful cry that rose up from Renata's chest sounded like a beast in a deep well. Hammer grabbed her and they held onto each other like the world was ending.

'We started this, babe. We gotta see it through now, we gotta.'

Shyla tore her eyes away and started to move.

KLOE STEPPED OUT THE DOOR and stood on the back deck for a moment. The back garden was mostly just a straggly lawn around the old Hills Hoist, but Shyla had planted a veggie garden and some herbs on the sunny side and Kloe had kept them reasonably weed free. Keg and Marty were close behind her. They'd let her take her bag, though fuck knows why she wanted it. Habit.

'Okay, Klo, let's get in the car, eh.' Marty again.

The car was Keg's, a big old American one, a rusty red with the steering wheel on the wrong side. Kloe thought she was in an old gangsta movie. She could see them all from high above. It looked cool.

'You gonna put me in the boot?' she asked.

'You gonna make us?' Keg sounded pissed off, as if taking care of Kloe was really fucking with the rest of his plans for the day.

She felt a hand on her elbow. 'You can ride in style if you behave yourself.' Marty's voice was soft in her ear, almost kind.

But as she took a couple of steps forward, she stumbled, missing the top step.

'Oh, fuck!' She fell down hard onto the concrete strip at the foot of the stairs, and something inside her shattered. She started to cry.

'Jesus fuck me,' said Keg, looking to Marty and starting to move. 'Let's just stick her in the—'

He never got to 'boot' because another voice cut in, shrill and loud. 'Stay away from her!'

Shyla was standing in the doorway, pointing a revolver unsteadily at Keg then at Marty then back to Keg.

'I mean it. Stay away from her.'

Keg shook his massive head. 'Little girl, you don't want to be doing that.' He took a step, but Shyla didn't back away.

'I will blow your fucking head off. Move away, now. I swear it, I will pull this trigger!'

Keg looked at Marty, who gave a little shrug as if to say, 'What can you do?'

'Mum! Mum! Get up. Mum!'

Kloe, bewildered, pulled herself to her feet.

'Mum, listen to me. Are your keys in your bag?'

Kloe still couldn't get her head around it. 'Shyla, what're you doing?'

'Are your keys in your bag? Just answer me!'

'I think so.'

134

'Look!'

Kloe fished around in her bag. Her hand closed around her keys. 'Got them.'

'Good, go and get into your car and drive away and don't come back.'

'What?'

'You heard me. Go!'

She was trying to think but it was hard. A minute ago it was all over — she'd got what was coming to her, and she'd been almost relieved, accepting. Now Shyla was saying she had another chance. But something was wrong with this picture, something niggling, and finally it found its way to her mouth.

'What about you? You have to come too, Shy. I can't leave you here with them.'

SHYLA HAD THOUGHT IT ALL through while she was sneaking out the front door of her auntie's place, riding her bike all the way home, seeing the big car pulling into the driveway, climbing in through the window, taking down the gun she knew Jase had hidden in the shoebox above the wardrobe. She was listening and waiting, afraid her thumping heart was going to give her away. And now suddenly Marty and Keg were taking her mum away, and it wasn't about thinking anymore, it was about doing.

'I can't. I have Tama and anyway I haven't done anything wrong. These guys don't want anyone to know they got fucked over by a girl like me, so they're gonna have to tell everyone that when they got here you were already gone. You can say that, can't you?' She was pleading even though she was the one holding the gun.

Marty and Keg looked at each other.

135

'Fucking answer me or I will put a bullet in your face. Don't think I won't.' She took aim at the larger target that was Keg's head.

Marty finally spoke for both of them. 'Yeah, works for us, Shyla, long as you never breathe a word. Otherwise we'll all be in deep shit.'

'Of course I won't, why would I?' She turned back to Kloe. 'Mum, for fuck's sake, go. Now. Go somewhere far away and never come back.'

Still Kloe just stood there with her mouth open, and for a flash Shyla saw herself shooting her mum.

'I'll be okay,' she said. 'You heard them. None of us want this to get out. Just go!'

It looked as if Kloe's brain finally sent a message to her legs and they started to move. She limped off around the side of the house. She'd left her car parked out the front, thank god.

Marty didn't take his eyes off Shyla. 'You got cojones, girl, I'll give you that.'

But still none of them moved.

'How long we gonna have to stand here?' Keg said.

'Shut up!' Shyla listened until she heard the sound of her mum's rust-bucket people-mover start up and take off down the road. She could picture the cloud of blue smoke pumping out behind it. The revolver was heavy in her hands and her arms were wavering now, but she gritted her teeth.

'We ain't gonna chase her now. Didn't even want to do it in the first place. It was business, that's all, Shyla. Just business.' Marty's voice was calm.

'You're supposed to be her friend!'

'She talked to the cops, Shy. Not just once, but regular. She was a rat, and you know what happens to rats.'

Shyla knew Marty was right. And when she knew she couldn't hold the gun on them anymore, she told them to go.

Keg and Marty headed off without a word. As they backed down the driveway the car's massive sound system kicked in, the bass rattling the windows on the side of the house, and Shyla found herself thinking what a stupid car to use to get rid of someone, talk about drawing attention yourself. Then she went inside, locked all the doors and windows, and put Jason's gun back in the box above the wardrobe. She never did find the bullets for it.

16

HONEY WORRIED THINGS MIGHT BE awkward in the light
of day, but everything was ka pai, as Marshall said when she
poked her head into the living room a little after eight. While
she made coffee, he scrambled eggs and they ate their breakfast at
the wrought-iron table in the back yard, sharing parts of the *Bay
Advocate* and laughing about local news and gossip. Honey felt
calm, happy even, and strangely relieved that she hadn't jumped
Marshall in the night. The blissed-out mood was like time travel,
taking her back to her childhood and teens when Marshall was like
a phantom leg or arm, a part of herself she took for granted and
wouldn't know was missing until the moment she had it back.
There was a *possibility* that sex would have made them feel even
closer, but she doubted it.

'What are you thinking?' Marshall was looking at her, and
Honey was aware she'd been staring into space for some time.

'Not a lot.' She shrugged. 'Just stuff.'

'About?'

'You know one of my least favourite questions?'

'What are you thinking about?'

'You got it.'

It was true. Tony had driven her mad with his questions, and
she'd always given him variants of the same answer: 'If I wanted
you to know, I'd tell you.' She was pretty sure it made Tony want
to thump her. But looking into Marshall's face, she felt he deserved
an honest answer.

'I was thinking over what we talked about last night, and also about how cool and easy it is to be here with you now. Kind of like old times, but also different.'

Marshall nodded, thoughtful, then matter-of-fact. 'You know what? For a while there, last night, I thought we might've ended up in the sack.'

Honey wondered if she was so transparent or if this was just another case of their being on the same wavelength.

'Me too, kind of.' A pause. 'Me too, absolutely.'

'Why didn't we?'

'You tell me.'

'I asked first.'

She gave him an arch look, but then decided, what the fuck. 'Maybe because you're more like a brother, or we already missed our moment, too much water, or just . . . it'd be wrong.'

'Because of Scarlett?'

'Yeah, that too,' she said casually, as if it hadn't been near the top of her list. And to cover the new surge of complicated feelings, added, 'Plus we were very shit-faced and we both know what a soft cock that makes you.'

'Fair enough. But really, what are my chances?'

'Slim, bordering on non-existent.'

'Thought so, but it never hurts to ask.' His eyes twinkled as he wiggled his eyebrows and smiled suggestively.

Honey decided to meet him head on. 'What would you do if I said, Fuck it, why not, come on, let's go inside now and tear off a quick one?' She tilted her head. 'Come on, what would you do?' She stared, her eyes green mirrors, challenging him.

'I'd say, well it's about time, Ms Honey,' he said.

'Sure you would.'

'I'd say I've lusted after you ever since I could lust, that my first and last most disturbing erotic thoughts were about you, and I think that in some ways every woman I've ever been with I was measuring against you, which is totally unfair because they never stood a chance.'

A smart-arse answer was already formulating when Honey realised that this time he wasn't joking. Then he leaned in and kissed her. She was so surprised she very nearly spilt her coffee.

'Hey! Watch out!'

His head snapped back. 'Shit, I'm sorry. I thought, I mean, I know, I should've asked, but—'

She silenced him by putting a hand over his mouth.

'I meant watch out, dude, you'll spill my coffee.' She gave him a mock-stern look, stood and took both his hands in hers, and pulled him up towards her.

The kiss was long. She dived into it; she felt as if she was travelling first to every part of his lips, nibbling with her teeth, feeling with the tip of her tongue, and then they were falling into each other, their whole bodies and souls were kissing, and everywhere they touched it was like they were crackling and surging with a living force field. It was every cliché ever written, every country song, and at the same time unique and real.

Finally they broke and looked at each other with awe.

'Jesus Christ,' he said, 'was that, I mean, did you . . .' He trailed off. 'That was freaky.'

She knew exactly what he meant but couldn't help teasing. 'Freaky? Get you with your fancy words.'

'Insane, amazing, unbelievable, fucking ace!'

She smiled. 'Could've been a fluke, a one-off.'

'Yeah, you're so right, probably never happen again.'

'Only one way to find out.'

She straightened, took his hand, moved briskly, as if late for an appointment. Which in a way, she supposed, she was.

IF SHE WAS BEING PERFECTLY honest, she would have said that the sex wasn't nearly as good as the kissing. They'd both been so excited, so over-eager, that when it came down to it, she'd have been happier just to cover his face and body in kisses and for him to do the same for her. Instead, there was the whole awkward fumbling at clothes, and for a condom (a relic in Honey's bag), the matter of timing, the need to find the right rhythm, trying too hard, the weight of expectations, and altogether too much intellectual involvement, when the kissing had been pure instinct and sensation. The blinds in the bedroom were still drawn, but even so Honey was self-conscious as she pulled off her top and got into the lumpy bed. Conscious also that Marshall's fingers had lightly skipped over her belly scars as he helped relieve her of her underpants under the bed covers, and that when he had run his fingers down her back, he had not said anything about the rosette of flesh that puckered around her lower spine. She'd got there, but it wasn't skyrockets so much as the relief of having a serious itch scratched.

As they lay there afterwards, inside their selfish little bubbles of afterglow, Honey decided to keep her doubts to herself. She figured they had plenty of time to iron out the kinks. A thought struck. *Sober sex.* When is it ever as good as sex when you've had a few but not too many?

Marshall had turned his head slightly. 'You awake?'

'Yeah.'

'What—?' He broke off, grinned. 'I was going to ask what you're thinking, but then I remembered that was a big no no.'

'I was thinking you should probably kiss me.'

It wasn't strictly true but the moment she said it, it made absolute sense. He raised himself on one arm, leaned over and kissed her. And whoa, again with the seismic activity. Honey felt as if her whole body was rising up to meet his, like she was going to unzip her skin and he'd enter the whole of her, not just . . . Then her phone rang.

'Fuck.'

'That's what I was thinking.' Marshall's eyes were wide, dark and shiny like two avocado seeds.

'It could be the hospital. Mum. I have to . . .' She motioned in the vague direction of the living room where her phone was buzzing on the glass-topped coffee table.

SHE DROPPED MARSHALL OFF AT the entrance to the hospice, a grouping of low, red-brick buildings on the perimeter of the hospital gardens, and continued on to the hospital car park. They'd driven mostly in silence. It went without saying that Marshall's presence wasn't required, but he had intended to see his Uncle Jim today anyway and it wasn't like his truck was going anywhere.

Honey said she'd come and find him when she'd sorted out what was going on with her mum but that it'd be really fucking useful if he'd see his way to getting a mobile phone sometime. Marshall just grinned in the annoying way he did, and said, faux *The Last of the Mohicans*, 'I will find you.'

Rachel was sitting up in her bed, arms crossed, watching an

American TV chat show, when Honey arrived. It was theoretically a two-bed ward, but the rest of the hospital would have to be stuffed to capacity before they'd intrude on Rachel Chalmers' space.

She's only sixty-eight, Honey thought, as she stood in the doorway, looking at her mother. A stranger, being generous, would probably guess somewhere in her mid-seventies.

'What are you doing here?' Rachel snapped. 'I told them not to call you, but of course nobody takes a jot of notice of me. I said I wanted to go home and they ignored that. I told them I wanted to be left alone. Ha! Chance would be a fine thing. What I need is an advocate.'

'I am your advocate Mum,' Honey said. 'That's why they called me.'

Rachel's look told her exactly what she thought about *that*.

'Anyway, I'm here now. How are you feeling?'

Rachel just shrugged and pretended to be interested in the television.

'Mum!'

With an exaggerated show of annoyance, Rachel turned the television off.

Honey braced herself. 'They said you tried to kill yourself.'

'That's not true.'

'Then why would they say it?'

'Because they're idiots.'

Honey tried to look her mother in the face, but Rachel turned away.

'I was preparing myself for the inevitable, that's all. It's my right to decide while I can, and they've got no right to stop me.'

'They said you were caught stealing drugs.'

'The girl walked in at the wrong moment, that's all. She's about twelve and wouldn't know her arse from her elbow.'

'But you were in the drugs room. You said you were organising a funeral.'

'It was a joke.'

Honey just looked at her.

'I was looking for insulin.' Rachel sighed. 'There's fast-acting and slow-acting. I need both. If you just use the fast-acting and they get to you in time, they can resuscitate using sugar solution. You need to trick them, so that even when they think they've saved you, the slow-acting insulin kicks in and you slip into a diabetic coma and then out of life. I've always thought it would be a pleasant way to go.'

'Mum . . .' Honey couldn't finish. Who was she to say it wasn't the smart thing for her mother to do, to stock up so she could decide when and how to pull the plug?

'I wasn't going to do it today or even anytime soon. I just wanted the option. I wanted to know it was there.' Rachel's eyes were bright with the tears that sheer will was holding back.

'I know.'

'So, now you'll have to do it. When the time comes, and you'll know when it is, you'll have to come in one night and put a pillow over my face, firmly and kindly, and hold it there until I'm gone.'

Honey was in no doubt whatsoever that she meant it. Her immediate, inappropriate thought was: It's okay, by then she'll have forgotten she ever asked you. But then came the counter-mand: The point is she asked you now, when she's relatively sound of mind. She's asking you for help and you just said you're her advocate, so what's it going to be?

She realised Rachel was waiting for her answer.

'I'll think about it.'

A moment, and Rachel nodded. 'Fair enough.'

Then she smiled, and Honey saw the years slip away; suddenly it was the face she remembered from her childhood, the one from long before her dad left and Scarlett died.

'I'm going to write it down so I remember. And in Mandarin too, to be on the safe side.'

'You do that, Mum. You do that.'

THE HOSPITAL WANTED TO KEEP Rachel in for a few more days for another psych assessment, and Honey was glad she wasn't the one who had to deal with the fallout. She had some sympathy for her mother; Rachel didn't need a shrink to tell her that if she persisted in having these thoughts, she could be sectioned under the Mental Health Act and be kept in a secure place and under observation until (if) she was deemed to be no longer at risk to herself or others. Kind Honey could have argued with the medical officer and had Rachel sent home into her care with some provisos and follow-ups, but she genuinely thought that it was better left to the professionals. Selfish Honey also had to admit she wanted more time to explore things with Marshall. She could imagine what Rachel would think and say if she knew she'd been lying naked with *him* beside her just a few hours earlier.

Honey found Marshall sitting with Gollum. She was so shocked at the sight of his uncle that she felt sure she was in the wrong room. The last time she'd seen Jim he'd been broadchested, muscular and straight-backed, his handsome face marred, or enhanced, depending on your taste, by a long pale scar that ran from the corner of his left eye almost to his chin. Stories about how he came by that scar varied, but all of them involved tales of the sea and near-death. Minus the scar, he'd looked a lot like Marshall did now.

He was lying in the bed with the cover pulled up just far enough to cover his crotch, with one coat hanger-like leg extended out to the side. His skin was a pale dirty yellow, stretched tightly over bones, his body was all sharp corners, and his face was a skull, nothing more. The room had a strange, cloying smell of decay, mixed with something else. It was sweat and death and hash oil.

'Oh, oh, here come the cops, hide the bong,' Marshall said, smiling, and Honey could see a vape with a mouthpiece and square box on the bedside table. 'You remember Honey, eh Jim? Honey Chalmers?'

Jim's eyes searched and came into focus, and Honey saw something awful in them, something like terror.

'Kia ora, Jim,' she said lightly, hoping she hadn't betrayed her shock, then adding unnecessarily, 'long time, no see.'

There was no doubt that whatever Jim was seeing, it wasn't completely of this world. He tore his eyes from Honey and looked back to Marshall.

'What's she doing here?' His voice ground its way from his ravaged lungs.

'I asked her to drop in, say hello. Is that not okay?'

Jim muttered something under his breath.

'What did you say?'

'Get her out, the fuck away, I don't want her looking at me . . . tell that cunt to go . . . don't look at me bitch . . .'

But Marshall was already on his feet and guiding her out the door. 'No worries, Jim, she's going now, it's okay, don't stress it.'

Out in the corridor, Marshall shook his head, bemused. 'Well,

I wasn't expecting that. What did you ever do to Jim?'

'Me? What? Nothing. Nothing that I know of.'

She'd last seen Jim the day after Scarlett's funeral. She'd been in the pub, hoping that Marshall would swing by, unaware he'd already skipped town. Jim was in the front bar, buying a bottle of something, and she'd gone through and asked him about Marshall. He hadn't been exactly friendly, but nor had he been particularly unpleasant. As far as she could remember, he'd just shrugged, said Marshall had headed back to Otago, and they'd gone their separate ways: Honey to drown her sorrows and deal with her guilt, and Jim presumably back to his shack or his boat.

'Probably got you mixed up with someone else,' Marshall said. 'Poor bastard's only got a couple weeks, maybe less. The staff say he has nightmares and screams at night. He's even been talking to Father Yun, which is a miracle for two reasons: one, that Jim's never had any time for the Church and two, because he's pretty racist.'

'And because maybe he's stoned off his tits?'

'Yeah, that too. You know Ariki donates it for free to the hospice on request? Now that's a real Christian.' He stopped smiling. 'I'm just about done here, but if you've got to shoot off—'

'I can wait for you in the car park.'

'Only if you want to.'

'I want to.'

'I could drop by later—'

'I don't mind waiting . . .'

'Are you sure?'

Christ, what was it about sleeping with someone that made every conversation suddenly loaded with subtext?

SHE WAS LEANING AGAINST THE Mini Clubman, revisiting the morning's activities, remembering Marshall's mouth on hers, when a voice hailed her.

'Hey Honey!' It was Gemma shepherding an elderly woman under a covered walkway. Honey waved back, but her heart sank as she watched Gemma say a few words to the woman and then click-clack in her heels across the bitumen.

'Honey! How's your mum? Is she okay? I've seen her in the day room, but I'm not sure she recognises me.' Gemma wiggled her hips, and Honey decided that drawing attention to her surgical enhancements had probably become a kind of protective tic.

'She's not too bad.' Honey shrugged. 'What about you, what brings you here?' She pretended to be interested but glanced in the direction of the hospice, hoping Marshall would take his time.

'Oh, I do some volunteer work with the old dears — you know, keeping myself busy. Gets me off the farm and you never know, maybe I'll meet another doctor!' Gemma laughed again, showing perfect teeth. 'I was going to say forget the coffee date, why don't we catch up properly for a girls' night, go to the pub, tie one on? I could certainly do with it.'

It was on the tip of Honey's tongue to say she'd been there only last night, but she didn't want to explain herself and she had to give Gemma points for trying.

'Yeah, why not, that would be fun.'

'Friday night?'

That still left her two nights with Marshall. She looked at Gemma again and recognised the loneliness. 'Friday night, sure. Sounds good.'

'That's great. Let's do the number thing.' She held up her phone to Honey, who hesitated just a moment before taking it and putting in her number. 'Don't tell your mum in case she tries to break us up again!'

'I won't,' Honey said, thinking Gemma would be the least of Rachel's concerns when it came to the company Honey was keeping.

A moment later a message crossed her screen: *c u Friday x.*

'Now you've got my number too, no excuses,' Gemma said, then trotted off back to her 'old dear'.

Honey was about to go back to an audio book on her phone when Marshall appeared from a different direction from the one she'd expected. 'About bloody time—' she began, but the rest stuck in her throat. Behind Marshall, partly obscured by the hospital pool and physio room, was the front half of the black BMW. Same tinted windows, same shadowy guys with caps.

Marshall's smile faded. 'Hey, what's up? You okay?'

'I'm not sure.'

'Look, don't worry about Jim. He's obviously in a very bad place.'

'It's got nothing to do with Jim.'

Marshall turned to follow her gaze. 'Who are they?'

'I don't know.'

But she intended to find out. She shifted to get a better view of the plates.

'Do you want me to ask?' He said it so simply and in such a straightforward way it took a moment for Honey to register. By then he was already moving.

'No, wait, it's too dangerous!'

'Dangerous, how?' He looked over at the car again. 'They gang bangers?'

Before Honey could answer, there was a throaty roar as the BMW fired up and pulled away with a Hollywood screech.

'Not very subtle.'

'You don't know the half of it.'

Honey was explaining how she'd seen the same car in the supermarket car park, and maybe it was a coincidence they were in Waitutū but then again maybe it wasn't, when some sixth sense made her glance around again. The Beemer was nowhere in sight, but someone was standing by the Reception sign, watching them with a face set like concrete. Gemma.

'Don't look now but we're being watched,' Marshall whispered, mock dramatic.

'I know. It'll be all over town by dinner time.'

'Honey and Marshall up a tree, K-I-S-S-I-N-G.'

'You can laugh, but she still makes me feel like we're back in school. Besides, she asked me if she thought she had a chance with you.'

'What did you say?'

'I said, go for it.'

'Gee thanks.'

They watched as Gemma turned and headed towards her own car, a late-model white Mercedes, unlocking it as she approached, pretending she hadn't been watching them. For some reason Honey felt a chill.

17

MARSHALL WAS PAYING HER SCARS some proper attention this time around. They'd made it inside, even pretended they were going to have a cup of tea, but then they'd kissed and that was that. She'd pushed Marshall back onto the couch and dropped her pants while he tugged his jeans down. Then she had knelt between his thighs and taken his penis in her mouth and gently worked it while she cupped his balls until he was groaning and squirming. Then he'd stopped her, lifted her head and kissed her again, gently guided her back onto the carpet and went down on her, softly.

Not a single rogue thought found its way into her head as she moaned and made tiny movements of her hips. She was about to die or come, and had to have him inside her. In a magic sleight of hand, he'd somehow managed to slip a condom on. She rolled him over, mounted him, hands pressed against his chest, in total control of the moment right up until she lost it. No pissy little skyrockets this time, more hypersonic missiles, right on target, the end of the world.

'I'm very glad you didn't die,' he was saying as he traced his forefinger over the scars. Honey couldn't help but think, the same forefinger that had recently been so wonderfully inside her.

'Me too.' She was pleasantly surprised she could speak.

Then Marshall said, 'I have to go soon.'

She was annoyed at how anxious that made her feel.

Marshall's lips explored her back for a long moment, then he propped himself on one elbow and tried to explain. 'I've got a neighbour who takes care of the milking and collects the eggs and looks in when I'm away, but they've got their own place to run and there's stuff needs doing.'

'That's okay,' she said as she rolled over onto her back. 'I've got stuff too.'

He stared at her for a moment. 'I know you better than I've ever known anyone in my whole life, and at the same time I haven't got a fucking clue what you're thinking. How can that be?'

'Back at you.'

'Okay, to be absolutely clear, I'm going back home to do what needs to be done so that things don't suffer and die, but I want to see you again as soon as possible.'

'Works for me.' Then a thought struck her. 'How does your neighbour know to do it — to look after your place, I mean — if you don't have a phone?'

Marshall sat up. 'You'd be a cop, wouldn't you?'

'Just answer the question, mister.'

'Maybe I kind of mentioned to them that I *might* be staying the night in town.'

'So you'd planned it all along, to get me drunk and take advantage of me. You cad.'

'Yep.'

Her hand snaked south to confirm. They weren't finished.

THEY STOPPED IN AT WIREMU'S garage to get replacement valves for Marshall's truck. Honey had toyed with the idea of parking around the corner, but then thought fuck it: Gemma seeing them together was as good as posting it. Might as well flop it out for all to see. Wiremu's face alone made it worthwhile.

Honey got out to fill up, while Marshall headed into the shop. But first she touched his arm and gave him a smile. Wiremu's open-mouth stare was comedy gold. Honey wanted to toot like Road Runner, and had a mental image of a giant anvil dropping on his head. She felt almost unbearably delighted as she filled the tank.

Wiremu was laboriously picking four valves out of a plastic container when she went in to pay for the petrol. She could just about hear the gears whirring: how was he going to get all the information he needed to plug the yawning gap in his intel?

'Hey Wiremu, what's up?'

'Same old, same old,' he said, though Honey had no doubt he was thinking something entirely different. Far too much was new. 'Marshall was just telling me someone took all four of his valves last night. From outside of the pub? That's not acceptable.'

'Yeah, some people, eh?' She was impressed he could sound so affronted on Marshall's behalf, the same Marshall he'd been badmouthing for over a decade.

'I'll say. There's been talk of getting some cameras put in around town, but you know the council, Waitutū is bottom of the list. I was broken into on Friday and it took two whole days for the police to get round to coming by. Didn't even look for fingerprints, said it wasn't worth getting a team all the way out here. Word of advice: if you're going to get robbed, make sure it's Monday to Friday between nine and five, and even then you might have to haul Constable Evans off the golf course.'

Honey made sympathetic noises. 'Look, I was wondering if you'd noticed a black BMW around town lately — tinted windows, couple of guys, one of them really big?'

Of course Wiremu had. 'I mentioned them to Constable Evans, because if it'd been local kids did the break-in, the first thing they would've gone for would've been the cigarette cupboard. But it wasn't touched. I remembered those two fellas stopped in the day before and something about the way they looked about made me think they were checking the place out. The giant looked PI but sounded Australian to me. The other fella was Kiwi, I'd say.'

'What did he look like?'

'Pākehā, about the same height as you,' he said, nodding at Marshall. 'Not exactly skinny, but muscly, you know, like a greyhound, if that makes any sense.'

It made perfect sense to Honey, and she had to take a moment to breathe as Wiremu continued.

'He had gold earrings in both ears, and a good head of hair. Might've been brown, but light. Seemed polite and friendly enough. If it wasn't for his mate, I might not have taken as much notice.'

He waited, but Honey took another moment to be sure she could speak.

'You know anything about them?' Wiremu pressed, clearly wanting to trade for his information.

'Not really,' Honey lied, pleased to hear her voice sounding in control. 'Thanks, Wiremu, you're a legend.'

He would have to make do with that. But then, just as she was leaving, she had one more question.

'The break-in. What exactly did they take?'

'Some new tyres, a compressor, some tools, Malcolm's still making a list.' Wiremu shrugged and didn't meet Honey's eyes. She was pretty sure that meant he'd be claiming for a few things on insurance that never existed or needed upgrading. 'What really got my goat was the mess they made, emptying my drawers, throwing about invoices. That's rude and unnecessary.'

Honey could feel Wiremu's eyes on them as they headed back to her car.

'I don't want to sound like a misogynist,' Marshall murmured, 'but he is such an old maid.'

'And a total hypocrite and a bitch,' Honey agreed.

'You okay?'

'Yeah.'

She wasn't, but she wasn't ready to talk about it either.

He finished pumping up the tyres with a nifty device that screwed into a sparkplug socket and used the Land Cruiser's own compression to do the hard work. Honey drily wondered if his tyres were let down so often he needed to carry it around. He said he'd got it when working outback in Australia, never left home without it.

Then came the awkward moment of parting.

'So,' said Marshall as he slammed shut the bonnet, 'I guess I'd better get a move on. Sourdough starter waits for no man.'

He went over and held her. She imagined the whole town taking a collective breath, but then admonished herself for being narcissistic. Ninety-five percent don't even remember you, her mother would say.

'Do you want to come out to mine tonight? I'll cook something nice; we could sit on the veranda and watch the little lambsies gambol.'

'I'd love to,' she started, and meant it, 'but—'

'Always with the buts.'

'But I have to be available for Mum, so unless you want to erect a cellphone tower this afternoon, or get a landline put in, you're going to have to come to me.'

Marshall barely hesitated. 'Will do. But I'll need to leave about five in the morning. I can't expect my neighbour to fill in for every booty call.'

'A booty call. Is that what it is?'

'I don't know, what do you want to call it?'

'Booty call is fine with me.'

He shook his head in mock sorrow. 'It's okay, I know you're deeply, madly in love with me and this is just a tough act you put on to hide the fact you're a squishy marshmallow of affection inside.'

'Don't wake me when you go.'

'No promises.'

Suddenly she wanted to cut through the bullshit. 'By the way. Thank you,' she said.

'What for?' He seemed caught off-guard.

'An amazing day. And the best sex ever.'

He hesitated.

Doubt came flooding in. Had it not been the same for him? 'Should I have not said that?'

'No, I mean, it's not . . . I just . . .' He smiled weakly. 'I guess I was waiting for the punch line.'

'I wasn't joking.'

'Christ, that's a relief. And yes, yes, the best day and the best sex. In fact, the only problem is, now the bar's so high, what if I let you down?'

'I guess we'll have to call the whole thing off.'

'Yeah, I guess we will.'

They stood grinning like idiots at each other. Honey finally broke.

'Go on, go and biodegrade or whatever it is you have to do. I'll leave the light on.'

Marshall's smile faded. 'Actually that's probably a good idea. And lock the doors and check that it's me first.'

She knew he was referring to the guys in the Beemer, and was torn between telling him everything and telling him nothing, and in the end settled on an anodyne middle ground. She told him that yeah, she had an idea who they were, but it probably had nothing to do with her, she was just being nosy, it came with being a cop and she'd be fine. She could see he was doubtful, but when it was clear she wasn't going to get specific he kissed her one more time, reluctantly released her and got into the Land Cruiser.

Honey waved him off, feeling silly and crazy happy. But a sudden thought brought her crashing back to earth. What if the break-in at Wiremu's hadn't been about stealing but about finding? The invoice for her car service, with her rego number, name and her mum's address on it, would have been there, written out, old school. Maybe it was a long bow. But as Michelle had told her, the Reapers had gone to a hell of a lot of trouble trying to track down Kloe Kovich. She couldn't for the life of her think what that had to do with her after all this time. But like most cops she didn't believe in coincidence.

The scar on her back was starting to itch. Less than an hour ago Marshall was kissing it. Her next thought made her shiver too, but not in a good way. If they were coming for her, just locking the doors probably wasn't going to cut it.

18

KLOE DOES EXACTLY WHAT SHYLA told her to. She drives. Her eyes are wide and wild, she's in a murky tunnel, heading for the light. She's on autopilot. She's lost contact with air traffic control. Maybe she stops at red lights, maybe she doesn't. Eventually she becomes aware she is on the motorway heading south. She's got half a tank of petrol and maybe two hundred bucks on her card. Part of her wants to take the next exit home, but she knows that would only put herself and Shyla in danger. Less than an hour ago she was resigned to dying; now, more than anything, she wants to live, and being alive means she really needs a smoke.

She fumbles in her bag for her tobacco. There is the arse-tearing blare of a horn as a massive SUV passes on the outer lane and she overcorrects, nearly flipping the unstable people-mover into the emergency stopping lane. A semi blasts an air horn at her as it weaves past. She pulls to a halt, grasps the steering wheel tightly and screams.

A few moments later a patrol car passes, the brake lights briefly flicker, and Kloe feels relief pass through her like a gentle breeze. Getting busted would take the decision out of her hands. She'll tell them about Honey, tell them what she did, accept her fate. But the cops must've changed their minds, or had better things to do, and the patrol car keeps going.

She is frantically searching through her bag for a lighter that isn't there when she realises what else is missing: her phone. Fuck! FUCK! She sees it sitting on the table and Marty picking it up and putting it in his pocket with a look of what? Resignation? Pity?

Her brain jumps to a parallel *what if* world where Jason never hit her, where she never called that pigshit. She pictures herself at the kitchen window, peeling spuds. She's watching the kids on the trampoline. She loves them fiercely, this much she knows, even if everything else is fucked up. And she knows that Renata will take care of them, and Shyla too, and they're safer without their mother. But then she realises something else. Her sister must have known about Keg and Marty coming for her. The order had to have come from Hammer, and there was no way in the world he wouldn't have told Renata. Kloe feels warm, sticky tears on her face.

Thinking about her kids helps Kloe focus. A few minutes later she pulls back onto the motorway and continues for a few kilometres before taking an off-ramp, turning around and merging onto the motorway north. She doesn't really know why, except that the North was where they were from, her people — at least that's what Renata told her.

She pulls into a service station in Wellsford, and it hurts like hell to put her weight on her ankle. The relief and humiliation of being saved by her daughter threaten to undermine her all over again. She limps to the cashier to prepay and briefly entertains the idea of trying to borrow a phone to call Shyla to make sure she's okay. But without her phone she knows nobody's number.

Kloe leaves the service station with eighty-four bucks and her pockets crammed full of stolen chocolate bars. Pretty soon she's convinced herself that North is where the future lies and the northern tollway is the yellow brick road. That's the thing about Kloe: she's always fucking up but she always bounces back; her superpower is in believing, despite all evidence to the contrary, that things *can* get better. As she drives on, trailed by a thin cloud of grey-blue smoke, she remembers the thought of the day, written in chalk on the open sign out the front of a neighbourhood café: *Today is the first day of the rest of your life.*

She's been given another chance and fucked if she isn't going to make the most of it. A Lorde song comes on the radio and she starts singing at the top of her voice her own improvised lyrics:

'Today is the first day of the rest of your life — fuck yeah!
After today, it's gonna be okay — fuck yeah!
It's a brand new day, you gonna find your way — fuck yeah!'

19

AFTER HONEY SAID GOODBYE TO Marshall, her next stop was the Waitutū police station. The 'temporary' structure had been there for thirty years and would probably be there for thirty more. It sat squat and uninviting on a flat piece of gravel on Dufort Street that ran parallel with the main road. She'd thought of paying a courtesy visit before, but knew the natural suspicion country cops have for their city counterparts. Especially of the female variety.

The woman behind the counter looked as if she was wearing a wig made out of Steelo pads. Honey guessed mid-fifties, but it was hard to tell. She was wearing a lime-green shirt and a lot of powder, and regarded Honey with bright, curious eyes.

'Hello, love. What can we do for you today?'

'I'm Honey Chalmers. I was wondering if I could talk to the officer on duty.'

'You're the detective, right? Rachel's girl?'

'That's right. Well, technically I'm on leave but, yeah.'

'I know! Rachel's told me *all* about you.'

Honey braced herself for another rave review of her mother's character. Instead, the woman clambered down off her stool and came barrelling through the security door to the side of the counter. 'Well, it's about bloody time you stopped by! I'm Rhonda, Rhonda Carlyle. Nice to meet you.' She came up to Honey's chin.

'Nice to meet you, too,' said Honey, shaking her hand.

'Now I'm afraid young Shane is out on highway patrol, and

Morrie Evans — let's see, what time is it?' She consulted the clock on the opposite wall. 'It's Wednesday, so there's a good chance Morrie had to do a lunchtime investigation out at the golf club. And depending how that goes, he might have to do a follow-up for nine holes on the green.'

A neat row of tiny teeth. Honey grinned back. She already liked this woman.

'Anything I can help you with? Would you like a cuppa? I know I could do with one.'

Honey hesitated only for a nanosecond. She'd bet on Rhonda being more useful than the two sworn officers combined. It was easy money.

'NOT MUCH I CAN TELL you about the break-in at the garage.' Rhonda stirred three teaspoons of white death into her tea. 'Morrie decided it wasn't a priority, and that's a shame, but to be honest Wiremu's only got himself to blame, the tight old bugger. He refuses to put in security cameras. Between you and me, every time there's a break-in, Wiremu gets some shiny new tools, so I'm guessing he's in no hurry to have the case solved.'

'Sounds about right to me.' Honey smiled. 'Do you know if there've been any other reports of a black Beemer, rego KWY 342?'

'A couple of phone-ins,' Rhonda said. 'You know what it's like, locals keeping eyes on strangers.'

Honey knew all right. If they were a couple of polo-shirted white guys in an Audi it'd be a different story.

'I believe they're staying out of town, down at Jagged Bay. Someone phoned that there'd been a break-in at one of the flash new baches, so Morrie and Shane did go down there for a chat.

They talked to a fellow called—' Rhonda rummaged around in her memory. 'Martin someone.'

'Martin Pascoe?' Honey's heart rate quickened a notch, though this merely confirmed what she'd suspected from Wiremu's description. Martin — Marty — was a lieutenant to Hammer, and unlike most of the Reapers had spent most of his life in New Zealand. She remembered the quiet Kiwi voice in her ear.

'That's the one. Apparently, he had a good explanation for being there, said the bach belonged to a friend of a friend, and there was no sign of a break-in. I can't guarantee that Morrie followed it up, but he will now.'

Honey had no doubt. She'd watched in awe as Rhonda dealt with endless distractions, never breaking the flow. At one point she was on the phone, sending an email and making more tea while fielding an enquiry from a walk-in wanting to get out of paying a speeding fine. The woman was the definition of multi-tasking.

Now, as Honey stood to leave, Rhonda asked, matter-of-fact, 'I don't suppose you're thinking of checking out the situation at Jagged Bay yourself?'

Honey hesitated, but Rhonda was already reaching for a pad and pen. 'Here, I'll sketch you the location of this bach. It's a bit hard to find unless you know where to look. Just promise you'll take care. By the sounds of it, these fellas aren't the kind you want to tangle with.'

'You've got that right,' said Honey. 'Thanks, Rhonda.'

Rhonda regarded her for a moment before speaking again.

'Your mum talked to me a bit about you being attacked. She was gutted, especially because she was worrying about losing her marbles and not knowing if you'd need looking after long term and if she'd be up to it.'

It was true Rachel had come to stay immediately after the assault, but when it became apparent Honey was in the clear and that she wasn't going to let Rachel take her back to Waitutū, Rachel had got sniffy and left, saying she had patients who needed and appreciated her. A few months later came the diagnosis and Honey was here anyway.

'We're not exactly close,' Rhonda said, sensing that Honey was put out, 'but she needed a shoulder. Sometimes it's a bit easier to talk openly to someone you don't know too well. All I'm saying is I know a bit of what you've been through and I've no doubt you've got the sense to be careful, but if you do need anything at all, call me.' She wrote her mobile number down on the back of the paper. 'Morrie sometimes doesn't answer his phone after hours in case there's work involved, and young Shane has a social life that involves trips out of town and sleepovers. I'm likely to be your best bet.'

JAGGED BAY, ABOUT FIFTEEN KILOMETRES by seagull south of Waitutū but twice that by road, was aptly named for the rocky, irregular cliffs and headlands on either side of the small bay. There wasn't a lot of sand, and it wasn't a safe place to swim, but the fishing and view were terrific.

Honey had attempted minor disguise with one of her mother's big floppy sunhats and eighties-style sunglasses. She was driving Rachel's elderly but serviceable Corolla. It wasn't nearly as much fun as the Clubman, but she had to assume the Reapers knew her car. The little silver-grey Jap import had been sitting in the garage since Rachel had finally acknowledged that driving might be problematic, and Honey was impressed that it had started first attempt.

There was only one way in and out of Jagged Bay, via a narrow bitumen road that wound for 12 k off the highway. The little settlement had come up in the world. Where Honey remembered jerry-built houses of faded weatherboard and recycled tin, much grander iterations now stood, along with faux pillars, well-kept lawns, gleaming galvanised garages and flash boats alongside the shiny new tractors needed for hauling them in and out of the sea. No doubt the owners in Auckland or Wellington still said they were 'off to the bach' for the weekend. The thought amused Honey. The rich could head to their palaces, and the poor could beg a week in some crumbling shack that had been in someone's family for generations, but both would be 'off to the bach'.

Whatever way you looked at it, there was serious money in Jagged Bay, and it was easy to understand why a couple of gang bangers from Auckland would prompt calls to the local police from concerned citizens. Honey too doubted that Marty Pascoe was here for the fishing.

The map Rhonda had drawn showed the main road changing from bitumen to gravel just the other side of the 'town', then branching off into several shared tracks leading to farms or houses. The place where Marty and his oversized mate — whom Honey guessed was Arthur 'Keg' Kahane — were reportedly staying was just a few ks back from a dead end. She couldn't access it on foot along the rocky beach because she risked being trapped by the tide. The narrow track in was the only way, but she knew that if she met Marty and Keg coming in or out her 'disguise' might not pass muster. Still, what choice did she have? Fuck 'em, she thought, yet again, and continued along the gravel road that soon turned into sandy track flanked with bush on the seaward side and open farmland on the other. Ten minutes later, she slowed to pass an incongruously large, shiny metal gate with a chain and big padlock at the entrance to the driveway but no fence on either side. The house, just visible through the mānuka scrub, was brick; ugly and new, in stark contrast to the surroundings.

She kept going and turned into the next driveway, continuing for fifty metres or so before stopping. The house up ahead was more modest than its neighbour, a basic pale-blue weatherboard bungalow on stilts with a million-dollar view over the ocean. There were no cars or occupants in sight.

To her right was a rough bush track leading back in the direction of the gang house, as she now thought of it. She bush-bashed her way along it in the little Toyota, coming to a halt behind the trunk of a large tōtara. She could just make out the burnt-orange side of the house through the trees.

Honey checked her phone: there was a flickering single bar of reception, so maybe it would work or maybe it wouldn't. Her plan, such as it was, was to get as close as she could without being spotted, and confirm the presence of Marty Pascoe and whoever else. After that she'd improvise. She had no doubt Michelle's information was good and the Reapers had gone to a lot of trouble to try to find Kloe. And *if* they were keeping tabs on Honey too, and *if* the break-in at Wiremu's was connected, then they must think she, Honey, could lead them to her.

But there were plenty of ifs, whys and buts to this theory. *If* Kloe was still alive, it was possible she could seek out Honey — but *why* now? It was nine months, closer to ten, since they had last spoken, so what had Kloe been doing in the meantime? Why hadn't she just called? How the hell had she stayed under the radar? And while it was true that Kloe was hardly Mensa material, she must know that Honey would guess that she had tipped the

Reapers off about where to find her. As if she'd be welcomed with open arms!

Honey started to open the car door but then stopped. Her heart was beating fast, and her hands were shaking; she was having trouble breathing. She tried willing herself to move, but nothing happened.

Before the attack she'd been quietly confident she could handle herself in most situations. She boxed, had taken a few intensive self-defence courses, and worked out at the police gym with weights and circuits. She had handled herself well in the field, dealt with domestic violence callouts and dangerous offenders, and tackled fleeing suspects twice her weight to the ground. She always felt in her bones she'd be a useful person in a stoush. Deluded.

From the moment the bag went over her head and powerful hands gripped her, she was frozen with terror, unable to think or to act. Her limbs and body felt like they'd been dropped in wet concrete. Her rational mind checked out and she could hear her tiny animal self pleading for its life. The memory of it embarrassed and disgusted her. Her counsellor had tried to get her to imagine it, to give it shape and form and to forgive it, and she'd played along — a necessary lie on the road to getting back to work — but she had never excused or pardoned it, *herself*, for being so weak at the very moment she needed most to be strong. Perhaps that was the reason she'd taken so well to running after *the incident* (i.e. code 1410 grievous assault): if she couldn't stand and fight, maybe she could outrun any attackers. Okay, it was cod psychology, but she knew, whatever else, she never wanted to experience that sense of helplessness again. And here she was, all alone and her body refusing to let her move. She focused on that one thing, her breath.

It seemed impossible at first; her body was so beyond her mind's control that she might as well have been watching from a satellite. She was panting, hyperventilating. *Just breathe.* But after an age that was probably a few minutes, her body responded. *Breathe.* Eyes closed, she pictured the air moving in, moving out, felt her chest expand and contract. The trembling subsided and then stopped. She opened her eyes, and the world was quiet except for the sound of the air coming in, going out. Gradually she became aware of other sounds. Rustling in the bushes, birds, a light plane somewhere. And, just like that, the panic attack was over.

Honey felt a rush of delight. Her rational mind knew it was just chemicals in her brain, endorphins, her body's response to fight or flight. She didn't care. She gazed with wonder at the bush around her. The edges of the trees were sharp against the thick grey clouds, the sea a quilt of green and dark shadows; the horizon made her heart feel like it was lifting out and up and soaring . . .'

She took stock. The mere possibility of being in the vicinity of at least one of the men who'd tried to kill her had caused a crippling anxiety attack. The sensible thing now would be to back up the Toyota and get the hell out of Dodge. That's definitely what the scared little animal was pleading for.

'Fuck 'em.'

Honey quietly pushed the driver's door shut and moved around to open the boot. She leaned in and took out a rifle. It was an old .22 semi-automatic Winchester with a five-shot magazine, basic scope and silencer. Her dad had used it for rabbit shooting, and it had somehow survived several gun amnesties since. Honey was nine when he'd taught her how to shoot with it, lying silently on her belly watching the rabbits come out to play on a grassy hill, slowly squeezing the trigger. She remembered the muffled phhhht of the bullet leaving the barrel via the silencer, and watching her target kicking up the sandy soil a moment and then stopping. He'd taught her how to skin a rabbit without a knife, pulling it in one piece like a wetsuit turned inside out. If you looked closely enough sometimes you could see the translucent lens over the eyes still attached.

Honey had found the gun, along with a couple of boxes of ammo, in a rusted metal locker in the garage when she was looking for Scarlett's diary. She'd put it aside, intending to drop it off at the station for safe disposal. Just before driving out, she'd located the key for the trigger lock on its rabbit-foot chain amongst about a hundred other keys of forgotten purpose in a kitchen drawer, given the rifle a clean and an oil, and transferred it to the boot of her mother's car, just in case — but she hadn't exactly been thinking clearly. In fact, from the moment Rhonda had mentioned Martin Pascoe, she'd been on the edge of panic. Now she felt the weight of it, looked at the dull barrel, the worn walnut stock. Nothing like a gun to start people shooting, she thought grimly. She put the rifle back, pushed the boot shut again, locked the car, and walked as quietly as she could through the bush.

20

KLOE NEEDED A PLAN. SHE'D been driving north for about five hours before pulling into a wayside stop on the outskirts of Kerikeri. By then it was well dark, and she was exhausted. She'd filled a Coke bottle with water at a toilet stop, got a brief sugar hit from a stolen Crunchie bar, but still she had to push back against the despair that threatened to overwhelm her. She thought again of turning around, throwing herself on Hammer's mercy, begging her sister to help her . . . But no, this was the first day of the rest of her life.

She could sleep in the people-mover, use public toilets to wash, scrounge food and necessities, steal clothes off clotheslines if she had to. She'd always wanted to see Cape Rēinga, the place where Māori believe the souls of the dead went before jumping into the sea and heading into the afterlife. Or something. Shyla would know. Jesus, she missed her already. She'd been so fucking brave, holding that gun on the guys, the look of respect on Marty's face. The kids would be asking about her, and Renata would be making up some story. 'Mummy had to go away' . . . She couldn't let herself wallow. *The first day of the rest of your life.*

But meantime she was bone-weary tired. She clambered into the back and lay down across the bench seat. It was awkward, trying to position herself where the seat belt catches didn't dig in, but eventually she got settled and closed her eyes.

She is running, trying to get out of the house that's on fire, but where are the kids? She can't leave without them, and now Shyla is here, saying it's all right, and leading her into a big white room. It's a giant fridge, like out the back at the butcher's, there are carcasses hanging, and she sees her kids are huddled in the corner, covered in a spider web of ice, crying.

She snapped awake. It was dark and really fucking cold. Then she remembered where she was, and why. With trembling hands, she put the key in the ignition and checked the time: it was just gone half past eight. Fuck! She had on just the clothes she was wearing when Shyla waved the gun around and told her to go — a thin cotton blouse and frayed denim shorts and a pair of jandals. For once there was no kids' clothing scattered in the back or even an old sack she could use to cover herself. Fucking typical, she'd paid the kids five bucks each to clean the car just the other day. Through the windscreen the dark dome of the sky was cloud free, filled with more stars than she'd ever seen.

But she wasn't in a mood to appreciate the view.

AT 9 P.M. ON A Monday night the main street of Kerikeri looked like the after-shot of the apocalypse. Bring on the zombies. The brightest spot seemed to be the Colonial Hotel, a rundown two-storey weatherboard pub with a sagging balcony all around. The main thing going for it was that it was open. Kloe parked the people-mover around the back. She put her weight gingerly on her ankle. It wasn't too bad, and her motivation was strong.

The ten-minute drive with the heater on full blast had thawed her out, and she felt herself relax a notch when she entered the side door to find a real fire going in the lounge, actual people sitting at tables and at the bar. It was a sanctuary from a cruel and lonely world. Well, okay, she'd only been alone for half a day, less, but she felt like she was coming in from the cold in more ways than one. The middle-aged barman was friendly enough, and moments later she was perched at the bar with a pint of beer and a packet of peanuts and let the chatter of the room and the TV screens wash over her like a fond memory.

The first half of the pint went down in one smooth, satisfying moment. She reminded herself that she had to make this last. But her thirsty self ignored the sensible one, and she was soon forking out another eight bucks she couldn't afford. *This* beer she was going to sit on. She glanced around her, feeling the need to get out of her head and talk to other people. In the front bar a younger guy with a straggly beard that looked like a cat had coughed up fur-balls over his face was looking at her. But something about his eyes gave her the creeps and she quickly looked away. She'd had enough dickheads to last her a lifetime. Why couldn't she meet a nice normal guy, for once? Kloe immediately answered herself. What normal guy would want her?

Since she'd been old enough, she'd rarely gone a day or two without a boy or a man of some kind in it. Already she was thinking her problems could be solved if she could find some guy to go home with tonight. A warm bed, somewhere to crash a few days while she sorted her shit. 'A bit of company and a fuck, what more could a girl want?' she pictured herself saying to Renata. Her smile froze. Not to Renata. That part of her life was over, gone. So was her second beer.

'You all right here, girl?'

She'd been so lost in her head she hadn't heard him come up beside her. She had to be more careful.

'Sorry, I didn't mean to startle you,' he said softly as he flashed a set of strong white teeth. He was broad faced, solidly built, and his skin was a deep dark-chocolate brown. Kloe guessed he'd be in his late fifties, too old for her really, but then again, beggars can't be—

'You on your own?'

'Yeah, I guess I am,' she improvised. 'I was supposed to be meeting a friend, but . . .'

'Well, it's only an hour or so till closing, but you're welcome to join us.' The man nodded in the direction of a table with maybe half a dozen people around it. 'I'm Samson, by the way.'

'How's it going, Samson. I'm — Maia.'

Maia was the name of a social worker who'd helped her get emergency housing when Shyla was small. It was a good name for her new beginning.

'Nice to meet you, Maia. What are you drinking?'

'Just a beer, thanks.' She smiled, keeping her lips pressed together. She didn't want him to see the gap where her front teeth used to be.

Samson's friends were a mixed crew, all ages and nationalities. Kloe found herself sandwiched between Joshua, a crate-shaped dude who barely glanced up from his phone and Mika, a chatty blonde woman with red cheeks who told her she was from Poland. Mika had spent every cent she had to come out to New Zealand to marry a Kiwi she'd met in Kraków who, it turned out, was already married. Nevertheless, she had fallen in love with the country and wanted to experience it firsthand and save some money doing fruit picking.

Devi, the young, rake-thin Indian man on her other side, seemed keen to explain. 'We have finished with the kiwifruit in Katikati for now and we are heading north to Kaitāia, did you know.'

'What about you, Maia,' said Samson, 'what brings you to Kerikeri?'

173

Good fucking question, thought Kloe, and no way to answer truthfully.

The group were looking at her with interest.

'I was a cleaner for six years but then the company got taken over and the new management let me go.' She was impressed with her lie, how easily it came to her. But fuck it, she had two little kids and Jason: she knew how to clean. 'That's why I left Auckland, there's nothing left for me there. And my ex, he was hassling me, wouldn't leave me alone. The cops said they couldn't do jack shit. I mean, sure, I got a restraining order, but that didn't mean anything to him, and if he did get it in his head to do something, by the time the cops got there, if they came at all, it'd be too late.' She looked down at the table, inspired. 'I come home this morning and he was waiting for me, real aggro, saying all this shit, so I guess I just freaked and took off.'

She was pleased to see the others nodding in agreement or understanding; even Joshua paused from playing on his phone. She told herself she wasn't lying, or not *really*. Jason did give her the bash, and the cops were useless in protecting her from the Reaps, so her story wasn't that different from the truth.

'Where are you going now? Tonight, I mean?' asked Samson.

'I've got a car, a people-mover, so there's plenty of room, I'll just park out the back, I'll be all right.' She tried not to sound too pathetic.

Another glance around the table, reading the mood, and then Samson said, 'Come to the camping grounds with us. We're heading off in the morning, but in the meantime you're welcome.'

'We've got plenty to eat,' added Devi. 'For breakfast, Rahl makes the best roti. He used to be a chef, did you know.'

'Are you sure?'

174

They were. The barman called last drinks and Kloe was hopeful, but her new friends readied themselves to leave. Rahl, it transpired, wasn't a drinker, so he was designated driver. Kloe insisted she was fine to drive herself, but Samson wouldn't hear of it: the police were known to wait until after closing to breathalyse incautious travellers, they had plenty of room in their mini-bus, they would drop her back to her car in the morning.

As Kloe stood, she felt her ankle give. She staggered a little and winced. Samson put out a hand to steady her.

'Are you okay?'

'I twisted my ankle, it's not too bad.' She liked how brave she sounded.

That night she had a hot shower and shared a tent with Mika who, as the only single woman in the group, had one all to herself. Mika cheerfully prattled on, and Kloe fell into a deep, dreamless sleep under a pile of borrowed blankets.

MIKA WASN'T IN HER SLEEPING bag, and when Kloe emerged from the tent, she found most of the camp had been packed up and the gang were enjoying a breakfast of roti and what looked like cat sick but was actually a mildly spiced dhal. It was quite possibly the best thing Kloe had ever eaten.

'Thanks, that was unreal,' she said at last, scraping her plate clean. Devi's partner, Sefina, silently took her plate and added it to a bucket of dirty dishes. Kloe sensed they were all keen to get moving. 'Are you okay to drop me back at my car?'

'Why don't you come with us?' said Mika.

'I . . . really?'

Samson shrugged. 'We had a chat about it this morning. We

could show you the ropes and carry you for a bit till your ankle's better and you're up to speed. We're going to be doing avocados and mandarins around Kaitāia, a bit of orchard maintenance as well, pulling up plastic and stuff like that — hard going, minimum wage, but some weeks we'll pull sixty hours so that's over a thousand clear a week.'

Kloe opened her mouth, but all that came out was a strange little gurgle.

'I'm sorry, I . . . shit . . . I don't . . . I—'

'It's okay, babe,' Mika said, putting her arms around Kloe. 'We'll take good care of you.'

21

HONEY HAD HERSELF A BIT of a situation. An hour and a half earlier she had set up her position about thirty metres from the house, lying down behind the scuted trunk of a large cabbage tree. From there she had a clear view of the exterior, as well as some of the living room through a set of picture windows. There had been no movement. The black BMW wasn't in the driveway, and she doubted Marty or Keg, or both, had gone to the trouble of parking it in the double garage, though there was no way of knowing for sure without taking a closer look. There was still no reception, but she'd taken a few photos and put her phone on mute in case.

As the day became heavy and the air metallic, tasting of impending rain, she decided it was now or never.

A cautious circuit of the house confirmed there was no one at home. She could see washed mugs and plates on the draining board by the sink. Some empty cans of Lion Ice were in a recycling bucket by the back door. For a couple of gang heavies, the boys were surprisingly tidy. The thick blinds were down on at least four of the bedrooms, but where french doors opened out onto a sheltered little fernery, open curtains revealed that at least one of the beds had been slept in. She wondered who maintained the garden, and noticed fine feeders and overhead sprayers that would be linked to an automatic timer. Whoever owned this house had spared no effort.

HONEY HAD BEEN PREPARED TO break something if she had to but was pleased to note a bathroom window slightly ajar. She quickly levered it open and wriggled through. She assumed there would be an alarm, if only for insurance purposes, but the state-of-the-art alarm system blinked unset in the hallway. She'd imagined getting in, having a quick look for anything to link the occupants to her or to Kloe, then getting the hell out again. This at least took the pressure off.

The house had a top-of-the-range wide-screen television and bluetooth speakers, along with a leather couch and some expensively comfortable chairs. A bookshelf along one wall contained a few bland *objets d'art* and holiday reading. There was a landline and Wi-Fi but no sign of a computer. In the bedroom she assumed was Martin Pascoe's (the leather motorcycle jacket was about a cow too small for his companion) she found what she was looking for. Under the bed, in a khaki canvas bag, was a folder containing printouts of documents and photos. One was a police surveillance sheet on Kloe Kovich dating back to the abortive Ōnehunga raid — stark confirmation of what Michelle had said about the Reaper mole.

As Honey spread the material out on the bed, she felt her heart racing. She was looking at candid photos of herself outside her Sandringham house — judging by her hair and general state, probably not long after her return from hospital. She shuddered to think the Reapers had been watching her even then. There were photos of her Clubman, of her mother's house, of Wiremu's garage, and even one of her outside the Waitutū supermarket. On the backs were written times and locations. Appalled as she was, she couldn't help but register the irony: she had entered Bizarro World, where the criminals were carrying out detailed, meticulous surveillance and the cop was breaking and entering.

Among the printouts was a high-angled CCTV grab of a woman in a baseball cap and dark sunglasses who may have been Kloe. It was time coded and dated only ten days ago. On the back was scrawled *Amohau Street, Rotorua*. Shit.

Honey had just pulled out her phone and begun to photograph the evidence when two things happened almost simultaneously. The skies opened in a subtropical deluge and a black BMW with tinted windows pulled up outside the house.

MARTY PASCOE WASN'T GIVEN TO sudden outbursts. He was usually polite, softly spoken, self-contained and capable of genuine acts of kindness. He wasn't afraid of his own company and, though he liked a game of pool or hanging out at HQ as much as the next member, he wasn't usually a participant in the gang's more violent recreational activities. His sexual needs were generally taken care of by a transwoman barely out of her teens who called herself Shakira and indeed bore an uncanny resemblance to her Colombian namesake.

Marty was helping to fund her transition and was mostly tolerant and even amused by the daily dramas that occupied her days and nights. Shakira often said she would die if Marty ever left her. Marty took that with a grain of salt. But he had proven without a doubt that he cared for her.

A few months earlier a creepy duo of subs had started stalking, raping and beating up sex workers around the back streets of K Road, and Shakira was terrified for her life and livelihood. So Marty waited and watched, identified, and then followed the shitheads back to their hole in Mount Roskill. They were playing a video game when Marty came in through the back door with his

179

favourite tool of trade, a baseball bat. They didn't even see him coming. Now the bigger one gets around in a wheelchair and his ratty little brother shits into a bag. You don't get to experience *that* on Xbox.

Marty came from a family of Cantabrian share milkers, but it was a hard fucking life for little return, and one morning, instead of milking the cows before school, he left for good. Christchurch skinheads took him in, and he learned about survival, but they didn't seem like any kind of master-race to him. A few years later he was freelancing as an enforcer for an Irish mob trying to get a toehold in the Pacific drug market when he was forced to take a sabbatical in Australia. Hammer threw him a lifeline, cleared the way for him to return to Aotearoa, and in return he was a loyal lieutenant. In that capacity he had murdered two men, not in the heat of battle but coolly and efficiently under orders. He had nearly killed a third — a woman cop — but she'd pulled through. This neither pleased nor displeased him from any moral perspective, but it had resulted in this extended Hegira in the wilderness, which was annoying. He missed his girl and his dog.

Right now, following his dash to the front porch of the house from the BMW, Marty was cursing quietly but profusely. He and Keg had sat in the car for a few minutes as an atmospheric river dumped half the Pacific on them but eventually made a run for it. Marty, in baggy shorts and jandals, had slipped on the steps, gone arse over, and let out a shout of shock and pain. Keg hadn't demeaned him by offering a hand up, but it was humiliating and it fucking hurt. Now he was sitting on his bed, holding a cold can of beer against his bloody shin and knee, unaware that at that moment the cop bitch he was meant to have offed was less than eight metres away.

HONEY HAD PLANNED AN ESCAPE route before she started her search. Assuming the occupants would come through the front door, closest to the driveway, she had unlocked the back door and figured she'd hear wheels on the gravel. But the rhythmic sweep of rain smashing against the roof had masked the arrival of the BMW, and it wasn't until she heard an almighty thump and a male voice cursing that she knew she had company.

She shoved the stuff into the folder, the folder back into the bag, the bag under the bed, and started to move, but heard someone already limping through the living room towards the kitchen. She risked a glance up the passageway and saw an enormous back blocking the front entrance: Keg Kahane. She ducked back and was pulling shut the sliding door of the wall-length built-in wardrobe in the adjoining bedroom when she heard the other one, presumably Marty, come through into the shared en suite bathroom and take a piss. It must have been the adrenaline, but she had to bite back a giggle, and almost lost it again when Marty flushed: she might be trapped with a vicious thug and murderer, but at least he had good manners. And struggling not to laugh was way better than a panic attack.

But the pissing and the flushing had brought up another issue. She was busting for a wee and had no idea how long the wait might be. As the men moved about, she tried to picture what they were doing: the air-lock sound of the fridge opening and closing, the crack and phttt of a beer can, the sound of Marty (she assumed) moving back into the bedroom. A soft scraping noise as she imagined him sliding the canvas bag from under the bed. She had no idea if she'd put its contents back in their original order. The flicking noise of him shaking out a pair of jeans, a thump that sounded like him changing weight from one leg to the other.

For the second time that day, she focused on her breathing, on relaxing, on letting go — but not of her bladder, although perhaps squatting and quietly relieving herself might not be such a bad idea . . . She was reaching to unbutton her jeans when she heard the jangle of the landline and the sound of Martin's uneven gait and his voice telling Keg that he'd get it. She slid the wardrobe door open and stepped out, trying to get close enough to hear: 'Yeah . . . Yeah . . . You sure? Okay. We'll go get (grab? go?) her . . . Yeah.' Marty hung up then, and he and Keg left in a hurry.

The moment she heard the BMW reversing up the driveway, Honey took a hurried but glorious piss and left through the back door.

She had to get on the road, *now*. The photo she'd seen put Kloe in Rotorua and Rotorua was only a couple of hours up the road. From what she'd heard of the garbled phone conversation, it was possible they were on their way to collect her now. She might, if she floored it, be able to pick up their trail. The other possibility, of course, was that they were going back into Waitutū to pick up Honey herself. Either way, she needed to be the hunter not the hunted. Another thought niggled, but she was in too much of a hurry to pay it much attention at that moment.

It was only after she had squelched and slid along the track that had turned into a quagmire, then tried to back out the little Toyota only to confirm that she was hopelessly bogged, that she remembered the other problem. She'd arranged to meet Marshall at her place once he'd put the chooks to bed and done the milking or whatever. If Marty and Keg were planning to do her some bad, and they found Marshall there instead . . . 'Fuck!' she yelled, as she revved the engine and the wheels just dug in deeper.

Twenty minutes later she was still cursing, and it was still raining. She had let air out of the tyres to increase their grip, laid down branches and old nīkau fronds — and had gained around ten metres. She checked hopelessly for cellphone reception again, and anyway, Marshall Luddite had no phone. She could go to the house and use the landline to call Rhonda to rouse the cops (not even Constable Evans would be playing golf in this weather) but she would have some serious explaining to do. Breaking and entering isn't generally considered a good career move. The folder couldn't even be cited, as she'd seen it very illegally.

'You right there, love?' A straight-backed elderly man was approaching down the track. He paused to take in the car, nearly down to its axles. 'Looks like you could use a bit of a hand.'

Honey gratefully agreed.

GORDON OWNED THE NEXT 'BACH' up the track, the blue place on stilts at the end of the driveway where Honey had turned in. He'd arrived home a while ago and noticed her car. As he hooked up his vintage boat tractor, Honey took the opportunity to quiz him about the big house.

Gordon regarded her from underneath eyebrows like big white hairy caterpillars. She was acutely aware that she was completely drenched and covered from head to toe in mud from her efforts to free the Toyota.

'Don't you know? I thought you were visiting.'

'No, I was just having a look around, a bit of a wander.' She met his stare.

'You're not a local?'

'From up the road, Waitutū.'

183

Gordon must have decided that made her all right, because he immediately suggested a towel and a cuppa. Honey wryly said she'd have to take a rain check. But once he'd pulled her up onto firmer ground and pointed the Corolla in the right direction, he answered her question.

'The owner's some bigwig from Auckland by the name of Bradley Morgan. Got rich playing with other people's money is how I heard it. He's got all the trappings. Wife number two's a bombshell and knows it, son is a right little shit. Caught him spraying graffiti on my boat, gave him a cuff around the ears and made him clean it off. Said he'd have a lawyer on me. I have to say I don't care for some of their house guests either.'

Honey was shivering now and regretted turning down the cuppa. Especially as there was no point in trying to pick up Marty and Keg's trail now. If they were heading to Rotorua, so be it. There was nothing she could give the Rotorua cops, even if she could find one of them interested enough to follow up. She was more worried about Marshall seeing the Reapers hanging around and forcing a confrontation. She bade Gordon farewell, cranked up the car's heater, jammed a Rolling Stones compilation into the CD player and pushed the poor little Corolla to its limited limits as she chewed over what she had learned.

The Reapers wanted Kloe badly (why?). They thought she might contact Honey (why?). They had gone to a truckload of trouble to find her, presumably to stop her (why?). To this end they had sent two experienced henchmen to watch Honey herself. This might mean that Kloe knew something (what?) the Reapers didn't want her sharing with her. She'd heard of Bradley Morgan, of course. A lot of investors had lost their life savings helping him ride out the last financial crisis and he'd gone from strength to strength. She remembered a newspaper photo of him holidaying in Hawaii with a past prime minister. It stuck in the mind because both the bastards had looked so grain fed and smug. But what the hell was someone like Bradley Morgan doing playing with the Reapers?

THE LAND CRUISER WAS PARKED out the front of her mother's house, but there was no sign of Marshall.

'Marshall? Marshall?'

He came around from the side of the house. 'Hey, what's up?'

She was ridiculously relieved but covered by nodding towards the bunch of greenery in his right hand.

'For me? You shouldn't have.'

'I just thought I'd give your mum's garden a bit of a weed while I was waiting.' He sounded uncertain. 'Is that okay?'

'That is totally okay!'

'Good,' he said, then looked her up and down. 'If you're going to have a mud bath, it's better to take your clothes off first.'

'You think?'

After a quick shower to wash off the mud, she ran a bath and let Marshall wash her back and then her hair while she told him of her adventures. He was unimpressed by the risks she had taken and relieved she'd escaped unnoticed, but that didn't prevent him taking the piss out of her Keystone Cop approach. Honey could see his point. Stuck in a wardrobe, dying for a piss while a potential killer was limping about a few metres away, cursing, then finding your car bogged, being rescued by an old bloke with a tractor . . .

Marshall couldn't keep a straight face. Honey splashed bathwater at him and tried to pull him in. He conceded and got in, fully clothed. She said he was crazy. He agreed: who else but a mad person would take her on?

Later, lying in bed, limbs entangled with Marshall's, she picked apart his words — who else would take her on, indeed? Was that what Marshall was doing? Taking her on? The thought made her idiotically happy.

She must have drifted off then, because suddenly it was pitch dark and she was sharply awake.

'Did you hear that?'

Marshall was also stirring. She motioned for him to be quiet.

Someone was moving around inside the house. Footsteps were coming up the hallway. Marshall didn't hesitate — he was out of bed and pulling his trousers on when a figure appeared in the doorway and the light flicked on.

'HOW I GOT HERE IS none of your concern. This is my house and what goes on under this roof is my business and that man is not welcome here.'

Rachel was sitting at the kitchen table and Honey had just brought her a cup of tea. Marshall stood in the doorway, shifting from foot to foot.

'I'm sorry you feel that way, Rachel,' he said fearlessly, or foolishly.

'Don't talk to me.'

'Mum!'

'No, fair enough. Do you want me to go, Honey?'

'No.'

'Yes,' said Rachel. 'And for the record, Gillian was visiting her sister and offered me a lift, and I had every right to check myself out. It's a hospital, not a prison. All their tests and observations are a waste of time. I'm not a lab rat. They just don't want to admit there's not a thing in the world they can do for me.' She sipped her tea deliberately, not looking in Marshall's direction.

Honey decided two could play at this game. She moved towards Marshall.

'Okay, if you go, I'll come with you. Is that what you want, Mum? To be here on your own?'

'Up to you.' Rachel was not giving an inch.

'Great.' She was her mother's daughter. 'I'll just grab my stuff.'

Marshall wisely kept silent while Honey gathered up her coffee and stovetop espresso machine and put them in a shopping bag. A stray thought intruded. It was just like Gemma all over again, her mother trying to control who she could be with.

'There's plenty of food in the fridge — milk and cheese, eggs and some bacon.'

'I'm off dairy, you should know that. And processed meats.'

'Suit yourself.'

Honey carried on at the kitchen table, packing up her laptop and cable. Marshall was looking at her in a way that screamed 'I should leave you with your mum', but Honey, bloody minded, shook her head.

Then Rachel said, 'I don't expect you to take care of me.'

'Mum, I came up from Auckland to care for you. Why do you think I'm here?'

'I'm sure you have your reasons.' Eyes narrowed in Marshall's direction.

'Yeah, I do. You're the reason.'

'Then why are you leaving?'

Honey wanted to scream.

Except that Marshall cut in. 'Rachel, I know you don't like me . . .' Rachel snorted, but Marshall was locked on target. 'And you've got good reason. I treated Scarlett badly, and I have to live with that.'

Rachel said nothing, just looked away.

'But that was a long time ago and this is now. I care about Honey a lot and we're not going to stop seeing each other, so you can either find a way to deal with that or you're going to make life way more difficult for yourself than it needs to be. You're sick and you need Honey, so the smart thing to do would be to suck it up. You don't have to like me. To be honest I'm not that keen on you. But if we can agree to get along, things will go way better for all of us.'

Honey waited for the explosion. Instead, Rachel stared into the middle distance for what seemed like an age.

'Mum?'

Rachel's eyes were unfocused.

'Mum? Are you okay?' Honey put her hand on her shoulder.

Gradually a light came back into Rachel's eyes and she looked directly at Honey.

'I want to go to bed now,' was all she said.

AS SHE SPOONED WITH MARSHALL, she ran her day over in her mind. The panic attack was the worst in a long while. PTSD, obviously, but giving it a name didn't make it any less real. She should report it to the police shrink at her next appointment. If there was an appointment. The last thing she wanted was to be assigned to a desk for the rest of her career. If she still wanted a career . . . Marshall was right, the break-in had been a comedy of errors and she still didn't know why she'd done it, apart, maybe, from the need to face her demons. But it had yielded results. She knew the Reapers were looking for Kloe, who was almost definitely still alive. And they thought Honey could somehow help them find her.

She doubted there was any point in going over to Rotorua or asking the cops there to check it out. If Kloe was living under her own name, the Reapers would have found her already. It was worrying that they had got hold of the surveillance footage of her in the first place. Assuming their mole in Auckland had provided it, how did they know where and when to look? Did the Reapers have a mole with the Rotorua police as well? She decided she'd put in a call to a mate in the Organised Crime Unit in Auckland for a strictly unofficial update on the Reapers and take it from there.

Finally, her review of the day's events took her up to the bit where Marshall told Rachel that he cared about her (a lot) and they weren't going to stop seeing each other. It made her want to purr. But on closer examination what did it even mean? Were they really not going to stop seeing each other *ever*, or just until Rachel was in a nursing home and Honey went back to her real life in Auckland? Did he think she would move back to Waitutū permanently? To be what? Country cop? Biodegrading at his place, baking loaves and doing interesting things with charcuterie? It was as ridiculous as the thought of self-sufficient, man-of-the-land Marshall in the city, content with tending a few potted herbs in her Sandringham courtyard.

Where did that leave them? Honey knew it was a conversation they were going to have to have. But as she lay there, listening to his gentle breathing, she remembered a puppy her father had brought home from the pub, a Labrador bitsa, too young to have been separated from its mother. Rachel had complained and threatened to take it to the pound first thing, but come morning Honey found the puppy in a blanket-lined laundry basket with an old alarm clock ticking beside it. She'd seen a rare softness around her mother's mouth and eyes as she explained that the ticking sounded like its mother's heartbeat and stopped the puppy fretting.

They had kept the puppy and he had become Legend, and when Honey's father left, Legend slept on the end of Rachel's bed and followed her everywhere until he was too old and arthritic to keep up. Honey put her head gently against Marshall's chest and heard his heart beating. He shifted a little but didn't wake. Yes, it was a conversation they had to have.

22

KLOE WANTED TO DIE, REALLY, just lie down under a bush, and close her eyes and never wake up. Her body hurt every day. Dust and grit got up her nose, in her eyes; sweat rashes ebbed and flowed like red tides of pain and discomfort. Her nights were just as exhausting — replays of iridescent green globes of avocado and bright orange mandarins hanging against a backdrop of mud-stained black plastic. Her back, neck, hips, shoulders and legs ached. Her calves cramped so badly it was like thick rope coiled under her skin, and she woke yelling.

'Don't worry, lovely,' Mika told her as she helped force her foot back, cruel to be kind. 'Everyone feels this way to start.'

They were sharing a room in an old shearers' quarters where the kitchen and bathroom facilities were basic but cheap. At the end of each day Kloe forced herself to stay awake long enough to eat. Later, Mika would natter away about the Kiwi boy who broke her heart, or how an uncle used to make magical sauerkraut that cured stomach cancer and how wasteful New Zealanders are with their bountiful gifts from the land. Sometimes she'd ask 'Maia' to tell her something about school or her childhood or family or boyfriends, and Kloe would carefully skirt the truth. Pretty soon, like a cheerful golden retriever, Mika would be reminded of a story of her own and Kloe could lie back and listen, tossing out an occasional 'uh huh' and 'shit eh' where appropriate. She marvelled at how someone like Mika could survive being so enthusiastic and open. Why hadn't life fucked her up already?

Kloe had always been cautious in revealing too much about herself — except maybe to Honey, but that was different, that was like a confessional and look where it had got her anyway. She knew instinctively that personal information was a weapon that could and would be used against her. It had certainly been the case at school, where she was bullied for her druggie, embarrassing mother who even came to class once, completely off her tits, and tried to drag Kloe out to retrieve the lunch money she thought she'd given her. She'd never really talked about her feelings to her friends, certainly not to her boyfriends, obviously not Jason. A good lie was safer.

Maia's story was a work in progress. She had been a successful cleaner, even owned her own small cleaning company, but then came Covid and, besides, her husband was a lay-about and gambler and spent all her money and gave her the bash and it had worn her down to the point she'd started drinking just to get through the day. She lost her job (or the company) and finally one day she knew she had to get away and clean up her act and had done just that, which was when she'd been lucky enough to run into Samson and his crew. Whenever gaps appeared she filled them creatively.

Early on she got caught out talking about children, so she fessed to having two who were living with her very successful sister and brother-in-law who couldn't have children of their own and gave them everything that Maia couldn't. The fate of her children had moved Devi to tears, and he insisted she could have his old phone for next to nothing, pay him when she could, he intended to upgrade anyway. He helped her set up a fake Instagram account so that she could stalk her real kids and keep up with their lives. Nico posted constantly and Aria was often in his photos. She also stalked Shyla on different sites, but knew better than to post anything herself.

As her stories about Maia evolved, Kloe came to think of her as the person she could have been if she'd made different choices. Maia wasn't a fuck-up. She was a victim of shitty circumstances. Things had gone bad out of the best of intentions. Maia hadn't tried to shaft her partner when he gave her the shits by tipping off a cop. Maia was never a coward. She hadn't dobbed the cop in to the gang who nearly killed her. Maia would never do that. She was staunch and principled. She'd left to make a fresh start, and fully intended to reclaim her children once she was on her feet and could give them the life they deserved.

Kloe wanted Maia to be true so badly that she was beginning to believe it herself.

But then Samson had quietly said to her one day while they were in a field harvesting green fingers of zucchini that he didn't care who she really was, or what she'd done. As far as he was concerned, she was a friend unless she proved otherwise. Kloe searched for a response but it was a slippery eel in her mind.

'I noticed your driver's licence when you opened your wallet to get some cash,' he explained a little sheepishly. 'Didn't mean to, but once you see something you can't un-see it.' He shrugged. 'We might hit a problem when the IRD figure out that number you gave them on your tax form belongs to someone else, or maybe it'll slip through. We can cross that bridge when we need to.'

'Thanks,' Kloe finally managed.

They'd got to the end of the row. Samson straightened up, stretching the kinks out of his back. 'You hiding away up here got anything to do with a motorcycle gang?' he asked.

Her shock must've been obvious.

'When we were in Kaitāia the other week and some patched-up fellas went roaring past, you kind of turned away and hid behind me.'

So, she hadn't been nearly as clever in covering her tracks as she'd thought. She decided that if she could trust anyone with her story — the truth this time, or most of it — it was Samson.

After she'd finished, Samson nodded. He took a moment, thinking it over, then asked the one question that Kloe couldn't answer — one big thing she'd left out of her story. Why would these Reapers still be after her? As long as she kept her head down, would they really bother looking very hard?

Kloe brushed some dirt from her hands, hoping he wouldn't see through her this time.

'Hammer can be a mean bugger, real vindictive, y'know. Probably wants to make an example of me for talking to that cop.'

If Samson had any inkling that Kloe was still hiding something, he didn't let on, just assured her that she was safe for now. They went back to work, carefully slicing off the zucchini and placing them in crates along the rows. There was one other thing Kloe hadn't told him, a real good reason Hammer might want to shut her mouth permanently. But it was also something she could use to set everything right. If she could stay alive.

SIX MONTHS LATER AND KLOE no longer hurt, or at least only in the way that anyone aches after a hard day's physical labour. The combination of exercise and good food meant she looked and felt better than she had in years, maybe ever. When she'd saved a bit, she even had all her fillings done and a plate fitted by an elderly dentist who had sold up everything and come to Northland to retire on a lifestyle block with his wife. The wife had left him for a yachtie and sailed off to Samoa and now he worked because he couldn't think of what else to do with the time that remained to him.

Kloe heard all this and more as she lay back in the torture chair, thinking that everyone is walking around with true stories that you'd never guess just by looking at them. But she guessed no one looking at her knew her secrets either.

She'd been months without a man and missed the feeling of falling for someone, of daydreams stuffed full of anticipation, of being wanted even for a few minutes at a time. There had been occasional come-ons from horny fellow workers, lonely men from all over the Pacific who were desperate to unload, but whereas Kloe could've easily let herself have a bit of fun, Maia wasn't like that.

There was another, deeper ache as she watched her babies, no longer babies, via social media, navigating school and moving towards their futures without her. Renata had taken them in, just like Kloe knew she would, and they looked happy, thriving. She felt a warm stab of affection for her sister. Renata hadn't been able to save her, but was doing her best for the kids. And they were way better off with her than with Jase, no doubt about it. The prick never appeared in their posts and Kloe figured he wouldn't be doing too much daddying now he'd slipped his leash. Shyla was killing it as well, flatting with some arty and musical friends and working in a café and studying, and had somehow got Tama into childcare — so, all good. It both cheered and pained Kloe to know that if Marty and Keg had taken her on that drive all those months ago, if she was dead and buried now, life would go on just fine without her.

She talked about this with Samson one day — she'd got in the habit of sharing confidences, knowing he'd not rush to judgement.

'That's liberating, don't you think?' he replied. 'To know we're so insignificant. Here today, gone tomorrow. Just like that.' He snapped his fingers and grinned.

'But isn't God supposed to care about everything, even the sparrow or some shit like that?' she said, dredging up a scrap of memory from the brief period when her mum was born again and took her and Renata to Sunday school.

'Some shit like that,' he agreed. 'But in the end we're just bags of meat with a bit of something — call it a soul or a spirit or Fred if you want to. We only get a little bit of time, and I figure it'd be better to do good with that time than bad.'

Kloe liked the idea of her soul being called Fred but she didn't believe in God. There was too much bad stuff in the world, and if there was a god with the power to fix things but didn't, he was a monster, and if he couldn't do anything about it he was worse than useless and didn't deserve to be called anything, much less prayed to. Samson laughed again and said she'd summed up the problem of evil pretty well.

LATER KLOE THOUGHT MORE ABOUT the 'problem of evil' and decided it wasn't anything to do with gods or souls. It was just basic ordinary people making fucked decisions they thought were right. Hammer wanted her dead because he thought it was right for the Reapers. Marty had been prepared to do the deed because he thought following Hammer's orders was the right thing to do. And, after her new, accidental family was broken up and scattered to the winds, and Kloe was on her own again, it was painful but nothing to do with evil. It was just bad luck and people doing their jobs.

The people from Immigration came for Mika first. She'd entered the country on a tourist visa and wasn't permitted to work and had got careless on her social media. They all had a good cry, but Mika knew she'd broken the rules and, anyway, Kloe could tell she was already looking forward to her next adventure. But Mika led to Rahl. He'd fled Pakistan years before because he was the wrong sort of Muslim, but his application for refugee status had been denied.

Kloe had felt a strange stab of guilt. If she went home she could be killed, but it was because she'd fucked up. Rahl could suffer the same fate for no good reason at all as far as Kloe could tell.

Their little gang struggled on for a while, but when Samson received the news from Fiji that his wife had been diagnosed with breast cancer everything changed. He had a working permit, but his wife was not able to join him and access the medical system that might save her life. It was at their sombre farewell gathering back at the Colonial Hotel that Sefina announced that she was pregnant. She was taking Devi to Samoa to meet her family for the first time and then who knew. Samson cried as he hugged Sefina and said that in this world the only hope was our children.

Joshua had an announcement too. He was heading over to the East Cape. Turned out that all the times that Kloe had seen him playing on his phone, he'd actually been playing the money markets — whatever that meant. He must've been good at it, too, because he'd made enough for a deposit on an orchard. And he'd met someone online and she was going to be a part of this new project.

'You're going to meet this person for the first time when you move in together?' asked Kloe in disbelief.

'Many arranged marriages work out just fine between two people who have never even corresponded,' counselled Samson.

Kloe could see his point. She'd made shit decision after shit decision when it came to blokes. Might be a relief to have someone take it out of your hands.

But it was Samson's comment about the children being their reason for being that clinched it for her. She had seen a posting that Renata was taking the kids to Rotorua for the upcoming long weekend. Nico was excited about seeing the hot pools and Shyla was going along as well. There was no mention of Hammer, so, as far as she could tell, it wasn't a gang outing.

IT WAS TIME TO MAKE a move. Kloe had long since sold her clapped-out people-mover to some German backpackers, so she arranged to get a lift south with Joshua. Of all the crew, Joshua was the one Kloe knew the least; he'd kept to himself and on his phone when he wasn't working, but now he seemed grateful for the company. The riskiest part of her plan was that she needed to stop in Auckland on the way. And not just Auckland but her old place, because the *thing* she needed was there — she hoped. It was the reason Hammer would still be looking for her. It was the thing he might kill her for and the thing that might stop him from killing her. It had always been in the back of her mind that she'd have to use it one day, and now, she decided, that day had come.

The house looked the same, only tidier, cleaner. The lawn was still patchy but it was mown, and there were some living plants in pots. The path along the side of the house had been weeded, the old engine block was gone, and the fence was no longer falling down. As Kloe watched from across the road, crouched low in the passenger seat of Joshua's old VW Passat wagon, she wondered if the new tenants had any connection at all to the Reapers. She knew Jason had moved into his new girlfriend's place. From the photos Kloe had seen she looked achingly young and happy, but who was Kloe to judge and, anyway, who posted pictures that showed their true self to the world?

'It doesn't look like anyone's home,' Joshua ventured.

'I can meet you somewhere later.'

'It's okay. I'll wait.'

'You don't have to.'

'I don't mind.'

The property looked so tidy Kloe worried that what she needed so badly might not be there anymore. She guessed there was only one way to find out.

'Be right back.'

'I'll be here.'

BACK BEFORE IT ALL TURNED to shit, when Honey was pushing Kloe for dirt on the Reapers and the Knights deal, it had kind of fallen into her lap. The gang was heading out en masse to Mount Smart Stadium for a concert. It was the kind of thing that used to rock her boat, the thunder of a dozen Harleys, the look of fear or envy in the faces of the masses, the way the crowd parted as the gang and the camp followers moved through to take up the best position. But by then she knew it would just stress her out, so she said she was feeling poorly and volunteered to stay behind and mind her nephews.

She was in the bathroom, rummaging through the cabinet,

checking out Renata's supplies of face creams and cosmetics, when she found a key on a leather cord and saw it was the one Hammer usually kept around his neck. He must've forgotten it after his shower.

After Renata's boys had fallen asleep, Kloe drove over to the clubrooms where she knew the security pass because she cleaned the place sometimes, and went into the poky little back room Hammer called his office. Kloe knew there was a safe there, hidden behind a framed, autographed Venom poster, and the key fitted the lock, no problem. Inside the safe were stacks of cash, and she was tempted but wasn't that stupid. There were also some letters from banks, and folders and other crap, and some photos in a folder. The guy in the photos was maybe in his fifties, square face, small mouth, puffy eyes, and obviously didn't know the pictures were being taken. In some photos he was wearing a suit and having a P pipe in a room Kloe recognised as out the back of the Reapers' nightclub in Fort Street. In other pics he wasn't wearing any clothes because he was fucking some Asian chick Kloe didn't know.

Kloe had no idea what any of it meant, or who the man was, but it was a fair bet that this was the kind of stuff Honey would be interested to know about. She used the light from her phone to take snaps of the photos, as well as of some of the other documents. She was shit scared and shaking so badly at one point she dropped what she was holding, and papers went everywhere. She tidied up, hoping to fuck she hadn't missed anything, relocked the safe and hung the poster back up.

Still trembling but feeling more alive than she had in a long time, she booted it back to Renata's place, checked the boys were still out to it, and put the key on its cord back where she'd found it. When Renata and Hammer got home she'd pretended to have a headache, mumbled a few words, and got the fuck out.

Next day, while Jason was sleeping off the after-concert party, she used Shyla's printer to print up the photos she'd taken, stashed them in a thick plastic duty-free bag and then deleted everything from her phone, just in case. She crawled under the back deck and hid the plastic bag under a broken flowerpot. Even if she didn't know exactly what it all meant, she figured it must be in Hammer's safe for a reason. She imagined herself dropping it in the middle of a conversation with Honey, real casual like, 'Oh yeah, I've got some stuff you might be interested in', but she never got the chance and, after the Ōnehunga raid, when Honey was nearly executed and Kloe was on death row, she knew better than to mention it to anyone.

Then one night, one stupid night when she'd been on the road only a couple of weeks and was still fucked up in head and body, she'd broken away from the group, feeling claustrophobic and resentful, with all this anger she couldn't contain or explain. She knew it had something to do with feeling real bad about what happened to Honey and shitty that she could no longer call her when she needed someone to talk to.

She'd gone to a pub and got wasted, and then for some reason her brain had thrown up a phone number she didn't know she could remember, and she had asked the bartender to let her use the landline.

Her sister answered. Kloe opened an artery down the phone about her kids, about how alone she was, about how fucked up it all was. Renata was short with her, telling her she had to stay disappeared and that this conversation never happened.

If only she'd taken the hint.

But it made her angry that Renata wanted her gone, and she'd told her that she knew, she fucking knew what Hammer had in his safe, about the photos and shit, she knew and she had made copies and if he came anywhere near her she'd make sure Honey got those copies, my friend the cop he nearly killed, the only person that ever cared, and that cunt tried to kill her, so you can tell him that, tell him that, bitch! She was crying now, drunken tears of self-pity, and it took a moment to realise the line had gone silent. Then she heard him — Hammer — on the other end, using his reasonable voice.

'How's it going, Klo?'

She froze.

'Klo? You wanna tell me what you just told Renata?'

Samson had found her slapping her head outside the pub, blubbering and cursing her stupidity and life. He had calmed her and taken her back to the campground and the next morning they moved on and the incident was never mentioned. But Kloe had no doubt whatsoever that Hammer had heard what she'd said.

KLOE MOVED QUICKLY UP THE driveway and across the front yard to the car, dusting off the dirt and cobwebs from her hair and clothes as she did so. She was touched to see the look of relief on Joshua's face. She would miss him.

'You find what you were looking for?'

'Yeah.'

He glanced at the bulge where the heavy yellow plastic bag was tucked under her shirt but he didn't say anything. Kloe appreciated his discretion.

'Ready to hit the road?' she asked.

'Sure.'

'Do you mind if we make one last quick stop on the way?'

'Not a problem.'

It went better than expected — just five minutes for Kloe to learn what she needed to know. Joshua put on a Celine Dion CD and they headed south out of Auckland to 'The Power of Love'.

23

JIM'S PLACE WAS A FADED timber and fibreboard cottage on a rocky rise overlooking Hōhonu Bay, a lonely hamlet a couple of kilometres north of Waitutū. It was rough but serviceable. The veranda was bleached but solid Lawson pine, and smelled of salt and smoked fish. A narrow shell driveway led down to a heavily padlocked boatshed close to the high-tide mark.

When Marshall had admitted he'd been putting off the job of sorting through Jim's things in preparation for the inevitable — which the hospice doctor suggested was only days away now — Honey had volunteered to help. He'd been surprised and grateful, but Honey was pleased to have the excuse of a day away from her mother. And she was curious to revisit scenes of their childhood adventures.

In the course of his life Jim had managed to piss off or push away virtually everyone who knew or was related to him — except for Marshall, who wryly acknowledged that being away from Waitutū for most of the last fifteen years had helped his relationship with his uncle immensely. Now Marshall was about to inherit the cottage and all it contained. He'd confided that part of him wanted to douse it in petrol, light a match and walk away, but he knew the worst memories would live on, regardless. The place was still a part of him, for better or worse.

They stood leaning on the shaky railing for a moment. The view was as wild as Honey remembered, the sea dark and choppy, the sandstone cliffs uncompromising. A perfect setting for a melancholy task. Finally, Honey shook herself and hoisted up her shopping bag full of cleaning products.

'Right, let's snap this puppy's back,' she said.

The minute they entered, Marshall stopped and put a warning hand on Honey's shoulder.

'Someone's been here,' he said.

'Are you sure?'

'It's too . . . tidy.' He gestured to an old armchair. 'And stuff's been moved.'

He motioned for her to stay where she was and advanced into the kitchen. It took only a few steps; the interior was just a front sitting room, a narrow corridor with a bedroom to each side, and a small kitchen with a toilet and bathroom off to the left. Honey, naturally, ignored his instructions and followed him through. She watched as he opened the fridge. There was a carton of milk and a cask of white wine.

'They've been here recently.' He checked the use-by on the milk container, nodded, then returned it to the fridge.

'Maybe Jim arranged for someone to take care of the place?'

Marshall's shrug said it wasn't likely.

'Kids?'

It wasn't impossible. When she and Marshall were teenagers, they sometimes used to break into holiday shacks in the off season and play house.

'Whoever they are, at least they're neat.' A pile of dishes, freshly washed, sat on the draining board.

Honey was reminded of the house where the Reapers were staying. That was surprisingly tidy too. It was hard to see a connection, but even the thought of one made her anxious.

She stepped back out onto the deck and took a couple of

calming breaths, then wandered back through the cottage and poked her head into one of the bedrooms.

'Holy shit!'

'What's that?' Marshall called from the kitchen.

Junk was piled on the floor and on the bed. Books, magazines, old furniture, abandoned or broken kitchen equipment, plastic bags stuffed with clothes, stacks of DVDs, discarded electrical spare parts. The wardrobe doors were wide open, revealing shelves stuffed full of towels, pillows, blankets and what might have been sports equipment. This had been Marshall's room when he stayed with his uncle, and she remembered it as being uncluttered, even monkish, with just the single bed and an improvised bookshelf. They'd sit on the bed and listen to music on his battered ghetto blaster when Jim was away at sea, in prison or wherever. It still amazed Honey that they'd never attempted sex or even a kiss when they'd had so much opportunity. With a pang she realised that this was where Scarlett had slept with him.

'Yeah, Jim turned hoarder the last few years.' Marshall was holding out a mug of tea. 'You sure you want to do this?'

'Bring it,' she said, and smiled.

A FEW HOURS LATER THEY had established three piles in the living room: stuff to keep, stuff to take to the charity store, stuff to throw out. The last pile was by far the largest. Marshall started jamming its contents into plastic garden bags he'd bought for the purpose and carrying them out to his truck for delivery to the Waitutū dump. Honey had pretty well cleared the bedroom and began turning her attention to the wardrobe. There was a brief distraction when she found and disposed of a nest of baby mice, but she was making good headway when she saw a familiar-looking black cover poking out from under a pile of threadbare towels. It was the missing journal.

Scarlett's record of the final months of her life.

Marshall had carried the last of the rubbish bags to the truck, and came through to tease Honey about slacking off. She was sitting slumped on the bed with the notebook beside her. Her face was running with tears.

'He raped her.'

'What?'

It took a moment for her voice to work again. 'Jim. He raped Scarlett.'

She held the notebook to him. Marshall took it and sat.

For the record of her seventeenth year, Scarlett had refined her usual mixture of text and sketches to create something like a graphic novel, albeit one based on fact. Some of those facts Honey already knew: Scarlett's growing sense of alienation from friends and her mother, her self-harming, her seeking refuge at the cottage with Marshall, her falling in love and trying to have sex with him, his drunken incapacity, then avoidance, her heartbreak when she learns that he's sleeping with someone else. But there was more. Several gut-wrenching pages showed Scarlett coming to the cottage because she'd heard a rumour that Marshall was back. Instead she found Jim drinking rum, his face dark with anger and bad intentions. He insisted she stay for a drink before he'd tell her the latest news on Marshall. The drawings show Scarlett's fear and her curiosity, her need to know balanced against her sense of danger.

The light grows dim. There is a sense of confusion and terror. Scarlett freezes. She can't move as Jim forces himself on her. There is blood. She tries to crawl away, and he does it again. Finally she

207

curls up and seeks refuge in sleep. In the first light of morning she finds Jim asleep, drool running down the side of his whiskered face, and she flees, goes home, showers and scrubs herself. Three weeks later she's missed a period and goes to the chemist to ask for a morning-after pill but she's refused and told to see a doctor.

A couple of pages covered Scarlett's inability to tell her mother what has happened and Rachel's irritation with her moody, unknowable daughter. Then there was a full-page illustration of Scarlett holding a phone.

Her face is contorted with grief and pain as she contemplates calling her sister. But she doesn't know what to say and fears it's her own fault for wanting to see Marshall so badly, staying when Jim told her to. Perhaps she's just bad and deserves to be punished.

Graphic Scarlett tries to get on with her life, but she is plagued by nightmares. She tries to tell her friend Barry how sad she is. She starts to explain that it's to do with Marshall, and Barry gets angry and tries to kiss her. Scarlett is repulsed and pushes him away. She thought he was her friend, but she got that wrong too.

The last page was incomplete.

Scarlett holds a scalpel stolen from her mother's medical kit and contemplates killing herself. But she worries about leaving a mess her mother will have to deal with. The text fills in the backstory. She knows for certain Marshall is back in town but hasn't come to see her. She imagines him riding horses out on Gemma's farm. He hasn't a care in the world. She wonders how to tell him not to blame himself, that she just can't see the point in living if it hurts this much.

Marshall looked at this last page a long, long time. Then he got up without a word and left.

24

SCARLETT, INCONGRUOUS IN A LONG green velvet dress, walks resolutely towards Hōhonu Bay. It doesn't really matter to her what happens. If Marshall is there or not, she has a plan and she'll follow it through. As she approaches the turn-off to the track that leads to the beach that leads to the cottage, the place where she found love and lost the will to go on living, a car approaches, slows, passes. She sees the disapproving face of Janice Scott, her husband Ian beside her, driving. She sees Janice's mouth move and Ian shake his head. Then they are gone, and all is quiet except for the distant sound of waves against the shore and sea birds and the distant buzz of a motorbike. She stands there for a moment, feeling the breeze against her skin. The sound of the motorbike grows louder but she ignores it, gathers up her courage and heads down the track.

IT'S JUST A SHITTY BATTERED old Yamaha 250 he's borrowed from a mate of a mate, but Marshall is enjoying the rush of riding it fast along the dirt road leading out of town. It's excellent for his hangover, that's for sure. Last night he really tied one on at the pub. There was a tense moment when Barry Snydon tried to go him, but that just added to the fun. He'd ended up going back to the campgrounds with a Spanish backpacker called Louisa or Lucia and having crazy sex in a pup tent. She was leaving that morning for Madrid and was happy for the memory. 'You are my first Māori!' she'd shouted shortly after he'd entered her.

'That makes us even. You're my first paella,' he'd said, which didn't make sense but she didn't seem to mind.

It hadn't exactly been comfortable on the hard ground, face against the dew damp side of the tent, so Marshall is looking forward to getting back to Jim's place for a sleep. Instead, he sees Scarlett ahead, unmistakable in her green dress, turning down the track leading to the cottage. He pulls up, mind and bike ticking over. Does he really need the drama right now? Or should he go the extra distance over to his dad's place and risk being nagged to do some work around the house?

SCARLETT HAS REACHED THE FOOT of the driveway, leading down to the cottage. She hears the sound of the motorbike again but it soon fades away in the distance. She knows the monster isn't in there; she saw his boat go out that morning. She is terrified but committed and wills her legs to move. She finally makes it to the front door and takes out a package from her backpack. Her final journal. It is addressed to Marshall. She hopes it will help him understand.

She knows where the spare key is kept and quickly unlocks the door. For a moment she freezes, remembering what has happened there, seeing the place, hearing the sounds, feeling her frightened self wanting to curl up again and close her eyes. She forces herself to move, places the package on the bed Marshall sleeps in, where they had almost made love. She stops for a moment to smell his pillow, but is afraid to lie down in case it drains her of the will to follow through, or the monster comes home to find her there.

Then she makes her way out to the heads. She imagines she'll stand for a long time at the cliff's edge. But it isn't like that. She just steps off.

25

HONEY STOOD ON THE DECK as Marshall drove away, his face set like a mo'ai. He hadn't said a word, so she hadn't either. She was pissed off, truth be told, that he turned it in on himself, shut down. Something Michelle had told her sprang to mind: the thing that attracts you to someone is the thing that breaks you apart. In this case, Marshall's man-alone self-sufficiency. But she knew her irritation was a smokescreen, something to distract from the revelations of Scarlett's journal. Hell, being shitty with Marshall was way less complicated.

She toyed with the idea of walking back to town, took a few steps up the driveway, but with no idea where he'd gone, or how long he'd be, she returned, busying herself with the job they'd started. Scarlett's journal had answered most of her questions and there was grim satisfaction in having guessed most of the salient points. Apart from the big one, the rape. She knew it was pathetic solipsism, but her mind kept going back to the image (a whole page!) where Scarlett considers calling her big sister but feels she has no right to intrude. Had Honey really been that distant, that unapproachable? Well, duh. She'd barely given Scarlett a thought in the five years between leaving home and her sister's death. She'd fobbed her off with shiny trinkets for birthdays and Christmas, patronising questions about school and boyfriends, throwing her occasional scraps from her own endlessly interesting life. Perhaps she should frame that page and hang it on her wall as a reminder.

THE CASK WHITE WAS SURPRISINGLY drinkable after the first glass, and Honey was on her third and the sorting more or less complete when she decided to take a lie-down in Marshall's old room. She doubted she'd be able to sleep, but her eyes were thick from tears and grit from the cleaning, and she was emotionally and physically drained. A few moments to get her head together, and if Marshall still hadn't returned she'd head into town before dark . . .

Suddenly she was wide awake. The room was completely dark. She'd been caught in a nightmare of being chased by a car that seemed to be able to go anywhere, over land, sea, in the air. If it reached her she'd be attacked just as Scarlett had been, and a voice in her head had been whispering, 'Do it, do it, you deserve it.' The car had cornered her against a church wall, engine revving . . .

There were footsteps, and the light in the front room came on. She was about to call Marshall's name, but stopped herself. She looked around for a weapon, a heavy object, anything, but she'd been bloody thorough and the room was stripped bare. The old bed creaked as she swung her legs around and planted her feet on the floor. Her mobile was in her bag in the front room.

Honey crept through to the doorway and peeked around the corner, down the hallway. No one was moving or making a sound. If Marshall was back, surely he would've said something by now. This was an intruder, and they were listening just as she was.

A dinged-up old frypan sat on top of a bag of stuff by the door. As she picked it up, something else spilled out and crashed to the floor. She waited a moment, but there was no sound from behind the door at the other end of the hallway.

She risked the few steps to the back door, hoping like hell the threadbare runner would mask her footsteps: all going well, she could creep around the outside and look through the side window to check out the front room. She had just reached for the back-door handle when she heard a noise outside, a crunch of shell grit, and she realised that whoever was in the front room had come up with the same plan in reverse. They'd gone out the front sliders, around the side and were now on the back step. Unless there was more than one of them?

Fuck it. She ripped the door open, frypan raised high, ready to damage, to kick, smash and scream — and came face to face with a petite woman about her own age. Honey almost didn't recognise her. A full head of shiny dark hair cut short emphasised her high cheekbones, big dark eyes and a full mouth of teeth. She radiated energy and good health.

Kloe was the first to break the silence with a nervous laugh.

'Jesus fuck me, you nearly give me a heart attack.'

'You and me both.' Honey waited a moment for her ferocious energy to drain away.

'You wanna do something useful with that?'

Honey stared at her dumbly for a moment, then lowered the frypan.

Kloe laughed again, more confidently this time, and raised the shopping bag she was holding.

'I bought eggs.'

JOSHUA HAD DROPPED KLOE AT a cheap motel on the outskirts of Rotorua. It had crumbling plaster pillars that didn't seem to hold up anything, and baby-shit yellow walls, but it was clean enough, cleaner than the air outside that smelled of long-dead things, sulfurous farts bubbling up through hot mud. Joshua had sniffed as he walked her to her room and joked that it wasn't him. She'd given him the bare bones of her plan to see her kids, watch them from a distance, spend a bit of time in the same general vicinity. She wouldn't approach them or reveal herself. She just really needed to see them.

Joshua seemed dubious, and it wasn't until Kloe gave him a fashion parade in her motel room — oversized baseball cap, big sunglasses and baggy pullover — that he agreed it was maybe worth the risk. He offered to stay another day, to be on the safe side, but Kloe knew he was anxious to meet his bride-to-be and wouldn't hear of it. She told him she knew from Nico's postings that her ex wasn't coming, and even if he did, he wouldn't try anything in public. Joshua was finally persuaded, and agreed to let Kloe buy him dinner before he headed out of town.

It was then that Kloe showed him the stuff she'd copied from Hammer's safe and hidden under the house. Not the photos, it was obvious what that was about, but the stuff about the banks and accounts that she couldn't understand. Joshua knew that shit; he bought and sold money (and Kloe still had no idea how *that* worked) and he might be able to give her an idea what kind of leverage she might have over Hammer. She couldn't tell him where she'd got the material from, or why she had it, but said it could be important in getting her ex off her back once and for all. She needed to know exactly what it meant.

Joshua took his time sorting through the papers, then pushed them back to Kloe and looked at her intently.

'I don't know what trouble you're in,' he said. 'But the only place for this is the police.'

'So it makes sense to you?'

'Kind of. In a general sense. Yeah.' He fidgeted with his napkin a moment. 'Your ex-husband is involved in this kind of thing?'

'Kind of, yeah.'

'He's a criminal?'

'He knows people who know people kind of thing.'

'I thought he had a cleaning business.'

'Kind of.' Kloe hated the lying but it was too late now.

'Have you ever heard of stuff like the Panama papers?' Joshua asked.

Kloe shrugged: not really.

He sighed. 'As far as I can tell, this is about setting up offshore accounts in different countries, using different front companies who could then buy property in New Zealand. It doesn't exactly say so, but I'm guessing this is a way of laundering money. You know what that is, don't you?'

Kloe shrugged again, but didn't completely skirt the truth.

'I heard some women talking, you know, involved in gangs. They were saying cash from drugs and whatever was hard to use 'cos the cops and the taxman would want to know where it came from.'

'Exactly right. So, if you deposit all that cash in banks with links to overseas countries where they don't let the taxman see their records, then you can use that money to buy places to rent or sell, and the money you get back from that is legal, so people say the money's been washed clean.' He indicated the papers again. 'On second thoughts, forget the police, just burn it.'

'Can't do that, mate, but thanks heaps.'

She was going to have to think carefully about her next move — that much was clear to her.

'You're not running from an ex, are you?' Joshua said at last. 'You're running from whoever that belongs to.'

'Maybe a bit of both.'

He stared at her a moment, then laughed.

'You're a dark horse, all right,' he said.

He was still chuckling when he dropped her back at her motel — though he reminded her again to be careful. He made her promise to stay in touch, and swore she'd always have a job and a roof with him (and his wife if everything worked out) if she needed it. He drove off, and for the first time in months she was utterly alone.

Lying on the miserable little bed in the miserable little room that smelled of damp and disappointment, her thoughts turned to the pub they'd passed a hundred or so metres towards the town centre. She could taste the beer and the bourbon and Coke. Her bad goblin whispered encouragements. *It's been ages, so long, you've been so good. What's the harm, the Reapers aren't going to some pissy little pub way out here, you can settle in, have a few drinks, maybe even find a nice fella and bring him back here, fuck me, girl, you've earned it . . .*

She got as far as getting changed into some jeans that showed off her butt and a tank top that suggested she still had a nice pair under her denim jacket and was applying some lippy when she took a good look at herself. Maybe for the first time in her life she understood what that saying meant. *Take a good look at yourself, girl.* She did, and for once she liked what she saw. Was she going to fuck it all up because she was too pathetic to spend a little time in her own company? Hell no.

But she was no saint either, so in her cap and dark glasses she went up the road to the bottle-o, bought a bottle of sav and took it back to her room to watch crap TV and get a little bit sloshed.

On late was a replay of a Kiwi series that was big years ago. She'd binge-watched it on DVDs from Blockbuster, stayed up for probably thirty-six hours or more, speeding off her nut with some mates, thought it was hard case. She changed channels and watched a mindless American action movie instead. At least it didn't bring back bad memories of a time when she'd lost weeks and still somehow managed to keep baby Shyla alive. She thought back over what Joshua had said. The knowledge that she had something big over Hammer made her feel powerful, more in control than she had ever been before. She could imagine a future in which she was safe to watch her kids and grandkids grow. All she needed was for her luck to hold.

The morning was chilly but clear and bright. She was up by six but the luge didn't open till nine, so she went for a walk and found an ATM to withdraw a bit of cash. Over a ham and cheese toastie and weak, milky coffee in a shabby café across from the motel, she planned her day and felt pleased with her detective work. Shyla had posted a pic of her with the kids, plus Renata's youngest, in their (way classier) motel last night. A line in gold was scrawled over it: *Luge here we come.*

Kloe had been there years before, with Jason, when she was pregnant with Aria and Nico was only three. Jase the arse insisted on taking the screaming child in the kart with him down the hill as fast as he could. She remembered it as a bit of a dump, but it had had a makeover since then — at least it looked flash on the promotional video.

She was on edge, hyper, almost tempted to walk into the main drag on the off chance she'd see the kids somewhere — but no, she had a plan and she was going to stick to it.

CONSCIOUS OF NEEDING TO MAKE her money last, and to blend in with tourists, Kloe had opted to catch a bus the five kilometres or so to the Skyline complex. Twenty-five minutes later, when the bus reached the stop across from the entrance gates, she detected a flaw in her plan. The road across to it was busy, and there was nowhere to hide. The only other remaining passengers, a couple of excited young backpackers, let out a shriek as they realised this was their stop, yelling out to the driver to please wait, wait while they gathered up their packs. Kloe was on her feet and moving before she was even aware of deciding.

Cap low, she followed the backpackers out and stuck closely behind as they crossed the road. It was just past nine and there were only a few vehicles in the car park. There was no sign of Renata's grey Volvo. Feeling exposed and with nowhere safe to wait, she bought a ticket and rode the gondola to the top. It cost a small fortune, but she felt a rush of joy as she soared over trees that seemed to be reaching their arms to her. There were even fucking deer and sheep grazing below, and the enormous grey-blue expanse of Lake Taupō in the distance. She felt a stab as she imagined being up here with the kids. Near the top was a café with a view of the gondola station. She bought a coffee and, screened by a low hedge, settled down at an outdoor table.

A COUPLE OF HOURS LATER she was still waiting, but with mounting anticipation. She'd followed them in real time as Nico had posted a vid of him doing a funny little dance in the queue to the gondola. Now there they were — Renata calling her three boys to heel as they strained towards the luge starting point, Nico and Aria, and Shyla bringing up the rear. Kloe was on her feet, moving towards them, trying to blend in with the crowd.

She watched them go into the luge station, a big open shed

where it would be risky to get any closer. It seemed an age before they came out, carrying helmets, and were guided by an assistant towards some free carts. There was a moment when her heart wanted to burst as she watched Nico helping Aria with her helmet. Then another moment when Aria wanted to ride with her brother but that was against the rules so she had to settle for going with her Auntie Renata. Finally, they were off, the boys shouting last one down's a rotten egg, and Shyla telling them to eat her dust, and Kloe was left wondering what to do next. Should she wait here for their next ride, or head down to the bottom and try to watch them finish. She finally decided on the gondola, and was standing at the crowded entranceway when a voice made her freeze.

'What the fuck?'

Turning, she saw a strongly built guy in a black tee-shirt and faded denims. He had his back to her and was talking on the phone, not to her. She'd have known him anywhere. It was Hammer.

'I know what I said, but shut the fuck—'

He was glancing about, instinctively cautious. Kloe tried to move away, but there were people pressing behind her so the only way she could go was forward.

'Don't talk to me about this now. No, fuck off—'

It was all Kloe could do not to turn around and look. She focused on the people getting into gondolas ahead of her, six at a time. The great horizontal wheel pulling the cable kept turning, the gondolas kept arriving. Six more. Six more. She started at a woman's voice in her ear: 'Excuse me, would you mind waiting for the next one. There's six of us and we'd like to stay together.' Her voice reeked of entitlement, and she was pushing past without waiting for an answer. Even had Kloe's life not depended on it, she wasn't putting up with this shit. She put her body between the woman and the next gondola.

'Sorry, it's my turn, you'll have to wait.'

She climbed in, keeping her face averted. The woman's face flushed, and her mouth opened and closed, but she stayed where she was and the assistant herded another five people in.

They were moving high above the canopy when Kloe risked another look. She could just make out Hammer at the rear of the crowd, turning away. He wasn't looking up, so she was in the clear. For now.

HAMMER WASN'T GOOD WITH QUEUES. He and a few of the boys had decided only last night to take a blast down to Rotorua, leaving early to avoid the motorway traffic. It wasn't their turf, so they knew better than to wear their patches. This meant he didn't get the respect he was used to; no one was moving aside. He was tempted to shove his way through, but there was park security, and he wasn't sure of what he'd seen anyway — a vaguely familiar figure in cap and shades. Kloe? Surely not. Why would she show up here, after all this time? And it didn't even look that much like her — it was more something about the way she moved. He was tempted to ring the boys still down in the car park, but nah, fuck it. He'd wait for Renata and the boys to get back to the top and have some family chill time.

KLOE DIDN'T NOTICE THE VIEW this time around; she was fretting about what to do when she got to the bottom. Would someone be waiting for her? Would she scream and make a fuss, or be too frightened? Maybe she could just stay on the gondola, going round and round forever . . .

But all passengers were required to get off, and she had no choice but to follow the others through the turnstile and under a covered area from where there was a clear view of the car park. And there it was. Over to one side was a line of Harleys, including Hammer's distinctive gold-plated one. Siz and a younger guy she didn't recognise were standing there, smoking, but going by the number of bikes there were other Reapers around somewhere. Kloe ducked her head, dodged around to the other side, and joined the queue going up again.

An hour or so later she was in the toilets of the café, knowing she couldn't stay there all day, feeling ill every time there was a knock on the door of the cubicle. Maybe if she made it back to the gondola, she could risk getting through the car park by finding another group and sticking with them. Siz and whoever wouldn't be hanging down there forever, surely? They'd be bored by now and have wandered off. And Hammer can't have seen her, or he would've kept after her.

At last she splashed some water on her face, gave herself a few words of encouragement in the mirror, clutched her handbag and exited. A white-faced teenager with an air of desperation dived in after her.

Kloe edged around the café, keeping a low border of shrubs between her and the start of the luge. Then she stopped. There they were — the kids, Renata and Hammer, and some of the other boys. They were horsing around, oblivious to getting in anyone else's way. An angry-looking man with a couple of tweens tried to get past them. One of the Reapers got out of his cart to confront him, but Hammer had words and they backed off. The man and his kids went down the track. Almost immediately, a couple of the Reapers took off after them, yelling and shouting. It was their idea of fun, but Kloe could imagine the guy was shitting himself.

She decided it was now or never. She had to get back down the gondola before Hammer decided to have another go on the luge and met her at the bottom. Even so, she snuck a last look at Nico and Aria, drinking them in, no clue when she might see them again. But she had to be smart and play the long game.

She'd just removed her sunnies for a moment to wipe her eyes when she saw her — Shyla — arms full of drinks and fries, rooted to the spot, staring straight at her. Kloe gave a tentative smile and took a step towards her, but Shyla gave a warning shake of her head as Marty appeared right behind her. Kloe jammed her glasses back on and turned away as Shyla shouted, 'Hey, Marty, a bit of help here! I'm gonna drop something!'

Kloe didn't dare turn around, just kept going until once again she was back in the gondola, this time with a family of loud Australians who named everything they could see. 'Tree. Sheep. Water. Wire. Ground. Boat.'

The luge track snaked below them, the karts and riders like toys. She had no way of knowing if any of them were Reapers. All she could do was get to the bottom, cross the open car park, and hope the bus was on the half hour as scheduled.

Outside the gondola station, she lucked into a tour group, Chinese or Korean, half of them in caps and dark glasses, who were being marshalled by a woman with a stick and an orange flag. She stuck with them most of the way across the car park. There was no sign of anyone at the bikes, so she walked briskly out through the gates and across the road to the crowded bus stop. Her luck held. Until the last minute. That last dumb minute.

SHYLA HAD DONE HER BEST to hide her feelings of — what? Shock? Relief? She just knew that the sight of her mother had cracked something open inside of her, and she wanted to cry. Marty must have picked up the vibe because he asked if she was okay, and she'd covered by saying it was maybe something she ate 'cos she didn't feel so good, but when they were heading back over to Renata and the kids she couldn't stop from looking around to make sure her mum had got away okay and she thought she could make her out in one of the gondolas passing overhead. Marty must've seen something too, 'cos next thing he'd said something to Hammer and Hammer had let out an almighty fuck and taken out his phone and shouted something into it. Then he'd grabbed a kart and headed down the track like his arse was on fire.

BY THE TIME HAMMER HAD got to the bottom and was meeting Siz and a couple of the other boys and scanning the car park and waiting outside the turnstile to check everyone who got off, Kloe was already at the bus stop. When the bus pulled up, Hammer was closest to the road, checking behind cars and tour buses, unaware that Kloe was shielded by the arriving bus. Anyway, it never crossed his mind that anyone would make an escape on public transport. Kloe's mistake was that when she was safely aboard, she couldn't resist crossing the aisle and taking one last look from the bus window. That was the moment Hammer saw her. And she saw that he had. He kept watching as the bus pulled away, then raced towards the bikes on the other side of the car park.

He, Siz and a couple of the other boys were pulling on their helmets, bikes fired up, when a police patrol car pulled up, blocking their way.

'You boys okay?' Constable Kahurangi Dickson was a slow and seasoned cop who didn't need to see patches to know who he was talking to. He took his time getting out while his partner ran the bikes' plates through the system. Always the chance of outstanding warrants.

'Yeah, no problem.'

'It's just we had a couple of calls, people a bit worried you weren't playing nice.'

'Us? We're just here with our kids, having a bit of fun.'

'Yeah, I've no doubt.'

Hammer smiled his best smile, though he wanted to smash him.

'Where are your kids now?'

'Still up top with their mum. They came in the car.'

'Nice day for it.'

Hammer scowled. Would this fucknuts ever get out of his face?

For his part, Constable Dickson was no fan of gangs but he understood their place in the ecosystem and as long as they put aside their patches he didn't see why they shouldn't have family days like anyone else. But there was something about these Aussies that got up his nose. His guts told him something was going on. And the last thing a good Rotorua cop wanted was anything smelling like a turf war in his town. The more these boys wanted to hurry, the more he felt inclined not to oblige.

'You down from Auckland?'

'Yeah.'

'Just for the day?'

'Probably, yeah. Be good to get going, it's a long ride.'

'No problem.' But Kahurangi nodded towards his partner. 'Just waiting to get the all clear. Shouldn't hold you up much longer.'

It was another ten minutes before the cops had finally pissed off and the Reapers could roar out of the car park and up Fairy Falls Road towards town. All the same, they made good time and caught up to the bus just as it pulled up to its last stop down by a pretty park on the shores of Lake Taupō. Hammer had it figured out. They would force Kloe onto the back of a bike, get her back to Auckland and deal with her there . . .

KLOE, OF COURSE, HAD GOT off at the first opportunity and taken off down a side street, where she'd found a sheltered spot and called a taxi back to her Rotorua motel. She'd slumped low in the back seat but there was no sign of the Reapers' bikes and she wasn't going to argue with that. There was no reception committee at the motel either. Back in her unit, she stood under the shower for a long time, worrying about Shyla but then consoling herself that the girl had already proven she could take care of herself. Then she let out a shout of triumph. The old Kloe would have crumpled into a ball, would have begged for mercy — shit, she'd have blown the gang and all their mates to save her pathetic neck. Not now, not ever.

There was a moment the following morning when, waiting for the bus to the coast, the sound of big bikes sent Kloe's heart into her mouth. But she was wearing a completely different outfit, with a floppy bucket hat over bobbed hair she'd cut herself in the motel bathroom. She melted into the shadows of the bus stop and the bikes thundered past. They weren't even the Reapers, just some weekend warriors out for a ride. She knew then she could do anything.

26

AT LEAST HONEY HADN'T SLAMMED the door in her face. Encouraged, Kloe had put on the jug and explained about being on the run from the Reapers and how she'd been hiding out, picking fruit and veggies up North, and how she'd gone to Rotorua to get a glimpse of the kids and had a narrow miss and decided to jump on a bus—

'Why are you here?' Honey interrupted.

'I wanted to see you, to apologise, y'know, for what happened.'

'You could've called.'

Kloe ignored the sarcasm. 'I lost your number ages ago.'

'So how did you know I was in Waitutū?'

'I stopped in at your place in Auckland. The American fella there told me you'd gone home to look after your mum. Don't blame him, eh. I said I used to be your cleaner.'

Honey didn't even crack a smile.

'I shouldn't've told them about you, the Reaps, I know that, 'course I do, I'm real sorry, but I was shit scared. They were gonna kill me, no bullshit, and they would have if I hadn't got out when I did. That's the honest truth.'

The words came tumbling out, but Kloe guessed it would take more than that for Honey to trust her, no matter how much it might look like she had her shit together.

'Actually, I meant why are you *here*? Have you been squatting?'

She clearly wasn't going to let Kloe think they were chums, not anymore, not for one second.

'When I got off the bus, I went to the supermarket and asked one of the checkout ladies if she knew someone called Honey. Not exactly the most common name, eh?'

Honey said nothing.

'She said you was staying with your mum, yeah? Gave me directions.'

'She told you where my mum and I live, just like that?'

Kloe shrugged. 'She didn't know you so much, but she said your mum was a great lady, a nurse, yeah? Looked after her dad when he was sick. Anyway, I stood down the road a bit from the house, saw your car parked there, and then — I dunno — it was getting dark and I was having second thoughts when I saw you come out with an old lady, and I chickened out and hid and watched you both get in your car and drive away.'

Honey appeared to be thinking this over. After a moment she nodded for Kloe to continue.

'Didn't know what the fuck I was going to do next, eh. So, I found the pub and sat down with a pint. Then I started worrying, the way you do, thinking it over. I was scared you blamed me for what happened—'

Honey opened her mouth, but Kloe held up her hands. 'Swear to god, I had no idea they were gonna do that. Not to a cop.'

'You gave them my address. You told them where to find me.' Honey stared at her.

Kloe stared back at herself in the green mirror eyes and flinched a little. 'Yeah, it was on an envelope I found in your car that time.'

'That time I drove you to hospital.'

'Yeah.'

Kloe understood the point Honey was making. She owed her, big time.

227

'Anyway, I seen this notice at the pub for the camping ground, so I booked into one of the cabins for a couple of nights, y'know, till I decided what I was going to do.'

'Doesn't explain how you ended up squatting here.'

'I'm getting to that. So, I was wandering along the beach next morning, 'cos it wasn't like I had anything better to do, and got chatting with this old Māori fella who was digging up pipis and I ended up helping him a bit—'

Honey sighed, which Kloe interpreted as get on with it.

'Anyway, this other bloke came along, walking his dog, and the two of 'em start going on about someone called Jim being up at the hospital on his last legs and if his place was gonna be put up for sale. Didn't pay much notice till one of 'em said about it being up to his nephew, Marshall, and then I remembered, y'know, the story about you and your friend and the time you nearly drowned?'

Honey was staring at her in disbelief, but Kloe just shrugged.

'I'm shit with numbers, good with names, eh? So, I asked the old Māori guy, Willy, and sure enough he told me Jim was your friend's uncle and that his old place was around the other side of the headland, so I decided to check it out, see if I could work out where your boat smashed on the rocks. Like I said, nothing better to do.'

'And you decided to break in and stay?'

'I never broke in. I found a key under the broken pot. And anyway, I only decided to stay here when I saw them in town.' She stopped, nodding meaningfully, leaving Honey to guess.

'Them being the Reapers?'

'Yeah, Marty and Keg. I guess they was sent 'cos they were the ones fucked it up the first time. Getting rid of me, I mean. I was getting a burger at the Chinese takeaway when I saw them in a

Beemer, cruising around. Figured the caravan park'd be the first place they'd look, so I grabbed my things, walked along the beach, and I've been here ever since. Apart from going back along the beach sometimes to the dairy. Bored off my titties, but it's out of the way, and there were books to read and some old vids — or there was until you cleaned it all up. Is he dead?'

'Who? Jim? Not yet, but it's close.'

'That's sad. How's your friend Marshall taking it?'

Honey's eyes flared like she'd forgotten something important. Without answering, she stabbed at her mobile, quickly searched a number.

'Hi, can you put me through to hospice?'

HONEY WAS SURPRISED AT HOW relieved she was that Jim was alive, if only just, though she wished him nothing but harm. It meant Marshall hadn't gone there to finish him off for what he'd done to Scarlett — at least not yet.

But meantime there was still Kloe to deal with.

'What do you want, Kloe? And don't give me any bullshit about wanting to apologise. You didn't go to all this trouble to say sorry, even if you are, and the jury's still out on that one, believe me.'

Kloe shrugged. 'I thought maybe I could talk to you about witness protection again. I miss my kids, eh, real bad. I'd do anything to be able to have them with me and safe.'

For a moment Honey was tempted to feel sorry for her.

'What kind of witness?'

Kloe looked surprised. 'Y'know, against the Reapers. All the stuff I know.'

'It doesn't work like that,' Honey explained. 'There was maybe a window when your information might have been helpful, but we're way past that, and you said it, you've been out of the loop for most of a year. How are you a witness to anything?'

Kloe looked at her a moment, blinking.

Honey tried to be clear. 'What can you give us that's worth anything? Can you testify that you've seen serious crimes committed? Have you got any proof? Is there anything that makes you the slightest bit useful?' She knew she was being cruel, but fuck it, this woman had done her a lot of bad and now she wanted her help? A cushy life at state expense, give me a break!

But Kloe looked straight at her and nodded. 'Yeah.'

'Yeah, what?'

'Yeah, I got something — evidence, photos and money shit. Dunno exactly what it means, but I know it's important.'

Honey stared at her. What the actual?

'That's why Hammer and them are still after me. They wouldn't've gone to so much trouble, only they want all this stuff I've got.'

It made complete sense. It explained why the Reapers had been watching her, why they were still hanging around, why they had gone to such extraordinary lengths to find Kloe.

'Where is this *stuff*?'

Before Kloe could answer, a set of car headlights swept the shack.

Kloe dived for the lights before Honey had even moved. 'Fuck!'

'It might be Marshall.'

'Bullshit.' She grabbed Honey by the hand. 'We gotta go!'

Honey stopped arguing.

Kloe led her through the front slider onto the porch and down the little track that led to the boatshed and the jetty. It was steep and difficult going in the dark; the moon was a no-show behind a thick grey sky, and the shell grit was loud underfoot. Back on more even ground, Kloe led the way along the shore towards another boatshed, the closest neighbour.

'I hid in there last time they came,' she whispered.

'You didn't say anything about a last time.'

'I hadn't got to that bit yet.'

Honey looked back at Jim's cottage, partly masked by a couple of cabbage trees jutting out from the hill. She saw a light go on.

'Keep moving,' hissed Kloe.

They continued on another fifty metres or so and crept under the little jetty leading to the neighbouring shed. A pile of rusting corro, really. Honey could see that stopping here made sense; any further and they'd be exposed to anyone looking down from the deck.

Kloe continued her whispered story. 'I was sitting out the front, having a smoke and a wine maybe three or four nights ago when I heard 'em coming. The lights were off 'cos, I dunno, I like sitting in the dark and listening to the sea. Thank fuck. Didn't know it was them, but to be on the safe side I took off. Then I heard them talking, Marty and maybe Keg — dunno, he only grunts like a pig most of the time. No offence.'

It took Honey a moment to get the joke.

'I hid down here too when you and your fella Marshall came and started cleaning up the place. When it looked like you was settling in, I walked around to the dairy to get some more smokes and something to eat. When I got back, the truck was gone. I thought you were too.' She paused. 'Just as well I was wrong, eh? Or you might still be there. Don't reckon a frypan would put much of a dent in Keg.'

Honey knew she was right, though the idea that she might owe Kloe anything was annoying.

The jetty creaked above them and Honey heard footsteps from the deck and indistinct voices. She prayed to no one in particular that Marshall didn't return for her. After about twenty very long minutes, the Beemer started up, and they watched the headlights rake the side of the hill as it headed back in the direction of Jagged Bay.

She decided it was both risky and pointless going back to Jim's shack, and with the tide on the way out it was a good time to walk over the headland and along the beach back to town. She was anxious to get moving, but Kloe kept banging on about needing to grab something she'd stashed in the boatshed and nipped off without further explanation. Honey could hear her scrabbling up the bank, then the sound of the sea swelling and relaxing away from the shore. She had a moment to reflect that once again she hadn't had a panic attack when faced with an immediate and concrete threat. The dangerous bit was the anticipation. That was progress, she supposed.

Kloe finally returned clutching a heavy yellow plastic bag. Honey assumed it was the evidence she'd been talking about, but didn't bother to ask: she had far more pressing concerns . . .

27

SHE FELT HARD DONE BY, totally fucked off, if truth be known. It wasn't like she was coming on to him — Christ, she wasn't mousey little Gemma anymore, she could have her pick of blokes, not that she wanted any of the losers around here, thank you very much. And everyone knew he was screwing Honey Chalmers, which was a bit rich, considering what he'd done to her sister. Not that Honey was a paragon. Gemma had gone out of her way to be a friend, they were supposed to meet here tonight, but of course she was a no-show, hadn't even bothered to message her. She was like her mum, a little bit too good for anyone else. And where had Honey been when Marshall needed her, anyway?

It looked to Gemma as if she might've dumped him. It would explain why he looked so miserable and in need of company. Well, pardon me for caring. Marshall had come into the pub while she was playing pool with Barry. He'd ordered a double whisky, and when the poncey little barman Craig gave him attitude, he'd told him that his money was as good as anyone's and if he wanted trouble he was going the right way to get it. Craig served him without another word, and Marshall sat down in the corner with his back to the wall and kind of glared until all the other punters went back to doing what they were doing before he came in.

After she'd sunk the black (Barry laughed like it didn't mean anything, like he'd *let* her win as he always did when there were other blokes watching), she'd gone over to Marshall, friendly as you like, and asked him if he was okay. Marshall had just shrugged, so she took that as an invitation, grabbed her G&T and sat with him. When he finished his whisky, she'd offered to buy him another. Marshall just nodded and Barry went off in a snitch, but that was his problem, she was a free agent. When she'd sat back down with their drinks she tried to get him to open up and talk, and finally he did. Boy, did he what. He was spewing. He said his uncle was still alive, and he wished the evil prick would never die but stay stuck like he is, in living hell, with pain and bedsores and no one to give a shit. That he wished he believed in an afterlife, because then the evil prick would be suffering eternal hellfire agony, but that was just a fairy tale to scare children and the ignorant, so the truth was, the shithead was gonna die and his suffering would be over proving yet again there was no fucking god.

Of course she had no idea what he was talking about, and he wouldn't elaborate, so she'd said let's finish up what we're drinking and go back to my place, where I've got plenty of booze and a Jacuzzi, I'll help you forget all about it. She was just trying to be clear and straightforward for the avoidance of doubt, as her divorce lawyer used to say, but now he looked at her as if he'd only just noticed she was there.

It took her a moment to understand he wasn't even looking at her. He was looking past her to where *she'd* just come in, looking like absolute shit, wearing old trackies and some pig-ugly holey pullover and her hair all over the place. Then the rude bitch came up, said exactly two words to her — 'Hi Gemma', as if they hadn't made plans, as if this wasn't supposed to be their girls' night out — before she took Marshall by the hand and led him out of the pub like he was a whipped dog. This had all been noticed by the Greek chorus up at the bar, of course, but she'd put on her best smile, like it was all totally cool, like she was just minding him till

Honey got here, like it had all been arranged between mates.

After that it got a bit fuzzy. She'd had a few more G&Ts and considered giving Barry a text: all is forgiven, something cheeky like that. She had no doubt he'd be keen, but she didn't want him to think he'd got to her — she wasn't gonna let any bloke get the better of her, not after all she'd been through. She went out to the car park, but knew straight away she was too pissed to drive.

That made her laugh. It reminded her of when they were about nineteen and Marshall turned up her place to ride the horses, and she could tell he was totally off his face and said so. Said maybe he should sober up a bit first. He said it was cool, the horse didn't drink or do drugs.

Well, it seemed funny at the time, maybe because she was so hot for him back then. Not anymore. He'd have to come begging on his hands and knees for her to give him the time of day. That thought entertained her for a while as she made her way down the main road out of town. At a brisk walk it was only thirty minutes to her place, and the fresh air was doing her good.

A few more steps and she broke a heel. Fuck. Now she was holding her shoes, hobbling barefoot on the road, trying to avoid gravel. The headlights came up behind, throwing her gigantic shadow onto the road ahead. She moved aside and heard the car slow. Maybe it was Graeme: the sad fat fuck had been trying it on and had offered her a lift, which she had 'politely' declined. She might reconsider in the light of her heel catastrophe. But now a black BMW slowed to a crawl beside her. The dude in the passenger side wound down the window, asked if they could give her a ride. She looked straight ahead and said no thanks. He laughed. That's when she took another look and saw he was quite handsome, in a dangerous kind of way. Wavy hair, big gold earring like a pirate, sharp cheekbones. About her age. She thought she could see a tattoo on his neck and sensed he had a tough, hard bod. The guy next to him, though, was something else. He filled the driver side of the car, slumping and ducking his head so he could see out of the windscreen.

'Come on, get in. We'll take you to a party.'

'What party?'

'At your place.'

'In your dreams.'

'You're so right, girl. You're in all my dreams.'

'Jesus, where do you get your lines?'

'Comes naturally to me, eh?'

'You need better material.'

'You mean, like, you're the only hot woman I've seen so far in this shit town so why don't you and me have some fun?'

She stopped and the car stopped.

'That's slightly better,' she said, cool as fuck.

'C'mon, get in. We got some excellent weed, coke, you name it.'

'I've got my phone ready to dial emergency if you make one stupid move. I mean it.'

'You're not gonna want to be calling anyone, word of honour.'

'What about your mate?'

'Keg? He's a pussy cat.'

Keg turned his massive head to look at her. 'Meow.'

Okay, she was pissed as, the world was swaying a little, but it made her laugh. She threw her shoes away and, hand in her bag, holding her phone ready to fast dial (emergency services were an hour away, but these guys weren't locals so how would they know), she got in the back. It was clean and comfortable; it smelled of leather and weed. She closed the door.

The good-looking one turned and smiled, white teeth in a shadow. 'Where to, beautiful?'

'It's up the road, just a couple of ks. I'll tell you where to turn off.'

The BMW accelerated away with a gentle purr.

28

APART FROM AN ANXIOUS HUNDRED-METRE dash from the beach and along the road to Rachel's house, the walk from Jim's shack had been without incident. Kloe had tried for conversation — the woman could talk — but when Honey made it clear she preferred to walk in silence, they let the sound of the waves fill the space. Honey had briefly considered ringing the Waitutū police after-hours number, but even on the off chance they responded, what would she have them do? She couldn't prove Marty and Keg had broken any laws, and she wasn't sure she wanted to put them on their guard just yet. She'd decide her next move after she'd had a chance to look at whatever it was Kloe had in that plastic bag.

Rachel said nothing about Honey being late, and when she introduced Kloe as a friend from Auckland who might be staying a couple of days, Rachel was polite bordering on gracious, as if she'd suddenly become a Southern Belle instead of an uptight Methodist. Honey was desperate to track down Marshall, but Rachel insisted they eat, and spooned out two bowls of very yellow tofu curry on brown rice. Honey was reminded why the rest of the world was deluded into thinking her mother was a saint.

Her thoughts turned back to Scarlett, Marshall, her, Jim, the whole rancid mess. There was nothing to be done about Jim — he'd die a shitty death soon, and good riddance — though the question of what to tell Rachel, if anything, was trickier. Honey was generally a believer in getting stuff out in the open, but would telling her mum that Scarlett had been raped — that it was almost

238

certainly the immediate cause of her suicide — do any good at all? True, Rachel might stop blaming Marshall (and Honey) for a while, but how long before she realised that Scarlett hadn't felt she could come to her mother at the darkest moment in her short life? There was also the terrible possibility that this new information wouldn't 'take' and that Rachel would forget. Would she have to keep being reminded? It was too horrible to contemplate.

Now Rachel was politely asking Kloe about her plans, and Kloe, butter wouldn't melt, said she was just hoping to enjoy the peace and quiet, walks along the beach, Honey has said such great things about Waitutū. Rachel raised a sceptical eyebrow at this and asked about Kloe's belongings. Kloe didn't miss a beat; she groaned theatrically and said she'd left her suitcase on the bus but she'd call them tomorrow. Rachel, reassured, said she was sure Honey could lend her a few essentials. Honey could only admire them both.

She tentatively brought up the sleeping arrangements. The easiest thing would be to put Kloe in her room and for her to sleep in Scarlett's, but after the day's revelations — Christ, was it only today? — she wasn't sure she could bear it. And that was without factoring Marshall into the mix. But Rachel was briskly no nonsense — well, of course Kloe could stay in Scarlett's old room, she'd put some fresh sheets on. Just like that.

Honey left the two of them chatting away like old friends and went out to her mother's Corolla.

AFTER ALL HER WORRY AND catastrophising, finding Marshall was a bit of an anti-climax. His truck was parked outside the pub. She went in, saw Gemma all over him. He looked about as miserable as a man could look, and when she told him to come with her he did as he was told. She was vaguely aware of filthy looks from Gemma, but she didn't have the will to explain, she just needed to get Marshall out of there.

He was so compliant she was in danger of losing respect. It was only when they got outside that she saw what a momentous effort he'd been making to stay upright. He staggered, and she only just managed to catch him.

'Christ, Marshall, how pissed are you?'

'Yeah.'

'Shit, you are not a feather.'

'S-ry.'

'Yeah, I know. Can you walk?'

''Kay.'

'Good boy.'

Somehow, she maneuvered him into the front passenger seat of the car. He slumped against the door the moment she closed it. By the time they'd driven the few blocks to Rachel's house, he'd fallen asleep or passed out. Honey was tempted to cover him with a rug and leave him, but a sudden image of him choking on his own vomit propelled her to action. She was going to need help.

She tiptoed inside to find Kloe talking a mile a minute about her kids, as if she saw them every day, and Rachel chipping in the odd encouragement.

'Kloe, could I have a hand for a sec?'

'Me and your mum was just talking.'

'Yes, I can see.'

Rachel sighed her long-put-upon sigh. 'Better see what her ladyship wants, Kloe, or she'll get all huffy. Don't worry about me. I was just about to put myself to bed. See you in the morning, girls.'

Who was this woman? Honey wondered. She'd read about changes in personality due to Alzheimer's but maybe this was just Rachel-with-company and she'd forgotten.

She'd obviously made a fan in Kloe. 'She's a lovely old duck, your mum.'

'She is when she wants to be.'

'What are we doing?'

Honey lowered her voice. 'Getting Marshall out of the car. He's very drunk.'

'Does he wanna get out of the car?' Kloe sounded nervous.

'He's pretty much out to it.'

'That's okay then.'

The two of them managed to drag Marshall out, prop him up and walk/carry him to the front door. Getting him through the doorway required more pushing and shoving. He half fell into the hallway before Honey caught him. They had got him as far as the door outside her bedroom when Rachel appeared from the bathroom at the end of the hallway. Honey, a teenager again, froze.

Rachel gave her a look of deep and abiding disappointment, turned, and went back into the bathroom, shutting the door firmly behind her.

Kloe was grinning. 'You in big trouble now.'

'Shut up.'

They tucked Marshall in — on his side, fetal position — and went back to the dining room, where they drank herbal tea and Kloe recounted what she knew about the contents of the plastic bag. Honey emptied the papers and photos onto the table. A couple of them slipped to the floor, and Honey glimpsed the naked back of a woman astride a man. She had a cat tattoo on one shoulder. Kloe's eyes were gleaming. She looked triumphant, smug even.

Honey was irritated. This wasn't a game. 'Okay, you can go to bed now,' she snapped.

'What if you want to know stuff?'

'I'll ask in the morning.'

'But—'

'I don't want any distractions.'

Kloe finally took the hint and said goodnight.

Honey decided the herbal shit wasn't going to cut it. She brewed a mug of industrial-strength black coffee, and began examining Kloe's stash. The photos were self-explanatory. The angle and quality suggested a hidden camera in the ceiling. The fifty-something bloke with the flabby arse snorting white powder off a pierced navel looked familiar; a quick Google search confirmed he was indeed Bradley Morgan. That would explain the availability of the luxury 'bach' for use by the gang. It wouldn't be great publicity for a high-flying moneyman like him to be known as a drug user and gang associate. Rooting a young Asian sex worker wasn't illegal, but the whole package would be enough for the Reapers to blackmail him into doing their bidding, at least up to a point.

Honey turned her attention to the financial papers, which seemed to confirm what Kloe's friend had told her. She was no expert, but the proximity of the photos to the banking details, company registrations and other legal gobbledygook suggested that Morgan was helping the Reapers to launder their ill-gotten gains.

It was the kind of information that could get Kloe killed.

Unfortunately, it wasn't likely to get her in witness protection any time soon. There was no evidential link between this stuff and the Reapers. Kloe claimed to have taken it (stolen it) from a safe at Reapers HQ. Good luck proving it. And Kloe as a credible witness? Doubt it. The defence (and Morgan could afford the best) would love her.

The papers showed various companies in offshore tax havens, along with suggestions for New Zealand investment opportunities. The investments themselves were probably legitimate, so unless the money could be proven to be dirty, Honey wasn't even sure there was a provable crime committed. Even if there was, who were the criminals? Unpicking the real owners behind myriad shell companies — who'd have the time or inclination for that?

At dinner parties with Tony's lefty liberal friends, Honey had got bored defending the cops, but the argument that really got up her nose was the comparisons between white- and blue-collar crime. She used to put it like this. Take a couple of under-educated, drug-addled dickheads with fetal alcohol syndrome who rob a liquor store. It's all on CCTV, they've probably got form — easy arrest. Low drain on resources. Compare that to some financial manager or lawyer, educated, careful, working in an area that requires specialist knowledge, squirrelling away millions in client funds. How many resources and person hours would it take to bring them down? What were the chances of a conviction? Honey guessed Morgan would be on the radar of the Serious Fraud Office, but they were seriously understaffed. They tended to work a few big cases, sometimes for years, and it didn't always go their way. And even if a legally admissible link between Morgan and the gang could be established, it would involve thousands of hours of tedious investigation. It was hard to see a place for Kloe in any of this.

She supposed she could release the photos anonymously to the media or put them online. It might hurt Bradley Morgan for a minute, it certainly wouldn't be good for his marriage, but he was unlikely clickbait. Or it might get swept under the carpet. The powers-that-be had a sad history of blaming the whistleblowers rather than the real villains, and the New Zealand media, with some staunch and notable exceptions, was hardly a beacon to investigative journalism. Morgan was more likely to get PR advice from them. She pictured the statement: he's sorry for the distress this has caused his family and has sought help for his drug problem, made a donation to the Drug Foundation blah, blah, blah. A former telco CEO had gone the same route not long ago, and was now making a very nice living as a consultant, thank you very much.

That's the way corruption worked in New Zealand. Not the kind that registered on international lists, more the 'you scratch my back 'cos our dads went to the same school and I married your cousin' kind. But it could be a death warrant for Kloe. Maybe not right away, but one day she might quietly disappear, a warning to other potential narks.

There was no way around it. It was on Honey. She was the one who'd pushed Kloe to inform on the Reapers. All she'd wanted was someone to talk to about her shitty little life. Honey had known this, and she'd exploited it.

She turned her attention back online, following the inglorious career of Bradley Morgan. Epsom upbringing, King's College, he'd scraped through an MBA, and escaped conviction for drink driving and drug offences. He had two children by wife number one; wife number two was the ex-girlfriend of an All Black, an influencer, and wrote an advice column for a Sunday paper.

Bradley liked to describe himself as a self-made man, and that was true in the sense that he'd taken his father's multi-million-dollar transport company and asset stripped it into insolvency, erasing hundreds of jobs for loyal employees in the process. He re-emerged as a hedge-fund manager and proceeded to make and lose several more fortunes, all of it money belonging to other people, earning himself the rather unimaginative business section nickname of the Phoenix.

A wave of disgust, salty and dark, swept over Honey. God knows she hated the Reapers, she had good reason, but she understood where they were coming from. They'd made choices, bad, violent, criminal sure, but from a much less varied range of options. Bradley had made choices from a position of privilege, and that's what really got up her nose. Why should Kloe die so that Morgan could carry on unscathed, as if his life mattered more than hers?

A germ of an idea lodged itself in her brain. It was seriously wrong — morally, ethically, she'd be crossing a line. She poked at it, though, examined it from different angles, and decided she could make it work. But could she live with herself afterwards? Once upon a time she would have said an emphatic no, but she'd already learned to live with more trauma than she'd known was possible. Could she justify it to herself as the lesser of two evils? Maybe. She groaned and leaned forward to rest her head on her arms.

'Howzit?'

Marshall was standing in the doorway, looking sheepish and unwell. He swayed a little.

'You should maybe sit down before you fall down.'

He plonked himself in the nearest chair, head bowed.

'You want some water?'

He nodded.

'Some coffee?'

He nodded again.

'Lost the power of speech?'

She didn't wait for him to nod again, but went into the kitchen, filled a glass from the tap and put on the kettle. She went back and handed him a couple of paracetamol as well.

'I woke up, didn't know where I was.'

'I'm not surprised. You were out to it.'

'How?' He seemed genuinely puzzled.

'The pub?' Honey prompted.

He shook his head, helplessly.

'Then Kloe and I carried you in.'

It took a moment to register. 'Kloe? As in? Fuck me.'

She resisted the urge to add the rejoinder, Not if you paid me. 'You missed out on quite a bit.'

She gave him the broad strokes of what had happened at Jim's shack after he'd gone walkabout. He was furious with himself for not being there when the Reapers turned up, but Honey reassured him it was for the best. When she got to the bit about finding him and Gemma at the pub, he winced and filled in the rest of the gaps as well as he could remember.

IN A RED HAZE MARSHALL had driven straight to the hospice to confront Jim, only to discover someone already there, beside his bed, talking softly about faith and redemption. Marshall was appalled. Jim Before Cancer wouldn't have given Father Yun the steam off his piss.

He paused in the doorway and watched Jim taking in every word, his dark eyes wide in his skull face:

'... who formed you from the dust of the earth.
May Holy Mary, the angels, and all the saints
Come to meet you as you go forth from this life.
May Christ who was crucified for you
Bring you freedom and peace.'

Like fuck, thought Marshall. Or maybe he said it out loud because Father Yun briefly glanced in his direction but didn't break from his work. Marshall considered waiting for him to leave, then putting his hands around Jim's matchstick neck and telling him to give his regards to the devil. But looking at him now, grey skin hung over angular bones, he just felt a great wave of hopeless sorrow — for Scarlett, for himself, for his uncle who had virtually raised him. With the back of the hand sometimes, sure. But Jim had taught him how to repair a net and strip an engine, how to read the weather and steer a boat by the stars. Given him the gift of self-reliance. Off the piss, Jim was hard-working, taciturn, a man who kept to himself. But drunk ... the thought made Marshall's throat dry. Who was he to argue with his legacy? If he asked Jim why he did it, what would Jim say? Because he could? Marshall quietly turned and left the priest to it.

More than anything he wanted to throw himself down a stairwell of oblivion. The scraps of wisdom and self-control painfully learned over the last decade seemed pointless. Who was he, anyway? Scarlett had trusted him, relied on him, and he'd let her walk into the lair of the beast. He could still see her back in the green velvet dress disappearing down the track towards Jim's cottage. Still remembered the moment of decision when he turned his bike around and headed off — to what? He couldn't even fucking remember.

But even as he was drowning in guilt, autopilot kicked in and he had used the phone at hospital reception to call his long-suffering neighbour on her landline. Something had come up, he'd make it up to her; if she could just take care of the animals, everything else could keep. Then he'd bought a bottle of bourbon and sat in his truck in the scenic rest area overlooking the bay, and drank. Sometime later (how?) he drove himself to the pub (why?), but all of that was gone, erased from his hard drive.

HE DRAINED THE DREGS OF his coffee, then looked to Honey, as raw and open as she had ever known him. He said it worried him that he could lose a few hours so easily. That was one of the reasons he'd quit hard drinking for a while in Oz — the fear of what he might be capable of while he was in blackout. Maybe he wasn't so different from his uncle after all. Honey shook her head and put her lips to his for a moment. He was nothing like Jim, she said. She put his cup aside, took him by the hand, and led him to her room. He apologised that he might not be up to much, but that was okay by her. She was exhausted. They spooned and fell asleep almost straight away.

Sometime after sunrise, with the rest of the house still sleeping, she brought them both a cup of tea and they made love as softly and as slowly and as quietly as they could.

They were quiet right up until the moment when they dissolved into each other, flesh into flesh, and Honey could hear cries coming from her own throat until Marshall, giggling like a school boy, clamped his hand over her mouth.

'Stop it, your mother will be in here with her broom to chase me away!'

When the giggling had subsided, in gradually diminishing waves, Honey lay back and gave Marshall an abridged outline of the plan she'd come up with overnight. He pursed his lips and widened his eyes and blew. Was she sure about this? She'd be sailing pretty damn close to the wind.

Honey deliberately underplayed the risks, shrugged and said it was the only way she could think of to keep Kloe alive. She could see he wasn't entirely happy, but he admitted he didn't have any better ideas and agreed to help.

That settled it. She was going to take it to her enemies.

29

HAMMER SHOULD'VE BEEN THE CAT that got the cream. That first big deal with the Knights and the Asians had paid off, everyone had made plenty of money and the cops had been left holding their dicks. The Reapers were putting in place the new business model, bypassing the Mexicans, onselling crystal meth to Oz, the money coming back as foreign investment in legit businesses. It was a sweet set-up and even if Renata was the brains behind it — he'd give her that — he was still the man in charge and riding high on the hog.

But he'd been to see the doctor again, and his blood pressure and cholesterol were through the roof. He was facing a lifetime of the pills that made him feel like crap. Some mornings he woke up wading through mud. In his guts, which were also giving him gyp, Hammer knew it all started with the drunken call from that fucktard bitch who told him what she'd seen in the safe. His fucking safe. At first he thought maybe it was bullshit: the bit about her taking pics and making copies sounded way too fucking bright for Kloe. But it kept gnawing away at him, what she could do with that information. That she could have got one over him. The thing that kept coming back to him was the cop who started all this. What if Kloe had given her the info?

What if the pigshit used it to pressure Morgan to back out on the deal? What if the cops started on the money trail and it messed up the plan? He'd no longer be the swinging dick who made everyone rich, he'd be the guy that blew it 'cos he let his brainless sister-in-law get one over him. The thought was humiliating, and it kept him up at nights, feeling sick as a dog.

He couldn't bring himself to talk it over with Renata. When she'd asked him what Kloe had said during that drunken call, Hammer had bullshitted, thankful he'd grabbed the phone off her when he did. He said Kloe must've overheard something but she didn't know what she was talking about. Renata was obviously suspicious but she didn't push it. He'd downplayed and said, 'Fuck her, long as she stays away from me, I'll stay away from her.' He didn't want Renata to know he'd buggered things up by leaving his key where Kloe could find it. Truth was he was hoping it would just go away if he ignored it. And it had, for months, until the bitch showed up in Rotorua and got away from him (again), sending him into a spiral of paranoia, a churning feeling that everything was sliding away from him.

Before his police mole got herself busted (another thing gone wrong!) Hammer had learned that DS Honey Chalmers was on leave and was staying with her mother in Waitutū. He'd not thought much of it until that fucked-up day he saw Kloe in Rotorua and it struck him that Waitutū was only a couple of hours away. Was Kloe hiding out there? Was she still in contact with her pigshit friend? Hammer figured the quickest way to answer those questions was to send Marty and Keg down to poke around and see what they came up with.

As chance would have it, his mate Bradley Morgan had a place down the coast a bit where the boys could stay away from prying eyes. Bradley was in no position to say no.

The hardest bit was getting this all happening without Renata twigging. She'd been bloody dark on him since the thing with Summer had blown up. The slut had been hassling him to dump

Renata and he'd told her to fuck off; next thing she'd appeared in a women's magazine with her celebrity ho of a mother, where she'd said her *ex-boyfriend*, who happened to be someone 'high up in organised crime', had introduced her to hard drugs — as if she needed any fucking introduction — but she'd seen the error of her ways and was in recovery. So much bullshit and he'd taken a ribbing, but it was Renata who felt she'd lost cred. The last thing he needed now was to give her another excuse to be dog on him.

When they first got back from Oz, Renata had enrolled at a business studies course at the polytech. Hammer had to hand it to her: his woman was always looking ahead. It had started part time, but now the kids were older she was focused on getting her qualifications and doing exams, and was pretty much lost to him, which mostly suited him fine. He gave her some bullshit about sending Marty away with Keg to suss out the drug scene down south with a view to future expansion, and she bought it. But it was another lie, another thing he was keeping from her.

Then came the call from Marty. Kloe had been sighted in Waitutū, and there was no good reason she'd be there if it wasn't to do with that pigshit. Whatever their game was, they were in Hammer's business, and he didn't like that thought one bit.

He'd wasted no time in ordering Marty and Keg to grab Kloe and bring her back, preferably alive. He'd work out what to do with her once he had the full story. But the latest report from Marty was that she'd given them the slip again! The bitch had more lives than the fucking one-eyed ginger moggy that hung around the clubhouse.

Hammer thought about heading to HQ to maybe spot some hash and pump iron. Nah, fuck it, they'd recently invested in a gym, a fancy new place with a pool near the university, and he already had a platinum membership. If he had another one of his dizzy spells on the bench press, at least the other guys wouldn't be there to see it.

HONEY HAD TAKEN THE COROLLA to Auckland and left her Clubman out of sight in Rachel's garage. Now she was parked down the road from a neat and unassuming suburban West Auckland house, watching Hammer throw a gym bag into the back of his shiny new Mercedes. He obviously wasn't trying too hard to hide his success, but Honey supposed it was like any business, appearances were important, and she knew the money trail from the Mercedes dealership would end up somewhere above board. She had seen the paperwork that proved a lot of thought had gone into making it that way. Even so, she felt a tightening in her chest as she watched him — she had no doubt that it was Hammer who had ordered her execution. Only when he drove off did she feel in control again.

LEAVING WAITUTŪ HAD TAKEN SOME hasty organising. Marshall had his animals and commitment to fermentation or whatever, and it was agreed his cottage was probably the safest place for Kloe in the short term. The Reapers knew where Honey was staying, but they had no reason to think Marshall was involved and his place was well away from town and prying eyes.

The clothes Honey lent Kloe were only slightly too big for her, and Honey had to acknowledge that she looked good in them. She had noted Marshall's eyes lingering a moment before he had gone over to her, a little solemn (or maybe it was the hangover), taken her hand and said how pleased he was to meet her. Kloe had blushed and said she was pleased to meet him too. Honey would never admit that petty jealousy made her linger a moment longer over the goodbye kiss with Marshall, but she was pleased when he looked at her seriously and told her to be careful and not to take any unnecessary risks.

'Back at you, buster.'

'I mean it. If anyone knows what these bastards are capable of . . .'

'Yeah, yeah. Been there, not planning on a repeat performance.'

She was keeping it light but knew he wasn't fooled. She touched a finger to his lips.

'Don't worry, I've got the New Zealand police force on tap. I'll see you in a couple of days, three at the most.'

It was a lie about the police, but if Marshall knew every detail of what she was planning she'd have to spend more time and energy justifying it, and she wanted to keep up the momentum. *Carpe diem.* Latin for fuck 'em. But they agreed she'd ring at a set time and Marshall would drive with Kloe's phone to the nearest spot with reception. If she had any messages for him, he could pick them up then too.

She gave him another, briefer kiss, and he joined Kloe beside the old Land Cruiser. Kloe gave her a cheerful wave and then said something to Marshall, briefly touching his arm as she did so. Honey guessed Kloe was the kind of woman who could only relate to men in certain ways. It made her feel mean spirited just thinking it, but that didn't mean she was wrong. She watched the Land Cruiser until it disappeared around the corner, and counselled herself not to be a dick. She and Marshall had just found each other again and he wasn't going to do anything stupid.

That just left the problem of what to do about Rachel.

Honey explained the situation to her mother as simply and vaguely as possible. Kloe was in trouble because of something in her past; there were bad people out to get her but she couldn't turn to the police for protection because of lack of proof. Honey was going to Auckland to try to sort it out, but in the meantime they had to hide Kloe somewhere else, and Rachel couldn't stay here on her own, so . . .

That was as far as Honey got. Her mother point blank refused to stay with any of her friends and admirers in the community or, god forbid, at the motel, and Honey had to acknowledge that her reasoning was sound. Rachel was frightened she'd wake up in unfamiliar surroundings, not know where she was and panic. She had, she said, coped fine before Honey's arrival; she'd cope fine a few days without her.

Honey mulled this over, then took her phone outside.

'Waitutū police station. Can I help you?'

'Rhonda, it's Honey Chalmers. I was wondering if I could talk something over with you a bit on the down low?'

Her plan had been to get the local cops to do some drive-bys; maybe even Morrie Evans could manage a couple to and from the golf course. She explained that she was pretty sure the men in the Beemer staying out at Jagged Bay were the ones who had attacked her, and she was worried about her mother while she was away in Auckland for a few days. She didn't see the need to mention Kloe and Marshall's part in all this.

Rhonda heard her out. 'Where are you now?'

'Still at home. I was planning on heading off soon.'

'Give me an hour to sort a few things.'

Fifty-nine minutes later, as Honey was putting her overnight bag on the back seat of the Corolla, the small but potent hurricane known as Rhonda was barreling up the driveway with a wheelie suitcase. She'd let Morrie and Shane know to keep a lookout. In the meantime, she was here to stay.

Honey felt like crying with relief.

Rachel looked puzzled as Honey explained that Rhonda would be staying for the weekend.

'How are you, Rachel?' Rhonda ventured.

Still Rachel said nothing.

'I'm Rhonda. From the police station.'

'I know who you are.'

Rhonda just smiled and pointed to the coffee table. 'You've got a jigsaw going. Looks difficult. That's a lot of sky.'

'Yes, it is.'

'Better you than me, I'd rather curl up with a good book any day.'

Honey breathed out and Rachel nodded. Jigsaws were a way to exercise her brain. She hated anyone interfering.

'I hope you like turmeric chicken for lunch,' she said.

HONEY WAS STILL WATCHING THE West Auckland house as she talked to Michelle on the hands-free. She had given her an edited summation of the facts thus far, up to the point where she'd left Waitutū for Auckland. She trusted Michelle implicitly, and it did her good to share. It made it real, less all in her head.

'Fucking hell.' A long pause. 'Fucking, fuck, fuck.'

'Well put.'

'See what happens the minute I let you go off on your own.'

'It's always about you, isn't it?'

256

'Of course it is. But how about we back up the truck a bit. This old boyfriend of yours—'

'He's not . . . he was never my boyfriend — I mean, not back then, but yeah, Marshall—'

'Oh my god, you sexed him?'

'A bit.'

'When?'

'A lot, actually.'

'And you didn't tell me?'

'I've been a bit distracted.'

'I need to know everything! Not over the phone, I need to see you. You have to meet me soon as you get up here. We'll have dinner, get drunk, tell all, not necessarily in that order. How far away are you now?'

Honey hesitated. 'I'm in West Auckland.'

A pause.

'Burning along the motorway on your way to meet me?'

'Not exactly.'

She felt obliged then to outline some of her plan. Just the bare bones. Not the details and certainly not the bit where someone could die. Even so, it was enough to have Michelle say firmly: 'No. Fucking. Way. No.'

'It's the only way I can see out of this for Kloe. If I make it official and involve Serious Crime or the SFO, she's dead.'

'And if you don't, you might be next. Why doesn't she just piss off somewhere and disappear?'

'She tried that, but these Aussies, they're not like the locals, they're organised and they've got a long reach. And she doesn't want to leave her kids.'

'She's not much use to them dead.'

But Honey had to cut the conversation short. 'Look, I'll call you again soon. I promise.'

'You'd better, and for god's sake be careful.'

'Absolutely.'

She disconnected as a newish seven-seater grey Volvo pulled into the driveway a few doors down. Safety first, she thought. Nice to know that in case of an accident the gang spawn would be well protected. She recognised Aria and Nico from the pics Kloe had shown her. The three chunkier boys must be Renata and Hammer's.

Renata took her time, unloading some shopping from the back and calling instructions to the kids along the lines of she'd fix them something to eat in a minute, no computer until homework was done, yes they could play on the trampoline but only two at a time! She sounded like any other mother. But Honey knew Renata was different. During Operation Pachyderm, she had studied Renata's profile in detail. She was smart, tough, high status, and the acknowledged brains behind the alliance between the Reapers and the Knights. Reading between the lines, Honey was pretty sure Renata had been in on the decision to take her out, although when she'd pressed the point Kloe had denied it. She was still loyal to her sister, even after everything.

Now Honey gave her a bit of time to put away the shopping and settle the kids, then she got out of the car, had a quick stretch, and went up the path to the front door.

30

GEMMA RAN HERSELF A BATH, but thought she'd never feel clean again. She put one foot in, had second thoughts, wrapped her gown tightly around her and moved cautiously through the house. It was too big, too many doors and windows. It used to feel grand, the way it sat on top of the hill, overlooking the stables and fields; now it felt exposed and isolated. A final circuit to check she was alone, and she slipped into the painfully hot water, trying not to think about the night before.

It was all going fine. The coke was primo, which meant she could keep drinking, and Marty — that was his name — was attentive and not stupid at all, but he kept asking her questions about Honey. Why was everyone so interested in her all of a sudden? She told him about seeing Honey in the pub that night and how Honey had dragged her boyfriend Marshall out, 'cos she was crazy possessive. She tried to change the subject then, but Marty kept coming back to it, so in the end Gemma told him about the old cottage along the south coast road, how Marshall had gone all back to the land with his carvings and goats.

Gemma didn't mention she had driven out there when she heard he was back, hoping they might connect for old times' sake. But he'd met her at the front steps and hadn't asked her in — said he was just on his way to fix something. She thought that was rude, but maybe he was just being honest, and she gave him the benefit of the doubt. Now it was obvious he was still up himself.

She told Marty that she was sick of the subject, and he seemed cool with that and the next thing he picked her up and carried her into the bedroom. She wasn't complaining, she was so out of it, and she remembered thinking she just wanted to feel something, anything, is that too much to ask. She pulled off his shirt and his pants, and his body was as hard as she had imagined and there were tattoos and scars, and then she was naked too and things were moving too fast and she wanted him to slow down and she tried kissing his chest, but then he forced her head down on him so hard she wanted to gag but she took him in her mouth anyway and then . . . something else was happening and that animal came up behind her and she was trying to squirm away but he held her butt like it was in a vice and she tried to scream as he ripped into her until finally it was over, and he threw her off him like a soiled towel. She just lay there, curled up, not feeling anything at all, except something wet running down her leg, and then maybe it was her mind's way of escaping, but somehow she fell asleep.

It was still dark when she woke and the house was quiet. She screamed out when she tried to move. It hurt so much. She knew she should get help, call an ambulance, but then the idea of having to explain, of anyone else knowing . . . She managed to get herself under the shower, and sat on the floor and let the semen and blood wash away. Then she crawled back to bed. She knew she'd have to get medical attention, get tested for HIV or STDs, get the morning-after pill. But right now, all she could do was escape again through a handful of Temazepam and sleep.

When she awoke again it was past midday. She rang her stablehand and apologised that she knew it was his day off but could he please come and see to the horses, she wasn't feeling well.

Lying in the bath, the tears finally came. One thing was certain. She was ringing an agent and having the property listed and she was never, ever coming back.

31

KLOE COULDN'T WORK HIM OUT. He was friendly enough, but wary. There was part of him she sensed was always outside the conversation looking in. She'd met loners before, some pretty fucking weird ones, the blokes in the corners of the pubs and bars, staring at their glasses or the TV or having conversations with themselves, and you could tell they were never gonna be joiners and everyone left them alone because fuck knows, extend the hand of friendship and they were likely to bite it off.

But he was different. He'd let her rattle on as he drove. She asked after his Uncle Jim, but he just shrugged and kept his eyes on the road, so then she talked about her kids, about how grateful she was for him helping her out, but he still hardly said boo, and as they got deeper into the bush and the road turned to gravel and then dirt she found herself giving up and just taking in the scenery. Truth be told, the raw bush gave her the creeps. She liked houses and streets and shops and especially people. Staying at Jim's fishing shack had been lonely enough, but she could at least watch the boats, the beachcombers, the bait collectors; she could walk to the shop, chat to strangers and feel a part of the world. The scary wooden carvings Marshall drove through as they turned in didn't make her feel any more comfortable, and the cottage itself was like something out of a horror film. *The Little Cabin In The Woods* was it.

Now she was sitting on the veranda with a mug of tea that tasted different 'cos of the goat's milk and honey, while Marshall took care of his shit. He'd said something about paying a visit to a neighbour, and had taken a few bottles of cider and some other produce to thank her for taking care of his place. She'd made not so subtle hints about quite liking a drink herself, but he'd just shaken his head and said it'd probably be good to keep a clear head eh, given the situation.

Ducks quacked, chickens roamed in a small pack on the field, somewhere a goat was complaining. It made her think of Shyla: she'd love the whole back-to-nature shit. Honey had said that if things worked out, Kloe would be able to start a new life somewhere else, not looking over her shoulder. Once upon a time she'd never have even dreamed of living in a place like this, out in the wops, but it'd be great for the kids, wouldn't it?

That's when she realised what was wrong with the rosy picture. Where was everybody? Didn't Marshall have a family or relatives, or what? The place was way too quiet.

After he had returned and shut up the ducks and chickens and put the livestock to bed and made them a dinner of stir-fried chicken and veggies and rice, Kloe finally coaxed a glass of homemade fruit wine out of him. He was still quiet, listening as she chatted on but not contributing much, so Kloe gave up trying to be subtle.

'So, you grew up around here?'

'Yeah.'

'Was this your family place?'

'My mum's family.'

'Where's she now?'

'She passed.' Marshall paused. 'A long time ago.'

'What about your dad?'

'Also gone — more recently.'

'Any brothers or sisters?'

'Nope. Do you want a cup of something, herbal tea?'

'A bit more of this would be good. It grows on you.' She held out her glass, trying not to look too eager. His own was barely touched, and for a moment it looked like he might object, but then he refilled her glass.

'So you're out here all alone?'

'Nope. I've got the ducks and chooks to talk to and the bloody goats — they never shut up.' For the first time all evening he laughed.

'What about the rest of your family? Cuzzies, uncles, aunties? You sure you're Māori, bro?'

For a moment she worried she might have crossed a line, but Marshall didn't seem offended.

'I grew up mostly with my uncle who was a bit of an outsider.' An understatement from what Kloe had heard. 'And my dad had ... um, mental issues.'

'Who hasn't? Everyone I know's fucked up some way or the other.'

'Yeah, I guess that's true.'

He was looking at her properly now, probably for the first time since they had arrived.

Kloe was encouraged. 'My mum was a druggie — P, heroin, you name it, which made her crazy anyway, but even before that she used to shut herself in her room and stay in bed for days when us kids were little. Renata would take us round to different friends and rellies to ask for food. There was a Māori lady everyone used to call Auntie Lil. She wasn't our real auntie, obviously, and she had a temper like you wouldn't believe, but she'd take us in and feed us. So, even though it was fucked up, we still weren't alone,

264

you know?' She wanted him to know it was okay to talk about whatever.

He scratched at a mark on the table for a bit, then finally looked at her again.

'I did a lot of shit I wasn't proud of,' he said. 'Then I was away for a long time, in the army and in Oz. When I got back I . . . I'd let people down, people who'd given me opportunities, and I guess I didn't want to have to engage with that, so I just went my own way.'

'Like your uncle, eh?'

Marshall flinched. 'Yeah, just like my uncle.'

He stared off into nowhere for a minute, then shook himself. It was nearly dark. He said he had to go up the road to where there was cellphone reception to check for messages from Honey. Kloe handed him her phone, told him the code and promised not to open the door to anyone. She was kind of glad he was going. She wasn't fond of being on her own, but the conversation was hard work and she'd noticed there was still half a bottle of wine.

She stood watching the Land Cruiser head down the track, then closed the door and locked it, as instructed.

RENATA HAD FINISHED SETTLING THE kids down to do their homework, was just turning her attention to dinner, when she heard the knock on the front door. It was probably a courier. Hammer was always buying crap on a whim, most of which he never used.

There was another knock, louder this time. Yeah, yeah.

Renata's first instinct was to shut the door in her face. She'd recognised her, of course — after all it had been Renata's idea to do surveillance on the pigshit's Sandringham place, and there'd been photos in the news. In the flesh the hair was more red than ginge, the eyes wide and green.

'Renata, hi, can I come in?'

'What for?'

''Cos I've got something to tell you that you'll find interesting, and if I keep standing out here someone might see me and that probably wouldn't be good for either of us.'

Renata considered. She didn't want her thinking she was scared, but the pigshit had a point. She took another moment, just to prove she couldn't be hassled, then opened the door and motioned for Honey to come inside. She sat her down at the kitchen table, flicked on the kettle, let the kids off homework to play on the PlayStation and computer in the living room, and slid the door shut. Told her to say what was on her mind.

Now Renata was kind of wishing she'd told her to piss off. But at least she knew why Hammer'd been acting weird lately, making phone calls when he thought she wasn't watching, being all secretive. She'd assumed it was another bitch on the side — she was gonna lay down the law this time, enough was enough. But it was worse than that. Much worse.

'You got balls coming here,' she said.

'I didn't think you'd want anything unpleasant to happen while the house was full of kids.'

So the pigshit had planned it this way. Of course she had.

Renata watched as Honey glanced at the back door and gave an involuntary shudder. She was pleased the cop wasn't as cool and in control as she was pretending.

'Still,' Honey said, 'I'd rather this was between you and me. Be good to know if Hammer is likely to be back anytime soon.'

So she knew he wasn't here, which meant she'd been watching the house a while. This pissed Renata off, but there was grudging respect, too.

'Far as I know, he's at the clubhouse, had business there.' She paused. 'As far as I know.'

Honey accepted this with a nod. 'I thought it would be better for us to talk, face to face, so you can decide where we go from here.'

Renata lowered her eyes, feigning modesty. 'If it's club business, I don't see what it's got to do with me. Maybe we should call Hammer, see if he wants in.'

'Well, that's bullshit.' Her tone was brisk. 'Everyone knows you're the one who calls the shots. Hammer's the muscle, you're the brains. But if you want to play games . . .' Honey started to get to her feet. 'By the way, Kloe sends her love.'

'Sit down. You wanted to talk, talk.'

Honey shrugged, sat back down. Renata stared at her coolly.

'What do you know about my sister?'

RENATA LISTENED IN SILENCE AS Honey laid out the bones of the story — the papers and photos, and Kloe's part in it. How Kloe had pinched them from under Hammer's nose, how she'd worked out what they meant. But when she got to the bit about Kloe arriving in Waitutū with the evidence of Bradley Morgan's involvement, Renata swore and held up a hand.

'So why are you telling me all this? What do you expect me to do?'

'I want us to work together to save Kloe.'

'Why would we do that?'

'Because everything Kloe has told me about you makes me think you've looked out for her, cared about her — her and her kids. Why would you stop now?'

'I'm talking about you. Why do you give a fuck?'

'This is all my fault. I started it.'

'Don't you think you paid your dues?'

There it was: not a shred of doubt that Renata had been at least aware of the decision to try to get rid of her. Bygones.

'I'm still alive. Kloe won't be if Marty and Keg get to her first.'

Honey noted Renata's surprise. She didn't know the Reapers were in Waitutū. Good.

'And you haven't shown any of this stuff to the cops?'

'Nobody.'

'Honestly? You seriously expect me to believe that?'

'Do you think they'd let me walk in here on my own if they knew? It'd be out of my hands. Bradley Morgan would call in some favours, hire the best lawyers, lie low for a while, then he'd bounce back like nothing had changed. The Reapers would suffer a serious financial setback and Kloe would still pay for it in the end. Neither you or I would be able to protect her.'

Renata appeared to examine her face for a long, long moment. Finally, she nodded.

'Okay, so what do you want me to do?'

HAMMER GOT IN LATE, WHICH was typical, even though Renata had left a message with him as soon as Honey had gone. The bitch was right: her plan gave Kloe the best chance of coming through this alive without fucking up their long-term goals. She still couldn't believe that a cop would come up with it, but she wasn't going to argue the toss. She'd tried Hammer again after she'd got the kids to bed, and this time she'd got through.

'Get your arse home, now!'

'What's up?'

'I'll tell you when you get here.'

She wasn't about to say anything over the phone. As it was, he must've stayed for a couple more drinks because he knew something was coming. Now he was looking at her, swaying slightly, beer on his breath.

'What's going on?'

'Sit down.'

She made him a coffee, made him drink it. Then she told him what she and Honey had agreed she would say. How she knew he was trying to have her sister knocked off behind her back, that Honey knew all about the photos and bank records and shit, and that it was all going straight to the cops unless they did something about it.

Hammer's first impulse was to have Marty and Keg finish the bitches, both of them, bury 'em side by side deep in the Waitākere Forest and forget they ever happened. Renata cut through his rant, told him that wasn't smart, that she had a plan. But first he had to phone Marty and call it off.

Hammer stared at her. His face was flushed, he was taking short sharp breaths.

'Well?'

'Hang on. Just give me a minute. Jesus, fuck me!'

He stalked through to the bathroom. Renata heard him open the cabinet, presumably to find his pills. She sighed. After a moment he returned with his phone to his ear, but it must have gone straight through to voice mail.

'Fuck!' Then he remembered: 'There's no reception out at Morgan's place.'

He called the landline. It rang out.

Renata was looking at him, a dangerous gleam in her eyes. 'If we're too late, this is on you.'

'Don't you think I know that?'

There was no point in riding him any further. He knew he'd fucked up, big time. Giving him shit wasn't going to change that. She nodded to the phone in his hand: 'Try again.'

32

HONEY WAS ENJOYING HERSELF, EVEN though she knew she shouldn't. When she'd reported back on her *interesting* meeting, Michelle had said she was insane for going in there without back-up and Honey had agreed it was entirely possible. But, she said, Renata had eventually bought her plan, even come up with a few creative suggestions of her own. Michelle believed this called for a celebration. Honey wanted a clear head for the drive back to Waitutū first thing, but Michelle wouldn't take no for an answer and Honey thought, bugger it, she'd been to the gates of hell and back, she deserved a blow-out. All she could do now was wait. The one thing she couldn't anticipate was how she would feel afterwards about the kind of person she'd become. But with Kloe safe, the Reapers off her back and Marshall in her bed, she was quietly confident she'd cope.

'What are you smiling at?' Michelle was looking at her knowingly. 'That's a shit-eating grin if ever I saw one.'

'Nothing in particular.'

'Yeah, right. Your *boyfriend* you mean.'

'Maybe.'

Over a Sri Lankan curry and a beer, Honey filled Michelle in about Marshall, from their first reunion at the golf club bar to their last phone call earlier in the day. She was so wrapped up in the story, she nearly overlooked the agreed time for their next phone-in. She went outside while Michelle vaped nearby, pretending she wasn't trying to listen in.

Marshall must've been waiting, and picked up immediately. He said he was parked in the truck on the rise near the cottage, hopefully the phone wouldn't cut out, no sign of the bad guys, Kloe can talk all right. A bit more chat about the drive to Auckland, and then she dropped it in, casually: 'Oh, yeah, I decided, I'm quitting the police force.' It sounded good and simple.

'Is that what you want to do?'

'I do. It's been a fine relationship, for the most part, but now we both want different things. It's not them, it's me.'

'How do you think your brothers and sisters in blue will take it?'

'They'll manage. The thing is . . .'

A lie, even a lie of omission, obviously wasn't a great start to a proper grown-up relationship, but she couldn't tell Marshall the whole truth: that her arrangement with Renata included action incompatible with being a police officer. Something she was sure he would object to for all the right reasons. Her only option now was to move on. Where to and how she didn't exactly know, just that wherever it was, Marshall would be there too.

'The thing is?' He'd taken his time.

'Ah, right. The thing. Well, the thing is, I just want to be with you.' She paused and waited. She still had serious doubts about turning hippie out the back of beyond, and she'd conveniently left her mother out of the equation, but one step at a time.

'Told you before. I love you, Honey, always have, probably always will. And not like a sister, eh. Unless we're talking the royal families of Europe.'

'I love you, too.' She cut in to stop him diluting his words with nervous banter.

272

A pause, then the relief in his voice made her smile. 'Just as well, eh?'

'Yeah.'

They lingered in silence a while, him in his truck under a star dome on the outskirts of Waitutū, her on the street outside a brightly lit curry place in Sandringham.

'I should go,' she said at last. 'I'm with my friend Michelle and the curries are getting cold.'

'Sure, have fun.'

'We always do. Can't wait for you to meet her.'

Michelle, casually gravitating closer, nodded her approval.

'See you tomorrow.'

'You will. I'll leave early to beat the traffic, should be there about one.'

She was about to disconnect, but Marshall wasn't going to make it that easy. 'Is it all sorted? The other thing, with Kloe? Are the cops on board?'

'Totally.' Honey was glad he couldn't see her face. 'Out of my hands now, and yours too. Just waiting for the final okay to put Kloe and her kids in witness protection.'

'Great. I'll let you go catch up with your mate.'

'You betcha, mister. Meantime, be careful, eh? Till this is over, we have to assume the Reapers still want Kloe.'

'Got ya, eyes wide open.' And he was gone.

'Damn, I'm gonna miss ya, girlfriend.' Michelle's faux American accent brought Honey back. 'If I thought the father of my babies lived out the back of beyond, maybe I'd consider a life of rural isolation too — no I wouldn't, you know it, I know it . . .' She broke off as she and Honey burst into tears and hugged tightly. Whatever happened, both sensed it was the end of an era.

Later, as Michelle was making up the pullout bed in her apartment, she startled Honey with a serious switch of mood.

'I was thinking about what you said, about going through Kloe's sister, getting the Reapers to clean up their own mess. I get you've got this dirt on them they don't want anyone to know about.'

Oh, oh, thought Honey.

'But wouldn't it be easier for them to clean up the loose ends and carry on, business as usual? The loose ends being you and this Kloe chick?'

'They know the papers and photos are in safe keeping and if anything happens to me or Kloe, they'll be passed straight to the police prosecutor.' Honey grinned, hoping to divert. 'I always wanted to be able to say that, but it's true. I delivered them to my mate Kevin, the lawyer, right after I talked to Renata. They'll copy and digitise them so, yeah, all good.'

Michelle wasn't so easily convinced. 'But if this Bradley Morgan person wasn't around to turn state's evidence, would anyone be able to prove anything?'

Shit, thought Honey. Michelle had worked out the fine print in the plan, or at least was well on the way. Stood to reason — she dealt with data all day. Honey always said she should be a detective.

'And if they did that, what's to stop them from taking you out, too?' Michelle was regarding her with concern but also suspicion.

Honey shrugged. 'What would be the point? With Morgan gone, I couldn't hurt them. And neither could Kloe.'

Michelle stared at her; Honey could see it clicking into place. Two plus two equals . . . ?

'That's what you want them to do, isn't it? Take out Morgan?'

Honey met her stare and raised her. 'Would that be such a terrible thing for the world? One less Bradley Morgan?'

'Fuck the world. You'd have to live with it.'

Honey had thought about it. A lot. In the process she'd discovered something about herself. Maybe it was the nearly dying; maybe it was the *how* of nearly dying.

'Let's not talk about this, 'Chelle, it's all hypothetical.'

'Is it?'

Honey just busied herself making up the bed. There was nothing more to say. Michelle shook her head. She didn't say anything either. She didn't need to. Honey knew exactly how she felt.

'I'll probably head off around six,' she said. 'I'll try not to wake you. Thanks for tonight — it was so great to see you.'

'Yeah. Night, hon.'

Disappointing Michelle was hard, but Honey had a feeling that this was only the beginning.

MARTY HAD HAD A SHIT night. It was fucking freezing in the car and Keg snored so loudly he'd had to keep elbowing him. The bush was quiet, and sound carried. Marty was sorely tempted to drive back to Jagged Bay and pick the whole business up again later. For one thing, the bed there was unbelievably comfortable.

He'd have to see about bringing Shakira down there sometime for a holiday. He could imagine her squeals of delight, sitting in the spa, sipping champagne. Just thinking about it helped him nod off for an hour or so. They'd partied hard with the blonde bitch with the big fake titties. Marty didn't need anyone to tell him he wasn't twenty anymore.

Her directions had been good, and it hadn't taken them long to find the place, even in the dark. But there was still the question of what to do about it. They'd driven past slowly but didn't want to risk another drive-by, so kept going a bit and found a place to turn off, another track leading fuck knows where. They'd inched their way through some trees to a high spot that had a partial view of the valley. Luckily, the cottage was nestled a fair bit back from the road. Unlikely any nosy neighbours or passing traffic would get involved. But the front windows and veranda had a clear view of the track leading up to it, and anyone approaching. If it was the Māori dude they'd seen outside the hospital with the pig bitch, he looked like he could take care of himself. The question was, how far was he prepared to go to protect Kloe?

Even if they didn't go all the way back to Jagged Bay, Marty figured they could go far enough to get reception and call Hammer and get an update. Maybe he had more information. His hand was moving towards the ignition when he noticed the time. What was Hammer gonna say about Marty calling him at 3.20 in the fucking morning? Hammer didn't even want Renata to know what they were doing, so how was that gonna go down?

Marty sighed and settled back again. They couldn't do anything more until they had a better idea of what they were dealing with, and that would only come from watching and waiting.

MARSHALL DIDN'T NOTICE THE BMW until just after nine o'clock the next morning.

He might've seen it earlier, but he'd been sidetracked by Kloe following him around, talking non-stop. It was obviously her way of coping with nerves, but it was driving him a bit crazy, however hard he tried to be Zen about it. He distracted her by giving her tasks to do, and was surprised to learn she had experience pruning fruit trees. As she launched into stories about her time with a team

276

of seasonal workers, Marshall again marvelled at her luck and survival instincts. He set her to work in the orchard, getting rid of dead wood. It was a bit early in the year, but the peace and quiet was worth it.

Marshall was just moving the goats to a patch of untapped blackberry when he glanced over and saw it: a glint of light off the chrome around one headlight, a dark shadow in the stand of eucalypts. Quickly, he looked away and busied himself making sure the rope on the stakes was moving freely and the goats weren't going to strangle themselves.

He considered his options. He couldn't be a hundred percent sure that the vehicle was the one belonging to the gang bangers. It was too far away and mostly hidden — he'd have to get back to the cottage and check it out with his field binoculars. But assuming for now it was — and fuck knows how they'd found him and Kloe so quickly — the most straightforward plan would be to get Kloe into the Land Cruiser and drive like the clappers. On the other hand, if the gang bangers sussed what he was up to, they might be able to get to the track entrance in time to block his and Kloe's escape. Even if they got past, the Beemer could just follow them till they got to the bitumen, when it would easily outpace the Land Cruiser and the guys could take potshots or force them off the road.

Marshall didn't have a gun. As a convicted felon he couldn't get a licence, and the laws were too strict to risk it. He did have a compound bow that he used for pig and deer hunting, but he had no doubt that the Reapers weren't fazed by legalities and would be much better armed. Never mind *Rambo* bullshit, Marshall knew what an AK-47 and its various poor relations could do.

The first thing was to get Kloe into the cottage in a way that didn't look suspicious.

'Let's have a smoko, eh? Cup of tea?'

'I've just got started.'

'I know, but there's no hurry.'

Kloe launched into a story about how she'd given up smoking because she wanted to be there for her kids, it was bloody hard but her friend Samson had been a great support and then his wife got cancer anyway which just goes to show. Marshall listened for a moment, then cut her off.

'I think they're watching us,' he said. 'Don't look, okay, just keep talking to me.'

Kloe did as she was told, but she couldn't have looked more obvious as she whispered, 'Fuck. Where are they now? What'ya want me to do?'

Marshall could see she was dying to look around: her body was rigid with fear and her eyes were wide. He only hoped their visitors didn't have high-powered binoculars.

MARTY ZOOMED IN ON KLOE and the Māori dude over by the fruit trees. He was using some fancy digital binoculars he'd found at the Jagged Bay place — only the best for Mr Morgan. Something was definitely happening.

Kloe had been yakking away, and Marty had felt a little tug of sadness for what he had to do. She looked fit, way better than she used to, and Marty remembered good times hanging out with her and the kids while that dickhead Jason was fuck knows where. He'd never wanted Kloe, not like that, but she was a laugh. Still Hammer had been clear about what needed to be done, and Marty wasn't going to argue the toss.

But he'd seen the dude look their way and then say something, and he'd seen a change in Kloe, and now they were both walking towards the cottage. Neither of them looked in his direction but that itself might mean something, like they were trying too hard not to look because they knew what was there.

Marty swore softly. 'Let's go.'

'Back to town?' Keg had food on the brain.

'No.'

Marty directed Keg to roll the Beemer silently back down the track, closer to the turn-off for the cottage. He felt behind him for his trusty aluminum bat but then reconsidered. The blonde bitch last night had kept going on about Marshall this, Marshall fucking that, and something about him being in the army. The bastard probably had firearms and knew how to use them.

He got out of the car and listened. There was nothing that sounded like people or cars, just bird noises and a goat bleating way off. He went to the boot and lifted up the spare tyre to reveal the modified tyre well hidden from casual inspection. The Kalashnikov knock-off would do for him. Keg preferred the sawn-off shotgun for close-range work. He slipped them onto the back seat and told Keg to swap places. Keg wondered if they were doing this, and Marty said he was still considering their options.

Keg was all for going into the little shithole, Waitutū, calling it in, asking Hammer what he wanted them to do. Marty knew it was his stomach talking. And what if they got orders to do what they'd been told to do in the first place and got back to find them gone? Keg agreed that Hammer would be mightily pissed off. He was glad it wasn't his problem; Marty was Hammer's sergeant-at-arms, so it was up to him. Marty told Keg to shut the fuck up, a man was trying to think.

THEY WERE GONE FROM THE stand of gum trees on the rise above the valley. In the shadow of the curtains in the front room, Marshall checked again through his field glasses, though he didn't need to. They had gone. But had they gone, gone, or were they just waiting down the road a bit? The scrub in a narrow strip between the cottage and the road was too thick to see through and there was a bit of a bank where the track cut through the sandy soil. Kloe was busting to have a look too, and Marshall had to growl at her to stay away from the windows. She looked hurt by his tone, but at least it shut her up for a while.

Marshall considered whether they should go bush, taking off out the back of the cottage and over the scrubby hill to the coast. They could walk along the beach back towards Waitutū. It would take at least an hour that way to reach the nearest cellphone reception. But he had to assume the Reapers had them under surveillance, and if they saw them go they could follow and pick them off once they were on the beach and out in the open.

He was still pondering his options when the BMW tore up the track leading to the cottage and came to sliding stop about twenty metres from the veranda. As the dust settled, he couldn't see any movement through the darkened glass of the windscreen. But they were there, and it was just a matter of time.

33

HONEY HAD PLENTY OF TIME for *what ifs* later. For instance, *what if* she hadn't stayed the night in Auckland, *what if* she'd driven straight through Waitutū and gone directly to Marshall's? All the *what ifs* that would haunt her for a long, long time.

She'd fallen into a deep, alcohol-assisted sleep moments after Michelle had said a curt good night, but a few hours later had snapped awake, thirsty and disoriented. She'd been dreaming but couldn't remember any details, just a vague feeling of dread. By 6 a.m. she'd given up trying to get back to sleep, had quietly gathered up her things, left a thank you love you note for Michelle, and headed down the southern motorway.

The horizon to the east was aglow when she pulled in at the truck stop at the Bombay Hills to fill up the Corolla and grab a coffee and limp sausage roll. Apart from a frustrating twenty minutes stuck behind a campervan that crept through all the bends and sped up on the straights, she made good time and arrived on the outskirts of Waitutū just after eleven. The temptation to keep driving the last 25 ks to Marshall's cottage was strong, but she forced herself to stop at her mother's place first.

'Successful trip?' Rhonda asked.

'I think so. How was she?'

They were sitting at the wrought-iron table out the back, having tea and cheese scones that Rhonda had baked (of course she had!). Rachel was gardening, and Honey watched as she slowly moved on the little mat she used to protect her knees as she weeded.

'Well, we had a lovely evening of parallel play. She did her jigsaw and I read my book. But in the early hours I heard some noises, so I got up to investigate. She wasn't in her room, so of course I was worried. I could just imagine having to call you and saying, "Oops, sorry, I lost your mum!" But then I found her in the bedroom next to the bathroom, the one that was your sister's?' Honey nodded for her to continue. 'She was curled up on the bed. I checked that she was okay, and she didn't answer me for the longest time. But finally she said, matter-of-fact, that she didn't want Scarlett being left alone. She said she'd had too much of that, that was the problem.' Rhonda shook her head. 'Outliving your children must be the worst thing. Anyway, I left her there, and this morning she was up before me, making some concoction in her blender.'

They sat quietly for a while, then Honey shook herself. She should keep moving, she said, she had stuff to do, but if Rhonda wanted to go, she was sure Rachel would be fine on her own. Rhonda wouldn't hear of it. She'd already organised to have all calls to the station put through her mobile. There was nothing pressing. Honey felt a sudden urge to cry with relief or gratitude.

For a moment she considered opening the garage and taking the Clubman, but she was in a hurry now, and the Corolla was out the front and pointing in the right direction.

IN HINDSIGHT, HONEY COULDN'T BELIEVE she'd been quite so thick, quite so bloody unprofessional. True, she had no reason to think that Hammer's boys knew where Kloe was, or about Marshall's part in it. But she knew they were looking and that they had been under orders to grab Kloe. She'd been confident that Renata was on board, but she still didn't know if Hammer had agreed to play along, or if Renata held as much sway as she'd said. When it came down to it, the real reason she fucked up so badly (she decided later) was because love makes you stupid.

She'd been as excited and unaware as a teenage girl as she'd swung off the road between the wooden carvings. She'd driven straight up the track towards the cottage without pausing for even a moment to check out the lie of the land. Then she slammed the Corolla to a stop. The black Beemer was parked at an angle a little distance from the cottage. She couldn't see any movement anywhere.

Honey got out of the car cautiously, shielding behind the open door that she knew would be worse than useless if the Reapers had high-powered weapons, and listened. She could hear nothing except the squawking of a hen and the insistent bleat of a goat somewhere behind the cottage.

There was glass all over the veranda, and the living-room window had been shattered.

On the ground near the steps to the veranda was a leg and a booted foot, toes pointing skyward. She assumed they were still attached to a body obscured by the Beemer. Nothing was moving. She leaned into the car, gave the boot lever a pull, paused at the loud click, and then moved slowly to the rear to retrieve her father's old .22. It'd been in the back of the Corolla since her trip to Jagged Bay, wrapped in a hessian sack. Now she removed the trigger lock, pushed the five-shot magazine into place and used the scope to slowly scan the cottage.

IT WAS BASICALLY A WHIM that had made Marty, finally, drive up to the cottage. That and Keg's constant grumbling. Fuck it.

He was sick of waiting and figured that the dude in there had no reason to stick his neck out for Kloe. Maybe he'd just hand her over. After all, what was Kloe to him? A nobody, as far as Marty could tell, just a favour to the pig bitch. Without even consulting Keg, he turned the key and gunned the car, fishtailing it. He figured the simplest thing would be to knock on the door and ask for Kloe. What happened after that was up to the fella in there.

He'd banged on the door for a bit, calling, telling Kloe to come out, that he wouldn't hurt her, that he just wanted to talk. Telling the bloke that they meant no harm, that this was nothing to do with him. But there'd been no reply, nothing. Well, that made sense. He was holding a fucking Kalashnikov knock-off after all. We come in peace. Yeah, right.

For a moment it occurred to him they might have gone out the back, be hiding up in the bush on the hill behind the cottage already, but he was pretty sure they would've seen or heard them. He decided to go around the back and leave Keg and his shotgun to stop them leaving via the front door, if that was what they decided to do. If Marty couldn't get the guy to open up, the next step was to kick the door down.

WHAT HAPPENED NEXT HONEY RECONSTRUCTED from Kloe's statement and the forensic investigation, and the shards of memory that cut into her dreams.

A moment after Marty went around the rear of the house, the front door opened and Kloe stood there as if this was a social occasion and Keg was a neighbour popping in. She asked how he was, what was going on. Keg said she was to come with them 'cos Hammer wanted to ask her a few questions. Kloe shrugged and

284

said she was sorry but she couldn't do that. Keg started to move towards her, pointing the shotgun like a revolver in one huge hand and saying that he didn't have time for this shit.

He'd got one foot on the step leading to the veranda when Marshall came for him from behind with an axe. Marshall had slid out of a bedroom window on the side of the house nearest the woodpile, and been waiting the whole time Marty had been asking for them to come out. He'd told Kloe not to say anything, not to show herself, just to wait. But she hadn't been able to leave it there. So she'd opened the door and distracted Keg long enough. It would have worked, too, if Marshall hadn't been encumbered with an unwillingness to kill in cold blood. He'd stood behind Keg and quietly told him to put down the gun, now. Do it. Instead, Keg started to swing the gun around, so that when Marshall brought down the axe on his head, splitting it like a dark melon, Keg's finger was around the trigger. When the shotgun went off, Keg was probably already dead. The recoil spun his body around, and he landed flat on his enormous back. The blast shattered the window beside Kloe but missed both her and Marshall.

'Let's go!' Marshall was yelling. There was no point in silence now.

Kloe stood there a moment, frozen in shock at what had just happened.

'Move!' he called out again, but then he saw movement out of the corner of his eye and started to run for the furthest side of the house.

Several shots rang out in quick succession, and Marshall stumbled and then disappeared behind the woodpile.

Marty came out from the opposite side of the house, gun forward, wary, and Kloe quickly slammed the door. He swore when he saw Keg like a beached pilot whale, a dark stain in the dirt around his head, the axe on the ground nearby. He thought he'd got the prick, but he couldn't be sure. And that bitch was still in the house.

'Kloe! Get the fuck out here!'

'No! Get fucked!' She was yelling through the hole in the glass.

He was tempted to shoot her through the door then and there, but Hammer needed her to answer some questions first. He had no idea why, just that it was important and Hammer was the boss.

'Kloe, I'm not going to hurt you. Hammer just wants to talk to you.'

'Bullshit!'

'For fuck's sake!' He'd had a gutsful of her shit. He stomped up onto the veranda and, using the butt of his gun, cleared the rest of the glass from the window and stepped over the sill into the front room. Should've done this in the first place.

He heard the back door slam. 'Fucking bitch!' He roared through the cottage and opened the back door in time to see Kloe running up a narrow track leading past the chook house. He swore again and set off after her.

HOLDING THE .22 AT HIP height, cowboy style, Honey advanced slowly towards the BMW. There was nobody in the car and there was still no sound or movement from the cottage. Finally she moved towards the body. She recognised Keg right away from his bulk and the patched leather Reapers vest. She knew it was pointless, the blood and brains from his head wound were all over the ground, but she still felt obliged to kneel and feel for a pulse in his huge bull neck. Then she noticed the drops of blood leading to the side of the cottage. She followed and rounded the woodpile.

Marshall was lying curled up, partially hidden by the giant stump that served as a chopping block. The autopsy would later reveal that two of Marty's bullets had struck him. One had passed through his shoulder, another through his chest. Bullets fired from a high-velocity weapon had enormous kinetic energy to share. The shot to the shoulder fractured bones and severed blood vessels. It might have killed him; at the very least he'd have lost the arm. But with the chest wound his liver had all but exploded.

But Honey knew none of this yet. She was leaning over Marshall, trying to shake him back to life, trying to feel for a pulse, trying not to fall into a black hole, not to scream, when she heard shrieks and yells coming from the rear of the house. She picked up her rifle and moved quickly. She wasn't really aware of thinking or feeling anything. She wasn't even numb, not yet. She knew that grief was already in her chest, wanting to claw its way out, and that it would have its day — but not yet.

Marty was half dragging, half carrying Kloe from around the other side of the cottage. His gun was strung over his left shoulder by its strap. Kloe was still protesting, begging for him not to do this, and he'd had enough. He smacked her, hard, hoisted her over his other shoulder and carried her the rest of the way to the car.

'The fuck?'

Kloe's body had obscured Marty's view, and he didn't notice the Corolla until he was almost at the Beemer.

Cautiously, he lowered Kloe to the ground. She started to crawl away and he stomped near her face: 'Stay the fuck there! Don't move!' She sobbed but stayed where she was, on her hands and knees, face down on the ground, as he unshouldered his gun and scanned the area. Keg still lay on his back. There were footprints in the dirt near his body. The footprints went around the side of the cottage, in the same direction as the splashes of blood.

Marty started to move around to the other side of the Beemer to give himself some cover.

He heard a shot and felt his legs give way at the same moment. He couldn't stop himself as he fell to sitting, his back against the right front wheel of the car. He couldn't feel his legs.

The logical part of his brain detached itself and moved away a little and considered. Whoever it was must've come around the other side of the house to get the drop on him. He must have been shot through the guts and the bullet had severed his spinal cord. He was gonna be a cripple, a para at the very least. He thought about the guy he'd put in a wheelchair, and the watching part of him laughed: that's karma for you.

He sensed movement then, and sure enough the pig bitch was coming towards him, holding a rifle. It was just a fucking peashooter, a .22, a bit embarrassing but the reason he was still alive. He was still holding his gun too, capable of making a far bigger mess, but the outside-himself voice analysed and rejected that option. Even if he could take her down before she got him, what was he going to do? He couldn't even fucking walk. Slowly he placed the gun down and pushed it away as best he could. He needed her, and she was a cop so she'd have to help him. He looked up and managed a crooked grin.

'Well, that's me fucked, eh.'

His outside-himself voice admired the understatement. He flashed to himself in his pimped-out wheelchair at the clubhouse, recounting this story to the bros and new recruits. In the same instant he thought of Shakira and the way she'd fuss over him. But now the pig bitch had stopped, and Marty felt something strange

288

and unpleasant rising. His outside-himself voice interpreted it as fear.

Her eyes gave nothing away, but she raised her rifle and from a distance of less than ten metres shot him in the heart and then through his right eye just to be sure.

34

KLOE WAS LYING FACE DOWN in the dirt, sobbing, when she heard one quiet 'pop' like a car backfiring in the distance. Then she heard Marty say something about being 'fucked, eh', but he was on the other side of the Beemer from her so she wasn't sure. It was silent for what seemed like an age before she heard two louder pops in rapid succession. She'd looked up in time to see Honey moving around the side of the house. That was when Kloe had got to her feet and slid around the BMW to find Marty sitting against the right-hand wheel, dead as. There was blood on the ground and blood and brains sprayed over the car door.

She'd found Honey sitting on the stump by the woodpile, staring at Marshall who was curled up like a baby. She'd glanced up at Kloe, a puzzled, lost look on her face. 'Is he okay?' she'd asked.

'No, darling, he's not,' was all Kloe could think of to say.

They'd stayed there, the two of them, looking at Marshall and the dark stain of his blood in the dirt and wood chips until Kloe had realised that Honey had no idea what to do next, how to behave.

'Should we maybe call an ambulance?'

Honey shook her head. 'There's no reception.' Then she added flatly, 'And there's no point.'

At last Kloe coaxed Honey to the car. She wondered if she should find something to cover the bodies, it seemed wrong to just leave them, but Honey said no, not to fuck things for forensics. She'd just sat in the passenger seat obediently and Kloe had started to back out, but then Honey insisted they turn in the next driveway and find Marshall's helpful neighbour and let her know what was going on, in case she stumbled on the scene.

'I heard some shots, I thought Marshall was probably dealing to the rabbits . . .' The woman trailed off and shrugged helplessly. 'Oh, god.'

'We're going into town now to let the cops know,' said Kloe, wanting to keep moving, conscious of how strange it was for her to be the one in charge.

'What about the animals?'

'The cops will be here in a little while. Maybe you could mention it to them.' She looked to Honey for confirmation, but Honey was staring off now, like she wasn't even there anymore.

Constable Evans proved remarkably competent. He sent his junior out to secure the scene, contacted Rotorua CIB and let things run their course. Kloe and Honey's hands were bagged and examined at the Waitutū station where they gave their preliminary statements.

Kloe had told Honey precisely what her statement would be, especially in regards to the timing and number of shots — had repeated it several times — on the drive back to Waitutū. She checked that Honey understood what she meant. Honey just nodded and stared ahead. Kloe hoped to hell she'd got through to her.

MARSHALL'S FUNERAL WAS AN ORDEAL and a surprise for Honey, for several reasons. When Marshall's body was finally released, it was Rachel who had swooped in and taken care of everything. She seemed to understand that her daughter was barely functioning. It was very different from how it had been after the beating that had nearly killed her. Then, Honey had wanted to fight, to survive. Now all she wanted to do was sleep and not wake up.

Rachel still had brief periods where she'd lose the thread, forget what she was doing or why she was hanging on the end of the phone, but her new best friend Rhonda helped smooth the way. Matters became further complicated when Jim chose to die the same day Marshall's body was transported back to the marae. As far as Honey was concerned, Jim's remains could be tossed in the rubbish dump on the outskirts of town, but she couldn't tell her mother this without revealing the truth about Scarlett. So Rachel helped organise the send-off not only for Marshall but also for the man who had raped her youngest daughter and probably caused her suicide. It was to be a double tangi.

'Life's pretty fucked,' was all Michelle said, when Honey had explained the terrible irony to her. She was the only one who knew the full story and understood why Honey blamed herself and would keep blaming herself for the foreseeable. She had arrived the night before the funeral and just listened while Honey picked over the bones of her mistakes. Honey didn't need her to say anything, there was nothing she *could* say. It was enough that she was there.

But Honey was astonished at the number of people who kept turning up over the three days of mourning. Jim had been a taciturn man, a mean and violent drunk who pushed everyone away from him. As far as Honey knew, the only visitors he got in the hospice were Marshall and Father Yun. She had thought of Marshall as a loner too, living out the back of beyond, off the grid, in the shadow of her sister's death. He kept surprising her, even now. Wiremu was there, of course, mouthing greeting-card biblical quotes and gathering information. A couple of nurses from the hospice and the good Father came, as well as Marshall's neighbour. But then Jim and Marshall's iwi had turned out, en masse.

Honey was called on to the marae with Rachel and Michelle on either side, hardly hearing the karanga, aware of little except holding herself up. She was introduced to relatives of the dead men, but they barely registered. Who were they? Where had they come from? Men in dark clothes and sunglasses stood around vaping, women in the whare kai cooked huge pots of food, kids ran about screaming.

The women took her as she was, a mute shell, and treated her as one of their own. At first Honey tried to resist, but it was pointless, so she let herself be pulled along in their keening. She tried to say who she was and why she was there, but her words got tangled until a tall grey-haired woman touched her gently on the arm and said that of course they knew who she was, Marshall had told them all about her. They sat around the two open coffins, holding photos and leafy branches, and sobbed. Part of Honey knew that it was all for show, prescribed, unreal, but it didn't matter. Make yourself laugh and you feel happy, make yourself cry, you feel sad: it was a chemical process in the brain and if the real emotions wouldn't come, if they were too locked up in her grief, then this was the next best thing.

Honey didn't look at either of the bodies. If she wanted to see Marshall, all she had to do was close her eyes. He was always there, his serious face as they made love, his face beside her as they drove in smiling silence, his studied face as he sliced and diced a meal, his machine gun laugh, and his kind, intelligent eyes. That Marshall was the one who kept her company while she went through the motions.

She must have eaten, had conversations, slept in the communal space, but she really had no idea, and if she'd suddenly woken to find it had all been a dream, she wouldn't have been particularly surprised. At some point Michelle had hugged her and bawled and said she was sorry she'd never met Marshall, he sounded like an amazing guy, but Honey couldn't remember how she'd replied or if she'd said anything at all.

On the final day of the tangihanga the koroua and master of ceremonies told about Jim as a younger man, the sailor and adventurer who'd travelled the world on merchant ships but had lost touch with his people and his mauri, his life force. His people had been waiting all along for him to come back but he had never done so while he was alive. Now, in death, he was with them again. Then he spoke of Marshall, a man in his prime, with still so much potential. His passing was a tragedy. Yes, he had strayed, made mistakes, as everyone does, but he had come home. Despite her numbness, Honey was surprised to learn that Marshall had been so involved in the marae, turning up for working bees, and had been advising on a local work scheme to get locals growing their own food. While most of the good (mostly white) burghers of Waitutū had spurned Marshall, he had been quietly going about good works. She'd only known the new Marshall for a few precious weeks. They'd talked about lots of things, mostly to do with the past and more recently the future, but the nitty gritty of the day to day — that was something they had expected to discover in time. Time that had suddenly and irreversibly run out.

KLOE HAD WANTED TO GO to the tangi; she owed her life to Marshall and she wanted to be there for Honey. The police vetoed the idea outright. Instead she had to wait it out in a hotel with a police guard, waiting to be allocated a new life. In her view, she was safe enough. The last thing the Reapers needed right now was more attention and, besides, Honey still had the dirt on them.

At least the kids were with her now. The police had gone with some social workers to collect Aria and Nico. They were upset at having to leave their auntie and cousins, and were shy and guarded around Kloe at first. She had moments where she wondered if she'd done the right thing after all. What if the kids were better off with Renata? Shyla told her she was being a dick and that Kloe needed to do what was best for herself and her kids, not what anyone else thought was right. Kloe thought that was a bit bloody rich, seeing as how she had to ask permission from the cops to stick her head outside the door. But Shyla was allowed to visit, and after they'd been in the motel a couple of weeks Kloe had borrowed her phone and broken the rules and called her sister.

'Shyla?' said Renata, surprised, because they'd agreed she wouldn't call.

'Hey, what's up?'

There was a long silence on the other end of the line.

'Hey, it's me.'

'What do you want?'

That was all. Nothing about being glad to hear from her, glad she was still alive, sorry for what she'd been through. There was a catch in Renata's voice, like she wanted to say something else, but instead: 'You shouldn't be calling me.'

'Yeah, just wanted to thank you, y'know, for taking care of Nico and Aria while I was gone.'

'They're good kids.'

'Yeah, dunno how that happened, eh?'

'That makes two of us,' Renata said lightly. 'Hey, big send-off for Keg and Marty last week. Brothers and sisters from all over, it was full on.' Her voice softened then. 'Why'd you do it, Klo? If you hadn't talked to that pig bitch in the first place—'

'Shit happens, eh?' It was all Kloe could think of to say.

'You could've talked to me.'

'Not really. But thanks again for looking after the kids.'

She hung up, and knew then that she'd probably never talk to her sister again. She had plans, real plans. She and the kids would go wherever the cops sent them until the fuss had died down, but she had no intention of staying in the long term. She'd already made contact with Joshua, whose orchard and new wife were both coming along nicely. In fact they were expecting their first kid. He said there was plenty of work on his place and around the district for an old hand like her, a good school nearby and even a cottage on his boundary that she could stay in rent-free if she did a bit of fixing up. Part of Kloe was still wary, like there had to be a catch, but fuck it. Maybe sometimes stuff does just work out. At any rate, she was gonna take Shyla's advice. She was gonna do what she thought was right.

35

HONEY, FOLLOWING THE ADVICE OF her lawyer and union rep, had said very little beyond her initial statement. Just the facts, ma'am. The shit hit the fan, of course. A police officer had been badly beaten once before and was attacked again, but this time she'd defended herself. Her boyfriend had tragically died but she had saved the life of a witness, a vulnerable victim of a vicious criminal gang. The Auckland Tabloid was predictable in the arc of its coverage. In the beginning, Honey was a real-life hero who could do no wrong. It didn't hurt that she was a) attractive, b) Pākehā and c) a woman.

Then after thrashing that tune for a few weeks, the mood turned. Was it self-defence or a calculated act of vigilantism? Had Honey abused her position as a cop to get revenge on her attackers? An online news outlet hopped on the bandwagon, figuring that police brutality was always good clickbait amongst its hipster subscribers. In this version of reality, there was a war between the disadvantaged underdogs (the 501 gang of displaced persons cruelly expelled from Australia) and the police (ACAB) who had the power of the state behind them.

Honey was mostly oblivious to the shifting opinions. She cancelled her social media accounts, stayed away from her house and didn't read newspapers. Michelle was a rock, as always, and did her best not to fill Honey in on the latest gossip. They had a few nights out on the piss, but they were more about self-medication than fun.

When enough time had passed, Michelle had tried to get Honey to open up and talk about what had happened, but Honey couldn't go there. The more she drank, the more sober she became, and eventually she did Michelle a favour and headed back to Waitutū. When a reporter and cameraperson staked out her mother's house, she threatened to shove the camera somewhere painful, and the two eventually decamped.

But it had prompted her to face facts. She arranged to put the house on the market and found a place for her mother in a serviced unit in a retirement village on the outskirts of Taupō. Rachel had once sworn that she'd never live in one of those places, had made Honey promise to kill her first. But now she clung to life and made the best of it — on the principle you only live long enough to go back on all the things you swore you'd never do. When she was no longer self-sufficient she'd be moved to the high-care unit, but if she ate enough turmeric and did enough yoga, who knew when that might be . . .

OF COURSE, THERE WAS AN internal investigation Honey could not ignore and the government was under pressure to hold an independent enquiry as well, but the Opposition gauged that there was little support amongst the general voting public in pillorying a cop who stood up to organised crime.

There was a long article in a bi-monthly glossy magazine. Honey still wasn't talking and Kloe, the 'mystery witness', was rumoured to be in witness protection, so the article was mostly based on what the police had provided and the odd person on the fringes. According to 'Shakira', a transgender sex worker, Martin Pascoe was a rough diamond and had come from a tough background, but that was in the past and he'd been trying to get his life together. The Reapers were involved in programmes to help 501s find their feet, had invested in legitimate businesses, and had even hired a PR firm to manage their social media. But the balance of the article was in Honey's favour and concluded that the gang members had pursued her to Waitutū, and that Marty would have killed Honey and the mystery witness if she hadn't fired first. A local television production company had optioned the article, but without Honey's cooperation and in light of New Zealand's libel laws, a highly fictionalised version was being developed instead.

Many of the facts for the article had come from Kloe's statement to the police enquiry, the bits that hadn't been redacted. She had never wavered in her story. She'd turned up in Waitutū without warning; Honey and Marshall had been trying to protect her. Martin Pascoe was dragging her to his car, had said he was going to kill her, when Honey had challenged him to stop. She had given a clear verbal warning. In response, Marty had fired his gun several times in her direction. Kloe had broken free from him and she had no doubt he would have shot her, but Honey fired first. There were three shots, maybe more, in rapid succession. Marty was killed instantly, and Honey was in shock, so Kloe got her into the Corolla and drove her to the Waitutū police station where they had called the after-hours number and waited.

RENATA KNEW THE REAPERS WOULD have to pull their heads in for a while, but then business would go on. If anything, this had been a wake-up call. There was a new way forward that didn't involve shootouts or gang brawls or putting chicks to the block. That kind of shit had to stop. Reapers Inc. was a business like any other with the potential for growth, dividends, asset accumulation and career paths for committed employees. The core business was still drugs, of course: that was where the demand and profit margins were. They'd use the proceeds to fund a better life for them and their kids.

But Renata had one last old-school problem to sort out. She'd had a text from an unknown number: *The deal still stands*. She'd tried to call back but there was no reply. It must have been from a burner phone that was dumped the moment it was used. But she had no doubts about who the text was from. The deal still stood, all right; now it was all about timing.

36

BRADLEY MORGAN HATED THE STINK from his sweat. He'd showered at the gym but as he made his way to the car park he could still smell himself. He'd hoped his sweat might start to smell less rank as he got fitter — something about toxins working their way out through your pores — but that was another thing they didn't tell you about getting older. He'd been on his health binge for nearly a year now and had lost ten kilos. The shit that went down with the Reapers and his place being used by the killers — it was the slap he needed. He'd explained it away, that the Jagged Bay house was rented out by an agency, that the Reapers had hired it through an intermediary, that it was nothing to do with him personally ... The cops hadn't exactly believed him, but they hadn't pursued that line of enquiry, so being who he was and who he knew still counted.

Apart from his personal trainer who was a complete fucking fascist, life was sweet. He had money, a great house, a beautiful wife, kids who were succeeding with a bit of backing and support from Dad, and this kick-arse yellow Lamborghini that still gave him a rush every time he saw it.

In the back of his brain it still niggled that the Reapers had something on him from that dark time when the P and the sex and the partying took over and he felt like he was on greased tracks that he couldn't get off, but he had come to terms with it. He'd helped them restructure the same way as he'd helped many other firms restructure, maximising profits, minimising tax. It might not be ethical but good luck proving it was illegal, buddy. There was nothing to show he *knew* he was helping them hide drug profits. Okay, yes, he'd been badly behaved and there were those fucking photos, but that wasn't him anymore, and if the Reapers released them he'd plead mea culpa and, hand on heart, could say he'd turned his life around and be ever so useful in helping the cops find the money and show which assets to freeze. He knew exactly how to fuck the Reapers over, and they knew that he knew, so it was a state of mutually assured destruction that kept everybody cool.

He'd already confessed all to his wife, who'd not exactly been surprised and had confessed infidelities of her own. At her insistence they'd done serious couple counselling and Bradley had to admit it had worked a treat. In fact, this weekend they were flying to Hawaii to look at a new holiday home. Jagged Bay was on the market, and if he ever heard the name of the place again it would be too soon.

Leaning in to deposit his gym bag on the passenger seat of the low-slung car, he groaned. Every part of him bloody hurt — he was definitely having a word with his trainer. He stood and stretched in preparation for the drive home. Just then a figure in a dark hoody came towards him, a silhouette backlit by the late-afternoon sun. Bradley registered that the person was pointing at him, and opened his mouth to ask what their problem was—

HONEY FLICKED THROUGH HER NEWS feed. The man gunned down in broad daylight in the car park of an exclusive Auckland gym had been named as Bradley Morgan. The article mentioned his rumoured ties to organised crime in general, but

302

was light on detail and made no mention of the events in Waitutū. There was online speculation that one of the thousands of mum and dad investors he'd ripped off over the years may have been biding their time. Honey tracked a couple more sites, but they all said more or less the same thing. If she'd hoped to feel some satisfaction, some sense of closure, anything at all, she was out of luck.

She was still on bereavement leave that had bled into mental health leave. The police looked after their own and it was all in the line of duty, after all. But the Assistant Commissioner had called her in for a chat, said there was a place for Honey in Wellington, in the National Organised Crime Group, where she could work a desk in intelligence coordination, safely off the streets. She'd experienced a hiccup in her career, that was all; in a few years she'd be back on track. Honey had thanked her politely, but she knew she wasn't a cop anymore and away from the streets was the last thing she wanted.

When she'd shot and killed Marty Pascoe she had told herself it was out of terror, that her PTSD had been triggered and she wasn't responsible for her actions. But Bradley Morgan was different. It had been a calculated act of revenge and still she felt nothing — just another box ticked off her to-do list. Was this her default position now? She'd had a job she loved and man she loved more and they'd both been taken from her. All she could do now was keep moving, stay ahead of the grief and pain, stay ahead of the other names on her list.

She turned off the news feed, pulled on her runners and headed out the door.

Acknowledgments

A shout out to Jacinda and Ashley's covid response for saving thousands of lives and gifting me lockdown time and space to write. To the anonymous detective who was the inspiration for Honey and shared with me her phone-in relationship with a gang WAG. The general background on 501 gangs was sifted from many news sources, but a big thanks to Carey Carter for letting me play on his wonderful (sadly not yet made) TV project *Chasing Pure* and for the chat with Jared Savage — the inaccuracies and fictions are all mine. Huge appreciation to my dear friends and early readers, Helen, Kath, Sukanya and my favourite sister Denise and niece Ruby. To Gloria, my consultant on all things contemporary, and to Rachel for the years spent correcting my mistakes in grammar and romance. To Michelle Hurley and the judges of the Allen & Unwin Fiction Prize for giving me this amazing opportunity; thanks to Michelle, again, and Leonie and Rebecca and all the A & U team for the terrific ongoing support. The wonderful Jane Parkin: how lucky can a first-time novelist be to have Jane as their editor. To Paula Morris and the late breaking (if not always observed) lessons of her MCW course. To Pete for Waitutū (Churning Waters) and Amiria for vetting my tangi scene so generously. And last, but definitely first, Adele for reading and re-reading and notes and enthusiasm and for relentlessly pushing me to submit *The Call* in the first place.